THE S

Chris Paling is the author of *After the Raid*, *Deserters* and *Morning All Day*.

ALSO BY CHRIS PALING

After the Raid
Deserters
Morning All Day

Chris Paling

THE SILENT SENTRY

VINTAGE

Published by Vintage 2000

2 4 6 8 10 9 7 5 3 1

First published in Great Britain by
Jonathan Cape in 1999

Vintage
Random House, 20 Vauxhall Bridge Road,
London SW1V 2SA

Random House Australia (Pty) Limited
20 Alfred Street, Milsons Point, Sydney
New South Wales 2061, Australia

Random House New Zealand Limited
18 Poland Road, Glenfield,
Auckland 10, New Zealand

Random House (Pty) Limited
Endulini, 5A Jubilee Road, Parktown 2193,
South Africa

The Random House Group Limited Reg. No. 954009
www.randomhouse.co.uk

A CIP catalogue record for this book
is available from the British Library

ISBN 0 09 928989 X

Papers used by Random House are natural, recyclable
products made from wood grown in sustainable forests.
The manufacturing processes conform to the environ-
mental regulations of the country of origin

Printed and bound in Great Britain by
Cox & Wyman Limited, Reading, Berkshire

For my mother and father

You shall hear their lightest tone
Stealing through your walls of stone;

Till your loneliest valleys hear
The far cathedral's whispered prayer

Daventry calling . . .
Daventry calling . . .
Daventry calling . . .
Dark and still
The tree of memory stands like a sentry . . .
Over the graves on the silent hill.

Alfred Noyes

It has been said that there are two kinds of loneliness: insulation in space and isolation of spirit. These are both dispelled by wireless.

J.C.W. Reith

I

Another element of great importance, though perhaps only of indirect interest to the outside public, is the loyalty which permeates the service. It is amazing to find how rare is esprit de corps, *how seldom real loyalty can be traced through all the grades of a great undertaking. Its importance can hardly be over-estimated, nor the magnitude of the detriment when it is lacking. Its absence is explainable in a variety of ways. The chief may be incapable of inspiring it or may have never sought to do so. Jealousy is common in business and, of all amazing phenomena, it is common from the top down – men are often jealous of their own subordinates. From the outset in the BBC we have endeavoured to establish these factors of confidence and loyalty, both from seniors down and juniors up.*

J.C.W. Reith, 'Broadcast Over Britain',
Hodder & Stoughton, 1924

ONE

MAURICE REID POKED a pencil through the closed blinds of his office and squinted through the narrow slat. 'I don't understand it,' he said. 'I just want to cry all the time.' Wincing at the bar of light, he withdrew his pencil. 'I can't help it. I think I'm going tonto.'

Maurice was standing in his small office which, had he opened the Venetian blinds, would have afforded him a view across the south end of Portland Place. Hidden from his sight was an eight-storey block of West End apartments, the windows of which were heavily draped. The one break in this grey, weathered uniformity was a brightly lit dentist's surgery in which a green-gowned man was leaning over the horizontal figure of a young woman.

'We're all falling apart one way or another.' Sitting at Maurice's desk and scrolling through a block of text on his computer screen was a tall man in his late twenties. He was dressed entirely in black with quiffed hair and teddy boy sideburns. The man's Christian name was David but, prompted by his aloofness, his colleagues tended to label him by his surname, which was Warde. Like the buildings opposite, the view into Warde's world was heavily draped. His green eyes were characteristically narrowed; he looked like an aristocrat who abused drugs. Warde had a tendency to appear always to be on his way somewhere else, his shyness masquerading as arrogance, which was safer. Warde was one of the few people who could make Maurice laugh, and Maurice was one of the few people Warde ever took the trouble to make laugh. Like Maurice Reid, Warde was a radio producer. Unlike Maurice, who was slightly overweight and prone to lethargy, Warde was whippet-thin and his concentration span was short. His hyperactive mind was currently engaged in attaching Maurice's desktop computer to the Internet.

'There.' Warde punched the return key with his index finger and the screen flooded from top to bottom with richly coloured graphics.

'What have you done now?'

'Just key whatever you want to search here and . . .'

'How do you switch it off?'

'Double click on this.' Warde clicked the mouse and the screen returned to Maurice's favoured backdrop, a sober view of Loch Lomond at sunrise.

'That's better. Much better.' Maurice looked up at the photograph pinned on the noticeboard above his desk: his son, Will, at his fourth birthday party looking towards the camera wearing a red paper hat and a troubled smile. 'I took Will to the circus yesterday and cried all the way through it.'

'Circuses are sad.'

'They're not supposed to be.' Maurice took up a pen and scribbled on a yellow Post-it note. 'Will. 6.00. Polly/bitch supper.' He peeled it from the pad and stuck it beside his computer screen. 'I think it was being with him, grubby little specimen. Bloody sticky ice-cream hands all over my trousers, twenty quid for two hours' worth of whingeing – then on the way out he wanted a hat with flashing lights on it.'

'And you bought him one I suppose?' Deposed from his position at the screen, Warde was now pacing backwards and forwards across the short distance of Maurice's office with his hands punched deep into his pockets.

'Of course I did. It was desperate. Absolutely desperate. I mean I fully accept it could just be the way that I'm seeing things, but I reckon everybody is on the edge, everybody: screaming point. Never mind road rage, this is life rage. You just had to look round the audience to see that. People in the cheap seats, straining to look round the pole things, screaming. People in the expensive seats, craning forward to get the most of it so they didn't feel cheated. And me in the side seats with my boy feeling sorry for everybody.'

The act of life itself burdened Maurice Reid. Since Will had been born, the gravity of his mortality had begun to weigh him down and this had a bearing not only on his demeanour but also on the way he carried himself through the world. He did nothing lightly because he no longer felt anything lightly, which made him good company for anybody (particularly female) who enjoyed long evenings of soul-searching. At parties and other social occasions he was often avoided. Apart from his failed marriage, Maurice was relatively successful with women. They found him sensitive, tortured and interesting, and also reasonably good-looking in a well-worn way. Those who knew him well (better, perhaps, than he knew himself) soon discovered that his interest in them and their traumas was one of his defences. It was also a strategy of self-analysis: he was drawn by pain because he recognised it, felt it, and therefore found it endlessly fascinating. Most men bored him rigid.

'It's you,' Warde said. 'You're having a compassion attack to make up for all your past cynicism.'

'No, I still feel cynical. I wish I could . . . I just wish I could believe in something. I just think that life is so bloody sad nowadays. That's all. That's why I want to cry.'

Warde opened the door. 'I don't see what you've got against the Internet. There's no point in being Luddite about it. I mean we'll all be using it sooner rather than later.'

'Listen. I've got better things to do with my time than e-mail a bunch of maladjusted morons who find it easier to talk to a screen than a human being. Anyway, I think anyone who can use the thing should, on that criteria alone, be excluded from access to it.'

'You just don't want to talk to anyone.'

'Exactly. And shut the door on your way out.'

'I just want to cry all the time,' Maurice said. 'I think I need help.'

'Sit down,' the doctor said, shuffling a pack of bulging manila envelopes. 'It's Mr Reid, isn't it?'

'Yes.'

'Sit down.' The doctor gestured and Maurice sat on the chair placed side on to the end of the desk. From the lower angle he could see out of the window to the whitewashed stockade of wheely bins. Maurice wondered what was in them: bloodied, bent hypodermics, soiled dressings, incontinence pads. Bins nowadays put him in mind of his own inevitable decay; the slow certain slide into senility.

'Let's have a look at you then, shall we?' The doctor looked Maurice up and down as if he could divine the root of his problems by a cursory appraisal of the state of his clothing. Maurice was wearing a creased powder-blue linen jacket over a white T-shirt worn one day too long, black Levis and balding brown suede shoes. What attracted people to him was the concentrated concern his face seemed to transmit. His ex-wife said it was the kind of face that could have earned him a living as a young, idealistic doctor in a TV medical soap. At whatever age you encountered him, you would always see in Maurice Reid's face something of the child that had run into his mother's arms after his first day at school: in his eyes, wonder at the world mitigated by confusion at its cruelty.

In the eight years that Maurice had been registered with Dr Soames, he had visited him on only five occasions. Once with the flu, once with piles, once with a strange lump on his penis that vanished shortly after the visit, once for anti-depressants after the break-up of his marriage (during which he had cried unconsolably for twenty minutes), and once, inebriated, with a yellow rash on his neck (two weeks after the visit for anti-depressants), at which time he had expressed the fear that he was turning Japanese. Whenever he went, Maurice always enjoyed the old man's surrogate paternalism, his crumpled-suited kindliness. Maurice had long ago decided that doctors held the secret of eternal life but never prescribed it for fear of the side effects. Hence their air of melancholy.

'Slip off your jacket.'

As Maurice slid out of his jacket, Dr Soames watched him closely, his brows knitted tightly, his head a little bowed. Maurice waited as Soames continued to stare.

'You're thirty . . . six?' Soames stood Maurice's envelope on the desk and read long-sightedly from it.

'Yes.'

'Do you drink?'

'Of course.'

'How many units?'

'Oh . . . twenty, I don't know, thirty, I don't know, fifty-odd units a week.'

'On the theory that one always doubles a patient's own

estimation I would say you've probably got something of a drink problem.'

'No,' Maurice said, 'I doubled it for you. I was going to say twenty-odd, then I remembered you always doubled it so I doubled it myself.'

'Smoke?'

'No thanks, I've given up.'

Soames smiled wearily. 'Drugs?'

'A bit.'

'Cannabis, heroin . . . *crack* cocaine?'

'Cannabis.'

'Roll up your sleeve.'

Maurice revealed his vein-marbled forearm. Soames leaned forward and slipped a black cuff up his arm, enveloping him in a bucolic aroma of pipe tobacco. A ledge of dandruff slipped from his wiry hair into Maurice's lap.

'How long have you felt this . . . depression?' Soames inflated the sleeve and watched the pressure gauge.

'It's not depression.'

'No?'

Air escaped and, as it did so, Soames lost interest in his gizmo. 'That seems fine. You say you're not depressed?'

'No. It's sadness. I know the distinction probably sounds a bit . . .'

'Undo your shirt.'

Maurice obliged. '. . . unusual. But I think it's more of a general world-weariness than depression.'

'I see.'

'Yes, it's . . .'

'Quiet please.' Soames listened to Maurice's heart. 'Thank you.'

'More a sort of existential . . .'

'Yes, well I can hardly . . .'

'Of course not. I wouldn't expect you to.' Maurice rested

8

his elbow on the desk and leaned his chin on his hand. 'Listen, can I tell you about a dream I had last night?'

'Please do.' Soames sat back and began crimping the short hairs on his earlobe between his thumbnail and first finger.

'It was, I don't know, evening I suppose. And I was walking along the top of a sea wall, on my own. And suddenly I was confronted by a tower − a mountain − a sudden incandescent mountain of water. Poised but shifting as though it was just waiting with its awesome, awesome power: hundreds of feet high and a mix of blues and transparent greens, sort of translucent, like . . . like glass I suppose. And then it teetered and crashed all over me and I held on to something; something metal. And I passed out. And when I woke up it was morning and I was dry but the path I was lying on was still puddled. But the sun was out and I walked for a while until I could find a taxi. And then I went home. And that was it.'

'Yes,' Soames said, slipping Maurice's envelope back into his pile: a delaying tactic. 'So, sadness you say. And a propensity towards tears?'

'All the time. Nearly. Unless, well, unless I've had a few drinks. Then it's not so bad. Most of the time. Except the following day it's worse.'

'Are you married? Remind me.'

'Christ, no. I mean I was. But I'm not now.'

'Separated?'

'Divorced. And separated. Not from the same woman. Well, not really separated, just apart. At the moment, anyway. I mean she's in . . . it's not important. I'm divorced from Polly, separated, I mean living apart, from . . . what was the question?'

'And your job. You're working, are you?'

'Yes. Sort of.'

'That's right. I remember. You produce, don't you? Radio?'

'Mm.'

'Yes, well that may explain it, then.'

'Might it?'

'Change. Revolution. The arrival of the market economy. It's no different, I imagine, from what's happened to those of us in the Health Service. Free-floating anxiety, that sort of thing, is it?'

'Absolutely, but I never imagined that would have anything to do with it. I mean you get used to change, don't you?'

'Like alcohol, food, and, ah, . . . sex, change is good in moderation. One can have too much of it.' Soames sucked the end of a drug company biro. 'I could offer you counselling but I can't see you going for that.'

'Oh, I don't mind. I'll try anything.'

'The alternative is . . . well, the new generation anti-depressants might help a little, but basically nobody has yet found a cure for sadness.'

'Counselling. Put me down for that.'

Soames opened a large desk diary and rocked backwards and forwards until he fixed the focal length of his eyesight onto the page. 'We have something of a waiting list. You're not intending suicide, are you?' He didn't look up.

'Not immediately.'

'Then I can't put you down as a priority.' He closed the book and smiled. 'Bear with it. We'll be in touch.'

'Thanks.' Maurice stood and slipped his jacket back on, Soames looked at him.

'Sadness is not necessarily a bad thing to feel. Believe me. Sadness, if you identify it correctly, is the converse of happiness. Depression is quite a different issue. Would you like me to prescribe you something?'

'No. That's fine. Thank you.' Maurice wanted to hug Dr Soames. He wanted to take him home and put him in an armchair by a raging fire, make him a milky drink and fetch his slippers.

'You could try a course of vitamins – cod liver oil – that sort of thing. It won't do you any harm: except I always find they make me belch foul fishy smells for much of the morning.'

'I'll try them.'

'Give it a week or so then come back and see me. If you do start to feel any worse come straight away. And don't worry about the drinking. Don't feel guilty about that as well.'

'OK.' Maurice hung by the chair for a second. 'Well, thanks.' He went out as Soames tried to read the next name on his patient list by holding the paper out at arm's length and squinting.

'Incidentally,' Soames said just as Maurice reached the door and opened it, 'how *is* your sex life?'

Maurice closed the door. 'Non-existent, really.'

'What about erection? Can you maintain an erection?'

'What, now?'

'No, in the usual . . . ah, course of things.'

'I've not really tried. There hasn't been much call for it recently.'

'Pop in to see the nurse on your way out. We'll have a specimen from you. Won't do any harm to check you out.'

Maurice went back to the reception desk and joined a short queue of curiously dank-smelling elderly women in tweed coats. Most of them were collecting repeat prescriptions which seemed to provoke a reflex in them to recall to the receptionist the symptoms of the condition that had first brought them there. When he reached the front of the queue, Maurice was sent back to the waiting room with a plastic number, green, and told to wait for the nurse. He picked up a two-year-old copy of *Cosmopolitan* to divert his mind from the worry of giving a specimen.

The nurse was young and antipodean, fresh in a very white smock and very very clean. Her den was papered with inoculation posters and postcards of Australia. The old wooden shelves were stacked with boxes of swabs and small bottles. Maurice was given a little plastic jar with a waxed paper label on it. 'There's a Jints beside the reception. Knock when you've finished.'

'Jints?'

'Jints lavatory.'

'Ah.'

The nurse waved a biro in the direction of the waiting room. Maurice slipped the bottle in his pocket and went out. Twenty minutes later, red-faced with exertion, he came back and knocked at the nurse's door.

'Mr Reid, I'd just about given up on you.' The nurse smiled and held out an envelope for Maurice to drop the specimen into. She was attractive, no nonsense, Maurice would have liked to take her to the cinema. She didn't look the sort who'd be happy to waste her evenings in a pub.

'Sorry.' Maurice closed the door behind him and took out his warm jar. 'There.' He held it out proudly.

The nurse put the envelope down and took the jar from him. She looked at it and coughed, though it could have been a stifled laugh.

'Is there not enough or something?' Maurice said wretchedly.

'It was a urine sample we were after, Mr Reid.'

'Urine,' Maurice repeated, swallowing dryly. 'Urine. Yes. I see.'

The nurse put the jar on the counter; it would have been inappropriate simply to have thrown it into the bin. But two cc's of sperm was of no use to anybody, however much labour had gone into providing it.

Warde was standing at the back of the studio cubicle and leaning against a tape machine as he looked through the programme script. The room was packed with the technical paraphernalia of radio: a long, sleek flight desk with thirty faders, hundreds of small coloured knobs, and two meters which registered the ferocity of the sound. Along the back wall were four substantial German tape machines, three state-of-the-art Swedish CD players and two record decks. There were also three computer screens with associated keyboards, and another one that was showing a number of cartoon fish swimming against a black background. To the right of the sound desk was a bank of telephones and a bay into which a number of blue cords were plugged. The room was air-conditioned, dimly lit, about fifteen feet wide and twelve feet deep, and had a wide triple-glazed window which looked into the empty studio – a room roughly the same size with only a blue baize table in it, laid with six microphones and six pairs of headphones, two six-foot-high acoustic screens on castors and a number of chairs. A window at the far end allowed those in the cubicle to see all the way through to the programme guests nervously sitting on the edge of the hospitality settees and sipping lukewarm coffee from poly-styrene cups.

The programme was due to begin in twenty minutes' time and Roy May, who was presenting it, still hadn't completed his journey to the basement from his office, ten floors above. Warde was diverting his anxiety by reading out Roy's spelling mistakes to his PA, an intelligent and hostile middle-aged woman called Beryl, and to the two studio managers: Barry, a grey-haired and elderly man in a tweed jacket, who had become increasingly dismayed and incompetent with age, and Jenny, who had just finished her training and was highly efficient but heavy-handedly over-enthusiastic with the machinery. Barry was sitting at the panel, Jenny was standing by the tape machines behind him.

'Here's one, Barry,' Warde said. 'Roy asked me for another word for hairy and I told him it was hirsute and the bloody idiot's written hair-chute.'

'Hair-chute,' Barry repeated. 'He wrote hair-chute, did he?'

'Yes he bloody did. Here's another . . .'

'Steady on. Full alert.'

As Roy May walked into the studio, Barry pressed the talkback key and said, 'Good afternoon, Roy.'

Through the glass they watched Roy wave as he deposited a pile of papers on the studio table, then pour himself a glass of water from a jug. He drank a little then, compressing his diaphragm with his right hand, belched loudly. 'All right for level, Barry?'

'Animal,' Beryl whispered to herself without looking up from the column of back timings she was adding up. Barry showed him the thumbs up as Roy pottered round the studio, moving the chairs at table and rearranging the four guests' microphones.

'I do wish he wouldn't do that,' Barry said. 'I've just set them up. Toddle in there and move them back, will you, Jenny darling.'

Jenny took a look at her row of tapes lined above the four machines, touched her script which she had put on the script rack, then took off her headphones and pushed through the heavy door to the studio. Roy was now seated and eating a sandwich as he corrected his script with a red felt-tipped pen. Barry opened the microphone as Jenny leaned over Roy, pushing his microphone back, and repositioning his clock.

'Nice perfume, pet,' Roy said, flustering Jenny who blushed, thanked him, and shrugged his hand off her back. 'I've changed the link into hair, Wardey. The cue's the same for the tape.'

'Fine, Roy,' Warde said over the talkback. 'I'd like to run through the top if you're ready.'

'Righty ho. Ready when you are.' Roy rubbed his hands briskly, laced his fingers and cracked his knuckles.

'All right, Barry?' Warde said.

'Certainly. We start with music, don't we? Do you have the gram set up, Jenny?'

Jenny, who had just crashed back through the door, was checking her tapes again. She switched her attention to her script. 'I thought he said "hello", first.'

'Oh,' Barry said, 'does he say hello? He doesn't say hello on my script.'

'Yes, he says hello,' Warde said. 'Then the music, then Roy starts talking after the fade at ten seconds. Keep it under. Let's go shall we?'

'Certainly. I'll just amend my script if you'll bear with me.' Barry reached down and lifted his scuffed tan briefcase onto the sound desk. He undid the clasps and took out a tupperware box of sandwiches, then a pencil case which he unzipped and poked his finger into. He drew out a blue crayon and squintingly examined the lead. 'So, Roy says "hello", does he? Then music.'

'I'm sorry, that's page two, love.' Beryl leaned across and patiently rearranged the script for him. The old schoolers always stuck together.

'Of course it is. Sorry. Sorry everybody. I seem to have my pages mixed up. Let me just rub this out.' Barry unzipped his pencil case again.

'Look,' Warde said. 'Can we just do it, please?' From the studio they heard Roy humming impatiently.

'Sorry. Sorry everybody. Whenever you like, Jenny.' After a brief pause, Barry craned round in his seat. 'Waiting for you, love. In your own time.'

'No, Roy says "hello", then I play the gram,' Jenny said.

'I'm sorry. I am sorry. Bear with me.' Barry laughed self-consciously. 'I'll give you a green light, Roy. Is it working? I'll just try it if I may.' Barry pressed the foot pedal and a small green bulb lit up on the table beside Roy's microphone. 'That's the one. Lovely. Right. Off we go then.' He pressed the talkback key. 'On my green then, Roy.'

Roy nodded.

'Oh forget it. Just bloody forget it, we'll busk it,' Warde said. 'I'm going for a slash. If I don't get back in time start without me.'

'Oh. Lovely. Time for another cuppa and a cake, then,' Barry said, opening his sandwich box. 'Anybody for a chocolate fancy?'

After visiting Dr Soames, Maurice decided it was too late to go back to work, and instead called in to see his ex-wife. Polly lived in Brixton with their four-year-old son Will and a woman called Val. She and Maurice had been separated for two years, and divorced for one, but Maurice still used the local doctor and dentist because he'd not yet got round to registering anywhere else. This, at least, was the reason he always gave to Polly. The truth, as they both well knew, was that one day he expected to be moving back home so there was little point in establishing himself anywhere else.

'Hello Pol,' Maurice said, holding out a bottle of white wine on the doorstep. Polly did not take it.

'What do you want?' Polly was wearing a long, rough woollen cardigan over a black T-shirt and faded Levis. Her black hair was considerably shorter than it had been when they were married. Maurice had always encouraged her to keep it long, Val however, liked it short. Polly was an attractive, attentive woman whose eyes radiated a smiling benevolence. She was slight and, although she was thirty-two, her precise age had always been difficult to estimate. She was ageing gracefully round the eyes and becoming more beautiful. Polly was the only genuinely kind person Maurice knew; and, as far as he knew, the only person she had ever hurt was him.

Maurice said, 'I've just been to the doc's. I thought I'd pop round on the off-chance, as I was in the neighbourhood. Thought I might read Will a bedtime story.'

'I wish you'd phoned.'

'Sorry. I just thought, you know, as I was in the neighbourhood.' Maurice already knew he was not going to be invited in.

'Yes, but you could have phoned. It's just rather awkward.' Polly reached out and rubbed his arm. 'You know how it is.'

'Yes. Fine. OK. Next time, then.' Maurice smiled wistfully, hung his head and began sulkily to walk away. Polly watched him go then looked over her shoulder into the hallway before pulling the door shut behind her. In four long strides she was beside him, hugging herself against the cold of the evening. The spectre of a wind rattled the branches of the street trees. A bus passed the end of the street, as absurdly bright in the dusk as a fairground carousel.

Maurice stopped. 'You'll catch your death. Here . . .' He unhooked his grey scarf and wrapped it round Polly's neck.

'You know it's not me,' Polly said. 'For me you could come in. I'd love for you to have tea with Will. It's just . . . well, we did talk about this, didn't we?'

'I know. I'm sorry. I just didn't, well, you know, as I was here . . .'

'Oh, Maurice,' Polly said fondly. 'I wonder when you'll start telling yourself the truth?'

'I do. Well, most of the time, anyway. But I never believe it. I mean I know I can't just turn up here. I know it's not on, but I tell myself that deep down you're quite pleased when I do: even though it makes things difficult with Val.' Then, after some consideration, 'Sorry.'

'Well, yes. Yes, I am pleased to see you, of course I am.' Polly stamped her feet against the cold. 'But you know how it is.'

'And how is Val?'

'Busy,' Polly said as though his question had been provoked by genuine interest rather than politeness. 'They're giving her a contract. Twenty-four pieces a year – guaranteed. Feature stuff.'

'Good. Good. I saw her thing on body-piercing. Was that her in the photo?'

'Yes.'

'How does she go to the toilet?'

'It's quite hygienic.'

'Is it?'

'Look, I'm sorry . . . I must . . .' Polly took a step back towards the house.

'Yes, 'course. Tell you what, have the wine anyway.'

'Don't be silly.'

'No. Go on.' Maurice forced it between her crossed arms. 'Tell Val you nipped out for it. Something to celebrate. Go on.'

'You are silly.'

'It's not rubbish. It cost me nearly seven quid.'

'Thanks.' They waited, looking at each other with a deep-seated fondness. Polly kissed Maurice on the cheek. He felt the contact deep in the pit of his stomach. She tied his scarf back around his neck and tucked it into his jacket.

'Go in. You'll freeze out here.' Maurice ushered her away; he could smell her perfume on the wool at his throat.

Polly began to walk backwards towards the house. 'Why did you have to see Soames?'

Maurice pointed towards his trouser fly. 'Todger talk.'

'Are you all right?'

'Yes.'

'Seriously?'

'Nothing serious.' Maurice saw Polly's front door open and his look alerted Polly to turn round. Val stood on the doorstep with her arms crossed. When Polly turned back Maurice was almost at the end of the street, his shoulders hunched against the cold.

Maurice was still thinking of Polly the following morning when Warde came into his office without knocking. 'Why is it always so bloody dark in your office?' he said and flicked the switch. Nothing happened.

'I like it dark. That way people don't come in uninvited. Anyway the bulb's gone.' Maurice looked round from his computer screen. The cursor blinked impatiently, wanting more. Warde leaned his drainpipe jeans against Maurice's cluttered table, brushed back his hair and smiled desolately. He was wearing his leather greaser's jacket.

'I'm sending an e-mail to "facilities" about my light bulb,' Maurice explained.

'Sorry. I didn't realise you were that busy.'

'These things are important. People don't think they are. But they are. It's the details that count.' He took a sip from a cup of cold black coffee.

'Well, what have you said?'

'Read it if you like. It's only a draft.' Maurice wheeled his chair aside, Warde craned his neck towards the text.

'I think it could be a bit more terse. Maybe a bit more ironic.'

'You don't think irony would be wasted?'

'Never wasted. Never. Shall I have a bash?'

'Go on then.'

Warde typed standing up and without looking at his fingers. Maurice watched him enviously. 'I thought your team were doing the programme this week.'

'We are. Lardhead's studio-producing so I'm letting him get on with it. Did you hear yesterday?'

'I heard the piece on set-aside.'

'What did you think?'

'It was all right. I wasn't really listening. Too many facts in it, perhaps. I lost concentration.'

'Mm . . . there.' Warde pressed the send key and 'Message Sent Successfully' flashed onto the screen. 'Oh sorry, did you want to read it?'

The phone rang. Maurice picked it up, then passed it to Warde. 'Lardhead,' he said.

'He doesn't like what? . . . No, we haven't got anything else. Look, just tell him if we don't run the sheep feature he'll have to have that five-minute column from the Welsh twat. That'll shut him up . . . right . . . no, I'll be up in a minute.' Warde put the phone down. 'Roy's being difficult. He doesn't want the piece on sheep.'

'It's awful. I heard it last week. I wouldn't use it. Give it to Elaine, she'll run anything.'

'I know, but we spent all yesterday afternoon putting farting noises behind the baas, and Lardy's mixed in some music: "Picketywitch". Roy likes "Picketywitch". It has absolutely no relevance to the piece but Lardy's made it sound as though it's coming from a tranny in the middle of a field. He's a genius. I know you think he's an idiot, but you just have to engage his attention. Anyway, we're running a farming theme this week so we have to have something. Wait a minute.' Warde picked up the phone and dialled. 'Lardy? Listen, did you tell Roy about the farting? . . . Of course you should, that's the whole point, he just wants to feel in on it . . . The column? Yes, it's in my office, on the shelf over the desk in the blue tray, it's marked "Welsh twat" . . . Yes, I think there's an edit in it. Right.'

'So what else is going on?' Maurice said.

'Nothing. Oh yes, did you see the new minority logging forms?'

'Somewhere.' Maurice poked through his wastepaper basket.

'Apparently they're doing a limb count: you're only allowed so many contributors a week with four fully functioning limbs. After that you have to make up the numbers with the partially abled. Equal Ops. That's how I read it anyway. I'm designing a new form. I'll send you a copy.'

'Ta.'

The door opened and two men in overalls walked in, each carrying a light bulb.

'Catch you later,' Warde said.

'I doubt it.' Maurice said.

On his way to the tea bar, Maurice passed Elaine in the corridor. Like Maurice and Warde, she was responsible for overseeing a small team of junior producers. She was clutching a sodden mass of bloodied tissues.

'What's up?' Maurice said, but kept on walking, pretending to be in a hurry.

'Phil's fallen over and cut his head.'

'Lardhead?'

'I think he'll need stitches.'

Maurice slowed then stopped. Elaine had that effect on him. She always made him feel like a juvenile in her schoolmarmy way and was undoubtedly wiser, nicer, and much more mature than he was even though she was only four years older. She wore cardigans and unfashionable jeans, and exuded a rosy sexuality that was picked up only by those men who were over thirty. Elaine's fair hair was tinted and cut in a bob and she wore black-rimmed glasses. Her eyes peered pensively from behind the lenses.

'Stitches?' Maurice said.

'Hello,' Elaine waved, 'anybody there?'

'Sorry, I was just thinking . . .'

Elaine leaned against the corridor wall, making a cushion of her hands.

Maurice said, 'Is everybody completely messed up?' Then he wondered where the train of thought had come from. Not quite knowing, he nevertheless pressed on, 'Or is it just me? I mean you're not.'

'What's the matter? Has something happened with Polly?'

'No. Nothing like that. It's just that . . . I think it's my ego or something.'

'Yes?'

'I think it's got some disease which has made it swell up. Like a prostate gland. But not all the time. It just means I want to be the centre of attention, and if I'm not I'm not interested.'

'Hence your lack of interest in Phil?'

'In anybody. Everybody, except perhaps Will. Polly most of the time. And occasionally, well, a few others.'

'Are you still living with . . . Tracey, is it?'

'Dawn. On and off. Off at the moment. I'm still in her flat, but it was off when she left for Brazil so I suppose . . . God, I bore myself sometimes with what I'm saying. Do you?'

'No. I only listen to other people.'

'That's because you're humane. You make people think you care about them.'

'I do. So do you. Shall we have lunch?' Elaine said.

'Yes.'

'Today?'

'Yes, sure.' Maurice racked his brains for an excuse. He enjoyed Elaine's company, but since he had temporarily escaped from the rigours of a daily programme, he had become a hermit. The longer he spent alone in his office, the less he found himself capable of mixing. When Warde was on leave he sometimes went for three or four days without speaking to anybody at all. He liked sitting in the dark and he didn't mind communicating with people by e-mail. But he left his voicemail switched on to intercept his telephone calls and he approached his mail with trepidation. He avoided all meetings.

'I'll see you outside the canteen, then. Say 12.45?'

'Fine.' Maurice began to move off. 'I suppose I do care about people. I mean I'm not completely cold-hearted. Say if Phil died or something, I think I would care.'

'Good.'

But it wouldn't make me cry, Maurice thought. As an afterthought he asked, 'How's your mum?'

'No better I'm afraid,' Elaine said, and was instantly on the verge of tears.

'I'm sorry.' Maurice had forgotten Elaine's aged mother was in the process of slowly dying.

He spent the rest of the morning going through the local papers looking for stories and found two headlines for Warde's amusement: 'BRADFORD MAN FOUND IN VAN' and 'FERRET CONMAN STRIKES AGAIN'. As evidence of his morning's industry, he scattered the remnants of the papers over his office floor, then spent the next hour reading a novel. At midday the voicemail light began blinking on his telephone and when he listened to the message he found it was reception alerting him that his 'contributor' had arrived. Shortly afterwards he was meeting a small overweight man in a linen suit as he came out of the lift. 'Going up,' the empty lift said to itself. The doors remained open. 'Mind the doors please,' the lift chided. An alarm began to beep. 'Going up. This lift is out of service.' The doors slid shut and the lift went down. A few seconds later Maurice heard it touting for business at the floor below.

'Hello, Professor,' Maurice said, holding out his hand. The professor transferred his briefcase, a folder of papers and a newspaper to his left armpit and they shook hands. The action loosened the wad beneath his arm and the papers spilled onto the corridor floor. The professor's short-sightedness manifested itself in a grinning squint which looked as if it might have been caused by his ears being tied together behind his head.

When they had retrieved the papers Maurice led him to the office making polite small talk about the regularity of the train service from Oxford. The professor gamely joined in. He was habitually enthusiastic and well-informed about everything, and everything received the same weight of scrutiny. All Maurice had to do was introduce a subject and for the following ten minutes the professor would launch into a detailed analysis of it. To prompt him through the rare pauses, Maurice chipped in an occasional 'Oh, really?', or a 'Yes, I thought that myself.'

'Did you get the script?' the professor said, sitting untidily in the spare chair in Maurice's office.

'Yes, it's ah . . .' Maurice glanced at the pile of papers in his bin, then remembered he'd put the unopened envelope beneath his in-tray. 'Very good,' he said, 'very good indeed.'

The professor said, 'Do you mind if we have a light on?'

'Sorry,' Maurice said. 'Bulb's gone. Sit by the door if you need to read.' With his left hand he shuffled through a sheaf of papers on his desk, camouflaging his right hand slitting open the envelope which was clamped between his knees. 'Yes, I thought, here it is. I thought it was fine.'

The professor pulled out his own copy from an envelope. 'How is it for time?'

'Fine,' Maurice weighed the sheaf in his palm. 'I made it about fifteen, maybe a bit longer.'

'Yes. I thought a little longer. I timed it twice.'

Maurice realised he'd forgotten his part of the ritual. The old man was fishing for compliments. 'I thought it was excellent. I particularly like the bit about . . .' Having forgotten the subject of the professor's talk, he opened it, and with a pretence at quoting him correctly read out a random sentence. 'Yes, here we are. *"And of course Laing's belief in the way we educate our children is paramount to the way in which we understand how he was educated. Differentiation between driving children mad, and simply driving them towards a given goal presupposes . . ."* '

'Yes,' the professor cut in, 'there's a repetition, isn't there? *Way*, way is repeated. I was trying to keep it loose, as you suggested. You told me to write less literally. Does it matter, do you think?'

'No. Not at all. Anyway, we'd better get down to the studio, hadn't we?' Maurice stood up and followed the professor out of the office.

'Incidentally, I haven't received payment for my last talk,' the professor said as they passed a series of large framed photographs of radio's famous faces. Roy May was the last in line with his dissolute smile and drinker's tan.

'When did we record it?' Maurice said.

'Oh, four, perhaps five months ago.'

'Early days yet, then, I'll give Contracts a ring.'

'And has it been transmitted yet?'

'Of course it has,' Maurice lied, wondering whether, during his last office clear-out, he'd accidentally thrown the transmission tape into the recycling bin.

'Yes. Oh, yes. There was just one other . . . Did you get a chance to have a look at the proposal I sent you?'

'Remind me.'

'Clerihews? A short series . . . the history?'

'Oh, yes. Very promising, I thought . . . I've passed it on to . . . ah . . .'

They disappeared round the corner of the corridor. Roy May's bloodshot eyes seemed to follow them as they went.

TWO

'ROOM FOR A little one?' Roy May forced his chair between Maurice and Elaine who were sitting knee to knee because the peculiar acoustic of the canteen made normal conversation almost impossible. In places it was easier to hear somebody sitting thirty feet away than one's immediate neighbour. Roy went away then came back with his tray of food. Having recently replaced an addiction to alcohol with one which involved eating huge quantities of carbohydrates, his plate was loaded accordingly. Roy was wearing his cream jacket, a white shirt, too small at the collar, and a striped school tie. He had been good-looking once, and still considered himself to be so. His best features were his lush, side-parted grey hair and roguish smile. His least endearing trait, and the one which date-stamped him most precisely, was his inclination to wink at the whisper of a double entendre.

Roy May began his career presenting a midday show on Radio Thames, a pirate radio ship, which was, in the mid-1960s, moored in the Thames Estuary. His irreverence was as refreshing then as it would become irritating later. When the stations were closed down and most of his fellow pirates came home and were absorbed into the establishment, Roy

May made his first career mistake. Rather than following his shipmates to shore to join the BBC, he held out for six months on one of the few ships still broadcasting. When finally the transmitter was also switched off there, he discovered that while the establishment had been happy to pardon the first wave of ersatz outlaws, those who had held out were considered to be genuine rather than opportunistic radicals, hence unemployable. The money he had saved (or not spent on binges ashore) was squandered on LSD, bourbon and kaftans and loon pants from King's Road boutiques with names like 'Granny Takes a Trip'. He spent much of the period that was later tagged 'the summer of love' getting high, coming down and, in between, very paranoid.

In 1969 he dried out, came down without going up again, and served a brief spell at the BBC on 'Where It's At!', supplementing his curriculum vitae sufficiently to lead to a job offer in Australia: Roy May became the Bloke from Blighty, the morning DJ on 'Good Morning Sydney'. The Australians took Roy May to their hearts. They liked him because the Brits didn't and because he seemed to have heart. He wasn't a ponce or a poofter, he didn't flaunt his wealth and he married an Australian girl. He was one of them. But Roy soon became bored of expat life and, convinced by his agent that he had strong career prospects at home, returned with his wife (Caz) and an accent now an unattractive cocktail of mid-Atlantic and Australian. But his agent had misjudged the market. The national radio stations wouldn't take him on, even for the graveyard shifts, which left him no other option but to sign up with a local radio station in the Midlands. With a rare display of humour he christened his afternoon phone-in programme 'Good Afternoon Sidney' and, again, built a respectable, if uncritical, audience. His strength lay in a demotic ability to talk to 'the punters' at their own level. It was imagined that this required a certain degree of skill, whereas, for Roy, it was the level at which he most comfortably operated.

Television finally sent for Roy May. Newsreading stints were followed by regional magazine programmes in which his ability to talk to the people without patronising them was noticed by a network controller who brought him in to co-host a weekday, later promoted to an early Saturday evening, 'people show'. Hearts were broken and tears were shed. Roy's shoulder was cried on even more regularly when he discovered the art of self-disclosure. His roots (working-class; father a steel-worker, mother a seamstress; poor but honest) were promoted in the *Sunday Mirror* and he began to earn in a week what many of his 'people' earned in a year.

Then the press got hold of a story about Roy May's hotel room liaison with an under-age girl. It was rumoured that money was spent on the girl and the Sunday paper, losing its only witness, did not publish. But Roy was considered too much of a risk for a family show and fired. For three years he opened the occasional supermarket or car showroom with the Dagenham Girl Pipers, was given a syndicated column in the *Yorkshire News*, and lived on the money that, this time, Caz had wisely invested. Then he was rediscovered by independent television. The floppy suits controlling the networks were now being worn by the middle-class sons and daughters of the families that had, in their millions, watched Roy every Saturday night. So he was again fêted, but this time with irony. And though he was wanted for what he had been rather than who he now was, Roy didn't care. It was regular work.

Which inevitably led to his current career in radio. Radio, of course, being the medium that breaks the careers that TV makes, and then catches those who fall (a sad, forgiving lover who loses her finest for the best years of their lives, then welcomes them back without a word of complaint). This was the latest incarnation of the man who was sitting next to Maurice, trying to eat, talk, flirt with Elaine, listen to Maurice and read his interview briefs at the same time.

'Anyway, I think I'm a serial quitter,' Maurice said. 'I give up for about six months of every year, living through complete hell, then I start again. I don't know why I bother. I think I've knocked it on the head this time though.'

'You were smoking last night,' Elaine corrected him gently.

'Yes, but night doesn't count. Pubs, anyway. You can't be expected to drink and not smoke. It's just not possible. You used to smoke, didn't you, Roy?'

Roy looked up from his plate and cupped his hand to his ear. Maurice repeated the question.

'Yes, all the vices, me. I had them all in spades, mate. In spades. But no longer. Clean as a whistle.' Roy patted his heart and breathed in deeply. 'Caz has put us on a new fitness regime. Low fat. I'm supposed to be eating a dry white roll and a bloody banana. I need my blood sugar building up. You can't do a show on a banana.'

'My mother never smoked,' Elaine said, laying down her yoghurt spoon. 'But she's dying of cancer. It's unfair. It's so unfair when . . .'

Maurice knew what she was going to say before she stopped herself, but Roy didn't. 'I didn't know your mother was ill, love.'

'Yes you did.' Elaine sighed. 'I've told you often enough.'

'That's right, that's right. I'm sorry.' Roy waved his fork round his ear. 'Too much going on. What about you, Maurice? Still poncing about making documentaries about dead poets?'

'No. I've finished all that.'

'So what are you doing?'

'Paperwork. Contracts, catching up on my mail. That sort of thing. You wouldn't believe the paperwork we have to do. All electronically, of course, but paperwork nevertheless. Of course the system is down for much of the day so all you can do is twiddle your thumbs. I'd like to be more busy, obviously, but that's how it's panned out.'

'Skiving then,' Roy said.

'Absolutely. Coffee?' Maurice said, standing up.

'I'll have a camomile tea,' Elaine said.

'Cup of Tetley. Leave the bag in. And bring me a couple of those pink low-calorie sweetener things, will you?'

When Maurice was out of earshot Roy said to Elaine, 'I'm sorry. I couldn't get away.'

'You could have called.'

'I couldn't. We had people round. Some bloody vegetarian friend of the missus.'

'What about tonight?'

'Not tonight. I'm doing a dinner in Swindon: computer do. Thousand quid. Taxi there, hotel for the night. That reminds me, I must write a speech. Any ideas?'

'A few,' Elaine said.

'Tomorrow, maybe.'

'No. I can't do tomorrow,' Elaine lied. 'I'm going out.'

'Are you?'

'Yes. Maurice is taking me to the cinema.'

'Right.' Roy looked over at Maurice who was standing in the till queue talking to the man behind him. His hands occupied in balancing the stacked beverages, Maurice was pointing towards Roy with his elbow. When he saw Roy had seen him he blushed. 'He's a smart-arse, that lad is. Typical bloody university ponce.'

'We all are.'

31

'No. He's different, him and Wardy. Think they know it all. I know they take the piss out of me behind my back.'

'They don't.'

'Course they do. I was in the bog yesterday and I heard them talking. Do you know what they called me?'

'I'm sure they weren't talking about you, Roy.'

'His Fadingness.'

Elaine snorted.

'Yes, very funny. Well I'll bloody have him one day.' Something came in to Roy's eyes that Elaine thought the girl in the hotel room might have seen. She had heard that the girl had been beaten quite badly. But it was just a rumour.

'Tetley.' Maurice put the tea in front of Roy who stared for a split second, then smiled.

'Ta.'

Maurice distributed the rest.

'I'll tell you something,' Roy said, pointing his knife towards his papers. 'Whoever's supposed to be doing these interview briefs wants a rocket put up them. It's absolute codswallop. I'm not interested in where this woman went to school, I want to know what she's going to say. It's all right for you lot, it's my bollocks on the line, not yours.'

'Next page,' Elaine said, carefully turning the paper over and squaring the pages together. 'Here: outline questions. Phil's very good with his notes.'

'Good,' Roy said, eating and reading. 'Well maybe the others could learn a thing or two from him.'

'How is Lardhead then. Still bleeding?' Maurice said.

'No. He's all right. Warde's making him do the programme. They should have sent him home.'

'What about the sheep piece then, Roy?'

'It's crap,' Roy said without looking up.

'Even the . . . you know.'

'Bloody schoolboy jokes, you mean?'

32

'Yes.'

'You lot want to get out into the real world. Get yourselves a proper job rather than fart-arsing around in studios half the day.' A projectile of minced meat from the wad in his mouth skimmed Maurice's ear.

'Proper job?' Maurice said.

'You don't know you're born.'

'Christ. You sound like my father, Roy.'

'You've got a father then, have you?' Roy said, through another mouthful of lasagne.

Elaine laughed but Maurice didn't.

'Joking,' Roy said. 'Just joking.'

Maurice excused himself and went for an afternoon nap wondering what was wrong with Roy. He was usually such an easy target.

'Em . . .' A cough. 'Em . . . I wonder if you could just . . .'

Maurice woke up. Due to the elasticity of sleep time he didn't know how long he had slept. It was dark, therefore probably night, but somebody was standing next to him and it wasn't Polly, Dawn or even William. His right leg was still asleep and seemed to be suspended higher than his head. His dream had been the familiar one: a lift carrying him to the basement of a building, the doors sliding open to reveal a darkness, complete as the silence, then his walking slowly and fearfully into the unknown. Once, in the far reaches of this place he had found William. Once he had stumbled over a body. Once he had walked through the night and come out the other side into the dawn.

Maurice's feet were resting on his desk. It was twenty to three. But it was always twenty to three in Maurice's office, the clock having broken. Vincent Edwards was standing at the door.

'Sorry,' Maurice said. He wiped his eyes and found them to be moist.

'Forgive me for disturbing your slumbers, Reid.' Edwards was called 'Peculiar' for no good reason anybody could remember. He was tall, graceful and given to vagueness; many of his pronouncements tailed off with a camp wave of his hand. He wore immaculately cut pin-striped suits, expensive shirts with gold cufflinks and highly polished black brogues. 'Peculiar' was the programme's editor. It was rumoured that he was a plant from MI5.

'That's all right. I was just . . . thinking really,' Maurice said with what he hoped was sufficient artistic whimsy. He lowered his legs painfully to the floor then knelt and began massaging his calf. 'Working up some proposals. I'm quite keen to do a series of Clerihews.'

'I see the light bulb situation hasn't rectified itself.'

'No. I'm waiting for a "Sparks" apparently. It's impossible to work in this darkness. Terrible headaches all the time.'

'Yes. You could, perhaps, open the blinds. I understand you have access to the balcony and a view of Portland Place which most of my producers find quite conducive to their endeavours.' Peculiar hovered. He seemed to be about to go. Maurice relaxed, not a bollocking after all.

'No, you see, opening the blinds would just be admitting defeat. It's the principle, really.'

'Actually it was the light bulb situation I wanted to discuss with you. I thought I should . . . It actually relates to your e-mail.'

'Oh, yes. Sorry,' Maurice said, then again. 'Sorry.' He hadn't read the e-mail before Warde had sent it off and could only imagine the worst.

'Yes. That language, hardly appropriate for an internal memo: even to that gentleman.'

'Yes, I am sorry, I didn't mean to send it. It was more of a draft really. Then, before I knew it, the bloody thing sent itself. I called computer support but they couldn't find a bug . . . I think I must have . . . in the dark, you know . . .'

'Are you all right, Reid?' Peculiar was looking at him with a pinched intensity.

'Yes, fine. Well, tired . . .' Maurice blinked. There was something in his eyes: tiredness burdened his thoughts. 'Probably a fashionable new disease they haven't come up with an acronym for yet.'

Peculiar offered him an immaculate handkerchief and Maurice wiped away his tears.

'I have to say I'm concerned about you.'

'Are you? Why?'

'You haven't taken any leave for a while.'

'Yes. I had three days in . . . at home, that was . . .'

'Three months ago.'

'You've been checking?'

'Yes.'

'I see.' Maurice knew he was in more trouble than he had first thought. Peculiar had no patience for human frailties; no discernible humanity. His concern always camouflaged ulterior motives.

'I've also been looking at your productivity.'

'Yes, I think I can explain that,' Maurice said, forgetting for a moment whose handkerchief it was and emptying his sinuses into it.

'I must say, for a producer who spends so much time in this building, I would be intrigued to be offered some explanation as to your . . . execrable productivity.'

'No, you see . . . you see, well,' Maurice suddenly stood up as though he was going to give a lecture. He ushered Peculiar into the room, looked up and down the corridor, then closed the door. 'I've been working something up on the sly. I think I may have come up with rather a good story.

35

It's . . . it's . . .' Maurice sat down as suddenly as he had stood up. 'Oh God.'

Peculiar laid a hand on his shoulder homosexually. 'Maurice, I'm not here to give you a dressing down.'

'Aren't you?'

'I know you've been going through something of a fallow period. That's understandable.'

'I thought we didn't have those any more.'

'Just take some leave. Go away somewhere. A month. A reasonable period of recuperation.'

'God, you make it sound as though I'm going . . . tonto or something.'

'Call it what you will. I'm signing you off as of a week Friday.'

'Right . . . thanks.'

'Come and see me before you go. And, ah, box your books up will you, I might need the office space.' Peculiar opened the door, but even the meagre corridor light was too much, and Maurice was forced to squint.

'You're not firing me, are you?'

'Of course not. Of course not,' Peculiar said, sizing up the office as he went out.

At 5.15 p.m., Maurice, Elaine and Warde went to the Gluepot together, a cigarette-fogged Victorian pub two minutes' walk from work. Actors used it, and city types. It was comfortable as an old coat; dark, and suitably womblike: a music hall place of gaslight shadows, ghosts and warm beer. Elaine, soon halfway down her second gin of the evening, was keeping Maurice company. He was slumped morosely on the bar over his pint, his elbows soaking up the spilled beer like a wick. Warde was playing pinball to an audience of three cheaply power-dressed office girls, Roy was already

36

there, holding court to nine or ten eager faces round the two small circular tables that had been pushed together by the door. He was doing a trick with a matchbox and a feather.

'They can't fire me, can they?' Maurice said.

'No, of course they can't.' Elaine had mellowed and reddened with the drink. She had taken off her cardigan and was watching Roy fondly.

Maurice was also watching Roy, but less fondly. 'He's a cretin, isn't he?'

'I like him. I like his . . . straightforwardness. He's different with women.'

'So I've heard. He's a symptom of just how far down the pan this place has gone.'

'I used to think like you. Then I began to realise how out of touch we were.'

'No,' Maurice said. 'It's not a question of being out of touch. You have to set the agenda, not follow it slavishly with idiots like Roy.'

'We can't go on making programmes that nobody wants to listen to.'

'Why not?' Maurice drained his drink; a lace doily of foam was left folded in the glass. 'It's never concerned us before.'

'Because we have to be accountable. I don't know anybody who listens to the radio as much as they watch the television.'

'Not the point, Elaine. Not the point at all. Anyway, politicians listen. And captains of industry. Anybody whose chum might be on.'

Warde sauntered over, rolling a cigarette in liquorice paper.

'You don't listen to the radio, do you?' Maurice said.

'Of course I do. Within reason. That's not the point, though.' Warde picked up on the familiar theme. 'Radio is like wallpaper. You're not aware of it unless it's not there.

It's a secondary activity, as I believe I was reading recently in a rather splendid pamphlet written by Peculiar.' Warde lodged the cigarette into the corner of his mouth and lit it with the petrol flame of a chrome lighter. Elaine reached over and took it out of his mouth. She licked the end and began toking on it.

'Anyway,' Maurice said, 'apparently we're suffering from the decline of the cohort effect. I mean if we do listen it's because we were conditioned by our parents listening to the Home Service. The druggy, clubby new generation were brought up on Radio Wonderful so they're only interested in music. We're in a dying profession, like mining and fishing. Perhaps they'll preserve the building and we can conduct tours round the basement studios wearing pith helmets and carrying canaries in cages.'

Warde slipped his tobacco pouch from his back pocket and dextrously, one-handed, rolled another cigarette. Maurice lit up his third of the hour from the packet of ten Camel Lights propped in a pool of beer on the bar. They smoked for a while in battlefront camaraderie, the chemicals loosening their precarious hold on the present. Elaine looked sexy when she smoked. Warde's performance merely enhanced his innate cool. Maurice smoked like a condemned man. They were all watching Roy.

'Still,' Maurice said, 'it's all changing, isn't it. They've done some market research. Now they know how many people listen to the radio when they're conducting a range of activities. Grouting, for example. We score very highly with people grouting the bathroom.'

'Hence the wholesale change in the schedule,' Warde said.

Elaine drained her drink. 'Can we talk about something else? I came out to get away from talking about the bloody Corporation.'

'I wonder who first decided to strip their floors?' Maurice said. 'Or wear a white T-shirt under a shirt?'

'Or wear a shirt without tucking it in?' Warde added.

'Or wear a shirt without a collar?' Maurice said. 'I suppose that next, people, men probably, will start wearing their underpants over their trousers. Or just not tuck anything in at all. Or, alternatively, and this is probably the most likely, start tucking clothes in inappropriately. Sweaters, for example, into trousers.'

'Trousers into socks,' Warde said.

The activity at Roy's table resolved into a flurry of pats, handshakes and goodbyes as Roy extricated himself from his audience. A uniformed chauffeur had arrived to take him to Swindon. Elaine excused herself and went off in the direction of the Ladies. Maurice, in the bar mirror, saw her make a last minute detour and leave the pub by a side door. Roy came over and said goodbye to Warde, slapping him on the shoulder.

'I might be late tomorrow, mate,' Roy said. 'Squared it with Vincent. Don't worry. I've got the notes.' He patted his jacket pocket.

Maurice waited for the same, the usual signal of being a part of Roy's inner circle. He fixed a smile on his face in preparation and worked up a rejoinder, but Roy turned his back and walked out.

'Bastard,' Maurice said.

'What?' Warde waved as Roy got to the door, turned smartly on his heels and saluted the room.

'Nothing.'

Maurice's disquiet solidified into anger and then self-loathing. When Elaine came back in two pints later he'd annoyed Warde sufficiently to provoke him into taking Roy's place at the table. Maurice watched Hardiman brush cigarette ash from the stool before Warde sat down, then hunker forwards when he began talking.

'Shall we sit down?' Elaine said, running her right hand lightly through her hair. The top button of her blouse was undone. Something had ignited her eyes.

'I'm not sitting with that lot.'

'Why not, darling?' Elaine leaned her head on his shoulder and looked at the image of the two of them in the bar mirror, though Maurice knew it wasn't he she saw herself with. Her red lipstick shone bright through the cigarette smoke.

'They don't want me. That's why. And don't call me "darling".'

'Darling,' Elaine said, nibbling his ear.

'Pack it in.' Maurice tried to brush her away.

'What's the matter, Maurice, am I giving you a stiffy?'

'You are, as a matter of fact. For God's sake, woman, what's got into you?'

'Nothing, yet.' She licked her lips like a chocolate advert and winked lasciviously.

'Listen, you're dealing with a man who's not had sex with anybody, including himself, for over a month. Well, with one exception. So watch it.'

'A month?'

'Yes. I've decided to become celibate. Well, not so much decided, it's more or less been foisted on me. I can't even get myself interested in myself. That's how bad it's got.'

'That's what's wrong with you,' Elaine diagnosed. 'You need a good seeing to.'

'I don't. I'm not interested in sex. I've decided to become an aesthete.'

'Even aesthetes have sex,' Warde said, coming to the bar after seeing that Maurice needed his help.

'Not this one, matey. Not me. Look, Elaine. I've got to go.'

'Coward,' Elaine said.

'I don't know what's got into you. I really don't.' Maurice picked up his briefcase and his cigarettes and walked out, ignoring the half-hearted farewells from Roy's table.

Maurice lurched to the tube station, humming. He was drunker than he'd thought, then realised that he'd drunk five pints of strong lager in an hour and a half, which accounted for it. It was raining. He meandered from café canopy to recessed doorway, waited for a while, then weaved onwards. The traffic swished past, rippling the yellow streetlights that gilded the gutter puddles. Maurice stopped to light another cigarette, wasting three matches as the night breeze snatched the flame away. He reached the steps of the underground and encountered the warmth and light escaping from its open mouth. He walked cautiously down the damp, steel-edged steps, slipped across the booking hall floor and bought a ticket from the machine. He fell in love before he reached the barrier with a woman in a short black skirt and long boots (all it took was a smile), then again with the woman he was standing behind on the down escalator: until, when they reached the bottom, he saw it was a man.

Maurice fell in love at least a hundred times a day. He knew that if only once he could find someone to reciprocate it, he'd never have to fall in love again. As it was he spent almost his entire life tortured by unconsummated and unreciprocated desire. Each jolt to his heart or his libido was followed by a cartoon of the life he would lead with each of the women he saw. With the black-booted woman, he was following her to a delicatessen counter pushing a loaded supermarket trolley. They shared the same taste in wine and light snacks, the woman was buying food for the dinner party they had planned with the nice couple from down the road.

In his daydream the woman swung her head to look at him, frankly and with sexual longing. Maurice's fantasies rarely strayed far from a domestic setting.

Maurice had loved Polly almost comprehensively, but she no longer loved him. Polly loved a woman so Maurice knew the hope of getting her back was remote. He often wondered if Polly had married him in an attempt to put herself back on the straight and narrow. In their most heated arguments this was his favourite line of attack. She claimed she hadn't. She married him because she loved him. But not enough. Val, she loved more than enough, as Maurice discovered when he arrived home early one day and found them on the kitchen floor together: performing cunnilingus complicatedly on each other. The kitchen table was coated in flour imprinted by buttock marks. They were both lightly coated with it.

Maurice tried to ignore the drunken tramp on the tube who pushed his beery face close and asked him for change. When the man launched into an implausible story about losing his wallet, Maurice feigned deafness. The man leaned towards the office junior on his left and repeated the story.

Maurice arrived home, let himself into the flat and, pausing to remove only his trousers and his shoes, dropped exhaustedly onto the bed. Something moved beside him. He heard a small sleep groan, felt a readjustment in the sheets, and found an arm flung loosely across his waist. Then, cutting through the stench of stale cigarettes on his shirt, he smelt the fresh, familiar smell of Dawn. He closed his eyes contentedly and slept cradled in her arms.

THREE

'MAURICE, YOU DON'T live here any more,' Dawn said, when he woke the following morning and found her staring at him. Her arm was triangulated by the line from her brow to her shoulder, her right hand lost in the dark tangle of her long hair. She was deeply tanned and naked; her breasts lay cappuccino and mocha above the white sheet.

'I can explain that,' Maurice said, pushing tentatively through the final veils of sleep.

'I'm sure you can't. But let's hear you try.' Dawn smiled indulgently.

'All right. But first let me clean my teeth.' Maurice stood, swayed unsteadily, then made it to the door where he clung to the frame.

'Make me a coffee.' Dawn rolled onto her back and stretched her legs. They rose suddenly and remarkably from the sheets like dolphins from the sea. Her tan was uninterrupted by bikini marks. 'I bought some back. From Brazil. Like in the song.' She cycled in the air.

'Fine.' The irritating tune insinuated itself into his brain where it would remain all day.

'And for heaven's sake, either take your socks, knickers

43

and shirt off, or put some trousers on. You look like a civil servant on his lunch break.'

'A what?' The song performed its first encore. 'Anyway, they're not knickers. They're boxers.'

'Doesn't matter. Just make me some coffee. Black. And bring me my cigarettes, will you. And stop looking at me like that.' Unexerted, Dawn stopped cycling, rolled onto her side and began scissoring her right leg into the air.

'Must I?' Maurice said as the bowstring of his libido stretched taut.

'You'll make a disgusting old man, Maurice. Hanging round playgrounds, trying to look up girls' skirts on buses, leaning just a little too close on the tube.'

'I do that already. Does it only become disgusting when you're old?'

'No, it only becomes disgusting when it is disgusting. It's all in the intent.'

'The intent's always the same. Old men can't help their sex drive. They can't help being old, either. I mean, it's pointless pretending you don't find women attractive. It's just more . . . are you sure I've moved out?'

'Yes. Absolutely. Anyway, I'm not taking on any more lost causes. I've decided to change my life.'

'Again?'

'Properly this time.'

Maurice had arrived as the result of Dawn's last change. They happened, on average, every three years. Dawn had lived with a rock singer in a Gothic mansion but left because she had become bored by him. She had lived with a penniless writer and deserted him before he bored of her, even though she claimed it broke her heart (a brittle organ, in constant need of surgery). Her impulsive trip to Brazil had been financed by a Dutch businessman she had met in a London club. The businessman's wife was part of the deal somehow, but Maurice was afraid to ask how. Dawn lived for change in the way the children of the rich do: her father's fortune underwrote the constant risk of failure.

Maurice pushed open the door of the lavatory, lifted the lid in deference to Dawn's return, reached forwards to lean his weight against the tiled wall, then, with his body cantilevered forward at an angle of forty-five degrees tried to empty his bladder. The first trickle pattered onto the foam in the basin, then he felt a contraction in the area of his prostate and the stream stopped. He tried again and managed to expel another millilitre. His bladder began to ache, his penis began to burn; Dawn called to ask him whether he was all right. He called back that he was, but the interruption broke his concentration and again the flow was stemmed. He ran the cold tap in the sink: this prompted a more satisfying response. It was then that he realised he was in for a good ten-minute session. These marathons occurred when he was suffering from sudden traumas, and often followed evenings of bingeing on strong lager. What seemed to happen was that the lager could only be expelled at the rate it had been consumed, but when he once tried this theory out on Dr Soames, he was told this simply couldn't be the case. He was, however, probably in for some prostate trouble later in life.

He emerged, exhausted, from the lavatory nearly twenty minutes later. Only then, in the small, well-equipped kitchen did he begin to despair over his loss of Dawn. He would have forgiven her anything, and often had. Dawn vacillated between boundless generosity and total self-absorption, there was little in the way of conventional behaviour in between. Maurice switched on the radio and cleared the drainer of take-away containers. 'When did you get back?' he called, snipping the corner from a blue stiff-papered pack of coffee beans.

'Yesterday afternoon. I tried to call you at work but you

had your silly answerphone on. I spoke to Warde instead. Didn't he tell you?'

'No.' Maurice trailed back to the bedroom door, inhaling deeply from the coffee bean packet.

'Well, perhaps he forgot.'

'No, Warde doesn't forget anything. He probably just . . . I don't know, wanted to embarrass me or something. Smell that.' Maurice sat on the bed and pushed the packet under Dawn's nose. She held her hair to her neck and breathed in, closing her eyes. When she smiled, every muscle in her face seemed to tighten. Dawn was beautiful, there was no other word for it. Joy, for Maurice, lay in brief moments like these.

'I can't possibly make coffee as remarkable as that smell so I'm going to chuck the beans away and make a cup of Earl Grey instead.'

'You're odd, Maurice.'

'And you're beautiful. And I'm now wondering what happened to make us split up.'

'Nothing happened. Not in the sense that relationships usually end. We just . . . faded out.'

'Fine. Just as long as I know.'

'Make the tea.'

Maurice went back to the kitchen. He switched off the radio when he heard Roy trailing the day's programme and poured a dusty waterfall of coffee beans into the bin. As he made the tea he heard Dawn get out of bed and go into the shower. At most, Maurice managed two baths a week, supplemented by the occasional shower. Dawn showered or bathed at least twice a day. On herself she hated any odour that was not artificially created. On others, she didn't seem to mind. Five minutes later she walked into the kitchen with a large white towel around her, accentuating both her tan and her cleanliness. The kettle had boiled. Maurice was watching the plume of steam escaping from its spout. Dawn joined him in his trance for a while, then took over and filled the pot.

'You threw the beans away.' Her blue–black hair hung in damp clumps. Where it clung to her neck tiny pearls of water slid off and down to her spine. Maurice watched two of them edge with decreasing momentum down her vertebrae. He reached over and cupped her head in his hand as though he was holding a seashell to her ear. She leaned into the contact.

'I'd really like to stay,' Maurice said. Dawn took his hand and held it to her breast. 'I'd try harder. I really would.'

'It's not that.'

'We could go to the supermarket together. Get married. Have children. Friends. Start again.'

'It's not you, Maurice. It's me. I need to make a proper commitment.'

'But that's what I'm offering.'

'No, I'm sorry. I need somebody who understands what that means.'

'I do know what it means. Of course I do. What do you mean I don't know what it means?'

Dawn slid out of his grasp, leaned over and picked up her Gitanes from the table. She lit one. 'Commitment is not just about going to the delicatessen counter together.'

'Is that what I said? Did I say that?'

'You're always talking about it.'

'Only as a symbol: a sort of emblem of domesticity. It was a joke. I thought you understood me.' Maurice went to the sitting–room and brought back his damp pack of Camel Lights. He lit one, then put it out because the first inhalation made him nauseous.

'There's no such thing as a joke. According to Freud, anyway.'

'Did he say that? Anyway, bollocks to Freud. The fact is that I seem to be spending all of my life at the moment fading out, as you put it, of people's lives. They're even trying to get rid of me at work.'

'Perhaps it's time to make a stand, then. I don't know, don't ask me how you should run your life. I'm the worst person to ask.'

'We've managed pretty well up to now, haven't we?'

'Look. I really don't want to get into all this again. I thought we had this conversation before I went away.' Dawn poured the tea and sat down at the table. She cradled the cup in both hands and focused her attention on the far wall in such a way as to indicate that the subject was now closed.

'Did we?' Maurice leaned on the fridge.

'Yes we did, but you only hear what you want to hear.'

'OK. But things change. I mean in the couple of months since you've been away you might have had a change of heart. Then it would have been inconvenient for you if I'd not been here when you came back. You might not have been able to trace me or something. We might have lived our lives unrequitedly, but secretly longing for each other . . .' Then, because Dawn didn't say anything, he added, 'That sort of thing.'

'Maurice. I've been away for eight months. Not a couple. Just before I left I told you to pack your things and go because I never, ever, wanted to see you again. Now for once in your life, listen and take in what I'm telling you.'

'OK.' He backed out of the room. 'Just don't come crawling back to me when you change your mind.' He waited but when Dawn chose not to answer Maurice knew that her mind was now on someone else. His three years were up.

Maurice dressed slowly then emptied his clothes from the bedroom drawer. His few records, books and CDs seemed so much a part of Dawn's flat that he left them on the shelves.

His clothes, which filled a suitcase and two plastic supermarket bags, he left by the door as he went back to the kitchen. Dawn held out a gift-wrapped parcel the size of a shoe box.

'I was going to storm out without saying goodbye,' Maurice said, taking the present and sitting beside her to open it.

'It's too late for gestures. You'd just end up feeling sorry for yourself and come back to apologise.'

'Well . . . thanks.'

'It's sort of a time capsule of our relationship. A hope chest. Is that what the Americans call it?'

Maurice sifted through his hoard like a miser. 'Not the lighter, though.' He weighed it in his palm: a gold object of conspicuous expense and beauty. 'I'll have to start smoking properly again now.'

'I saved the theatre ticket from our first date.'

'The Bush? Yes, that's right. Some Irish thing with people shouting and running around naked. We went out at half-time, didn't we? You saved the ticket?'

'You came here and moved in. Poor Adrian was left wondering where I'd gone.'

'And the photo . . . blimey, it wouldn't do to leak that to the tabloids, would it . . . CD, copy of,' he held it the right way up, '*Candide* . . . packet of . . . tea?'

'Grass.'

'Smashing . . . cuddly toy.'

'I bought it for you on our first anniversary,' Dawn took the small rabbit back and held it to her cheek.

'And you call me odd.'

'I didn't want you to go without something to remember what we had together. What we did together. It was important for me.'

'And me,' he said quickly. 'For me too. But it still has to finish?'

49

'Yes. Things are happening for me. I can't go into it all now. I wanted this goodbye to be about us. That's all. That's all right isn't it?' Dawn was unused to behaving well. This was less to do with her inherent selfishness than never having been shown how to do it. Working this out quite early in their relationship, Maurice could never hate her for it, but she was not a woman who would ever provoke sympathy.

'Of course it's all right,' Maurice reassured her fondly. Encountering such a profound feeling of loss amongst his habitual sadness made it hard for him to know how he really felt about losing Dawn. It mattered almost as much as losing Polly. The brief contact of their hands as Maurice took back the ridiculous blue rabbit tipped first him, then her, over the precipice of misery and they cried together intermittently through half a pack of cigarettes. Exhausted with the emotion of another goodbye, Maurice took his suitcase and carrier bags and went to work.

Warde was sitting on a tall stool in the window of a café just outside the underground station, two minutes' walk from work. He was drinking a small cup of espresso coffee and reading a newspaper. Warde was fashionably unshaven, wearing a long leather coat with the collar up, and looked characteristically wrecked by the activities of the previous night. Maurice, catching sight of him through the window as he passed, backtracked and went in to join him. He cluttered the limited space round the stools with his carriers and suitcase. Warde folded his paper with an irritation Maurice was too miserable to see and went to fetch another coffee. Maurice positioned himself back-on to the high stool, grasped it from behind and mounted it. When Warde offered him the coffee, he took the cup in his right hand, still tenuously holding on to the seat with his left.

'Turn round,' Warde said as he would to a geriatric, taking back the coffee. Maurice shuffled round the stool so that he was facing the window. A narrow shelf ran across it. Maurice used it to balance himself in the same way he used the handlebars when he was learning how to ride a bike. Warde put the cup down onto the counter. 'You look like a tramp.'

'Thanks.'

'So what happened?' Warde said.

'Dawn chucked me out.'

'Right . . . right.'

'I said she chucked me out.'

'I'm sorry. I was . . . anyway, look, probably for the best, etc., etc., plenty more fish in the sea.'

'Thanks for your support.' Maurice patted his pocket and felt for his new lighter. 'She gave me this: like a gold clock I suppose. Something to remember her by.'

Warde took it. 'Nice. Italian. I should think she paid a couple of hundred quid for it.'

'So there we are.'

Warde continued to weigh the lighter, he flicked the electronic switch and a tiny blue flame leaped up. 'How do you feel about it?' Warde watched the flame, let it burn.

'Oh . . . I don't know. I knew it was coming. I suppose I should have done something about it before.' Maurice knew he could no longer look to Warde for help. Something about his predicament had triggered a similar trauma in his friend. He moved onto safer ground, protecting himself from the contingent misery of rejection. 'I have to say she looks quite astonishing. Astounding. I felt almost . . . I don't know, humbled by her.'

'You're too soft,' Warde said slowly.

'Am I?'

'I don't know what's happened to you. Sometimes it's like knowing somebody who's suddenly decided to become a registered charity. You give everything away . . . I don't understand it.'

'I don't give things away. They just go. Of their own accord.'

'Nothing goes unless you let it go. You have to use energy to keep hold of things that matter.'

Maurice gave up wondering what the conversation was really about. 'Yes, well energy is something I definitely don't have. It's gone . . . perhaps I am fading out. Anyway, buggered if I know where I'm going to stay.' He looked beneath the counter at his meagre possessions. 'Polly won't have me there . . .' He toed his plastic carrier. 'I don't suppose . . .'

'Certainly not,' Warde said.

'I'll have to find a hostel or something. Doss house. Somewhere full of drunken labourers and rampant ring jousters . . . I imagine they'll all feel it incumbent on themselves to pleasure themselves with my lithe young body. Still, if you haven't the room.'

'No, slightly delicate domestic arrangements. Next time.'

'Right. Thanks anyway. Any time I can do the same for you . . .' Maurice finished his coffee and, leaving Warde to read his newspaper, walked the short distance to work.

Vincent Edwards was, at the same time, crossing Hungerford Bridge, swept along on the gentle tide of suburban commuters. His view of the grey river was serrated by the latticed metalwork hedging the walkway. A pleasure-boat laden with early tourists flickered like an old movie in his peripheral vision. To his left, the trains rumbled huge and loud into Charing Cross Station, but his eyes were fixed straight ahead. On a whim, as he left the house that morning, Edwards had decided to take the train to Waterloo rather than Victoria and have breakfast at the Festival Hall. He felt better for the change in his routine. His step sprung as he pom-pommed along, the rhythm of his poms counterpointed by the dry click of his brass umbrella tip on the ground. Morning was a good time for Edwards, the day was rampant with possibilities and there were at least ten hours to go before he was back in Tattenham Corner. Beyond his gardens, his small collection of clocks, and his motor mower, there was little in his home to engage his interest. He barely saw his wife, except at the weekends. They slept in separate rooms and on the rare occasions they did encounter each other (sometimes in the kitchen in the insomniac hours of the night) they were polite but distant. Alison Edwards was a painter with a small reputation as a watercolourist. Her husband hated her fey compositions (the colour barely visible on the paper), and her pallid approximation of subject matter which she argued was style and her critics (such as there were) that it was poor technique. They had no children and no desire for them. Edwards was homosexual and gay in the old-fashioned sense of the word. Making love to women he likened to stirring paint in a pot. He preferred the straightforward compost delights of sodomy.

Edwards was fifty-four, a survivor of many purges at the Corporation. He now managed a team of twenty-three talented producers, all of them hand-picked over the previous five years. In the past, Edwards had equated his job to that of an orchestral conductor: standing at the podium, waving his baton to guide his players through the finer points of a score that they all knew by heart. Now there was a resigned hackery among some members of his staff. The newer producers didn't seem to feel it, but a number of the older ones were, in Warde's expression, 'jobbing it'. To them, loyalty, a common cause, a shared belief in some sort of public service ethos were notions as quaint and irrelevant as the old photos of dinner-jacketed announcers.

Nevertheless, Edwards remained optimistic, if only because he was intending to announce his retirement within the month. When he retired he was going to live in Istanbul with a man called Charles and never speak to his wife again. He had decided to mark his retirement with a grand gesture to summon the spirits of MacNeice and Parker, Gielgud (Val) and Grisewood, Thomas (Dylan and Wynford Vaughan), and the other ghosts of the Gluepot. Edwards wanted Maurice Reid to have his job, which is why he wanted him out of the building for a week or so.

He pom-pommed across the concourse of Charing Cross Station, was briefly diverted by the sight of the flanks of a boy, proud as a mare, emerging into the sunlight from the lavatories. But he decided to save himself for lunchtime: a decent meal at the Garrick rounded off by cheese on toast, then a quick one with a Lebanese friend in Soho before he caught the train back to Tattenham Corner.

FOUR

Maurice arranged his bags in the crannies of his cramped office and opened the blinds. Beyond the fall of his narrow, cigarette-end-strewn balcony a convoy of black cabs queued at the taxi rank in the centre of Portland Place. Occasionally one would be whistled up by a hotel porter and another would fill in behind. Two lines of traffic proceeded slowly towards Regent's Park. The southern stream was halted in its progress towards Oxford Circus. An open-topped tourist bus with a solitary Euro-couple in ample shorts, hats and scarves was gridlocked. Maurice opened his balcony door and the noise of the city suddenly roared in as though he had tweaked the volume knob on a radio. He stepped outside and, leaning his elbows on the balcony rail, lit a cigarette and flicked the spent match into the tourist bus. Behind it, a Porsche driven by a woman in a short skirt and long legs took his attention. Through the sunroof he could see her left hand toying with the gearstick, her fingers drumming impatiently on the steering wheel.

Seeing the woman provoked him into thinking about Dawn, already a part of his past, and now accorded the myth-like status of all the women he had lost. He remembered the night they had met. A rare evening which had begun when he had looked at himself in the mirror and saw a reasonable approximation of a decent-looking man. His jacket had just been to the dry cleaner's, his hair was well-cut, the bags under his eyes lent him an air of wisdom rather than ill-health, and, due to a recent bout of chronic food poisoning, his weight was down. With the false bravado of three bottles of Carlsberg Special lager, he propositioned Dawn at the bar in the Bush Theatre. She was wearing a white linen dress. Her date had gone to the Gents. By the time he was out again they were on the way to her flat.

Having left Polly six months before, his life at the time was sufficiently empty to be filled wholly with Dawn's. So they completed each other, tying their emptiness together to make a whole. But now Dawn's life had been removed and Maurice could only reacquaint himself with what was left of his own.

The traffic moved on. Another line of cars ingratiated itself in the shadow of the tall building. Exhausts puttered white fumes into the chill of the December morning. Maurice went back into his office to find his telephone ringing. He fitted the receiver into the crook of his neck and, as he answered, began opening his mail.

'Maurice?' It was Polly.

'Hello.'

'You don't sound like you.'

'Well I am me.' He laid down his wad of mail, shifted in his seat and switched on his computer. The computer wished him good morning, Maurice whispered an obscenity at it as he did each day. One day he fully intended to smash its stupid face open with a house brick.

Polly said, 'What's the matter?'

'Nothing.'

'Well why did you swear at me?'

'I didn't. I swore at the computer. It told me to have a

nice day. I mean you can just picture the cretin who spent months coming up with the stupid graphic, can't you?'

'Yes . . . how are you, Maurice?' Polly was not alone. She had used his name in the way that she did when she wanted to maintain the formality of their transactions for the benefit of Val.

'I'm all right, Polly. And how are you, Polly? And how is the dismal Val, Polly?'

'I was calling to confirm tonight.' In response to his, her tone had become reasonable, even warm. This was why Maurice had fallen in love with her. She put his comfort above her own.

'Tonight?'

'Tonight. Yes.'

'Oh. Tonight.'

'You've forgotten.'

'Of course I haven't . . . well, actually, yes I have.'

Something was shouted from the far end of the room. Polly covered the receiver, smudging the sound. After a pause, she said, 'You're having Will until Sunday. We're going to Paris.' A door slammed. '. . . I think.'

'Sorry. Look, I'm sorry. I didn't mean . . .'

'Sorry what? Sorry you can't do it or sorry Val's in a shitty mood?'

'Sorry full stop. Of course I can have Will. I mean I'm not sure where . . . no, look, it's no problem. I'll pick him up at sevenish.' Maurice's mood see-sawed upwards; there was only ever room for one of them to be down.

'Six. And stay for supper. Those were the arrangements. Val's cooking something.'

'Right. Six, then.'

'You know how she is,' Polly whispered.

'Yes.'

'She does try to do the right thing.' The old Polly now,

her vulnerability drawing him closer. 'She's just not very flexible. But she honestly does try.'

'You don't have to explain, Pol. You don't have to justify anybody but yourself.'

'You know I wish, sometimes, that other people could see her the way she is when we're alone. She's . . . she is kind, and decent, considerate and . . . look, I'll see you later.'

The line into Polly's life was cut, leaving an echo of sadness in Maurice's head. He had thought that as time passed it would get easier to live without his wife. But it had become harder because the further away she got, the more clearly he could see her and the more transparent her motives became, the more he loved her.

Maurice had reapplied himself to the tedium of opening his mail when the door was shoved open and two men in blue overalls came in. The taller and broader of the two looked at him but didn't say anything, then gestured to the empty light socket. The second man, in pressed overalls and with a beard which looked like iron filings clinging to the bar magnet of his square jaw, whistled, shook his head, and led them out again. Maurice was shocked but sufficiently irritated to wheel his chair to the door and shout after them. 'At least have the courtesy to shut the door!' At which point Vincent Edwards passed along the corridor, smiled tersely, and walked on as though he was propelling himself along an invisible railway-line using his umbrella as a lever. Maurice slammed the door, closed the blinds and threw his mail in the bin. Then he got it out again and confronted the inane screen-saving logo on his computer, hideously technicolour in the dark room. He switched the machine off and looked away before it wished him goodbye. It was a small but satisfying victory, and he basked in the glory of it as the phone rang again. This time it was Elaine informing him that Warde had called in sick, that she had a meeting all morning, and that he would have to get off his backside and edit the afternoon's programme. Maurice put down the phone wondering what could possibly have happened to Warde in the short time since he'd left him at the café. But, more importantly, wondering how he was going to put up with working with Roy May for the rest of the day.

'I don't like this at all.' Roy, having missed the morning's editorial meeting, was looking at the running order for the programme while he ploughed through a fried breakfast. Maurice suspected it was his second of the morning, the first having been taken at the hotel in Swindon.

'What don't you like?' After shouting down the corridor for Hardiman to come and sort everything out, Maurice sat down beside Roy.

'That piece about the sheep. I told you yesterday I didn't want it.'

'Well I'm not wedded to it, Roy. If you don't want it then we'll find something else. Won't we, Phil?' Maurice said, handing the problem to Hardiman as he walked through the door.

'Sheep?' Hardiman said brightly, dealing both Maurice and Roy fresh sheets of paper. He looked tired, and kept blinking, but each blink caused his entire face to spasm. Phil Hardiman was tall but stooped in apology for his height, and used up a great deal of his energy to maintain the facade of a smile on his pitted, doelike face. He wore a diamond-patterned jumper and brown cord trousers and smelt of fresh sweat. A born middle manager, he would rise slowly but inevitably through the ranks and finally find a female sufficiently similar to his mother to take him on. His mother and the woman would argue and fall out because of these similarities (cooking, the sharing of other household duties, and the fact that she made him go to the cinema when he was obviously too tired from being at work all day, would be the main bones of contention). But apart from the family conflicts, like many physically unprepossessing people, they would be blithely happy and have a number of odd-looking but well-adjusted children.

'What are you running instead of the sheep piece?' Maurice said.

'Something's come in from Manchester about a new video surveillance scheme.'

'Good. Well done, Lardy,' Maurice said patronisingly.

'That's more like it,' Roy said. 'Bit of fibre. I knew I could rely on you, Phil.'

'Then again,' Maurice said, 'that's surely not new, is it? I mean, they've been putting cameras in the public crappers for months to stop acts of gross . . .'

'No. It's about them vetting the people who monitor the video cameras,' Hardiman said.

'Good. Well I'll leave you to get on with it, then.'

Hardiman took Maurice's place at Roy's desk, depositing a pile of tape spools and a folder of draft cues in front of Roy's breakfast. Roy waved his eggy knife at the tapes and Hardiman, reading the signal, dutifully laced one of them onto the machine.

'Right then,' Maurice said, edging out.

'Got better things to do, have you?' Roy said. Hardiman paused by the play button.

'I'm sorry?'

'I said, you've got better things to do than listen to these tapes? I mean that's what they pay you to do, isn't it?'

'I've heard them, Roy,' Maurice lied. 'And now it's your turn. That's what they pay you to do, isn't it?'

'Phil. Go and fetch us a cup of tea will you, mate. Tetley. Bag out. And a couple of those pink sweeteners.' Hardiman slid out of Roy's small office and closed the door behind him. Roy put down his knife and fork and pushed his plate aside. He laid his elbows on the desk and gestured to the chair. Maurice queasily sat down; Roy was an easier target with an audience around. 'Well?' Roy said. 'Let's have it, then.'

'I don't know what you mean, Roy.'

Roy tilted his head to one side, looking at Maurice from the new angle. '. . . You think you're so bloody clever, don't you?'

'No.'

'I'd really like to know what your problem is. Because I'll tell you straight, I'm sick of you looking down your nose at me.'

'You're imagining it.'

'No I'm not. I know your sort. Telly's full of them. Bloody clever bastards who sit around while you buy them drinks all night then slag you off as soon as your back's turned.'

'I've never worked in telly.'

'That's just what I mean, you see. You can't resist a clever little comment.' Roy punched his forefinger towards Maurice. 'If you were any sort of bloke I'd take you outside and give you a bloody good hiding.'

'I don't think violence would solve anything, would it?'

'Actually, Maurice, you might be surprised to know that it does. Especially with little tits like you. Now I don't want a fight with you. If it comes to a choice between you and me I know who'll end up going, and it won't be me.'

'Really?'

'Yes. I do. But I'm not going to put up with you sniding it over me. I just won't tolerate it. It's your job to keep the talent happy. And I'm not happy. So what are you going to do about it?'

'Talent?' Maurice, spotting an exit line, stood up. 'You said it. Mate.' He walked out, setting the seal on the day, but feeling better than he had for weeks.

Hardiman met him in the corridor, bringing Roy's tea. 'He's all yours,' Maurice said.

'Is he all right?' Hardiman said nervously.

'Quiet as a lamb, Lardy. I'm in the smoking room if you need me.'

There were three smoking rooms in the building. One in the basement, used for the nervous toking of pre-programme cigarettes. One on the sixth floor, used by actors anecdotalising over budget price king-sized and one on the eighth for the terminally bored, looking for an excuse to kill ten minutes or so each hour away from the office. The walls were a nicotine yellow, squared with the white ghosts of removed posters, the extractor fan was oiled with the black tar of countless Silk Cuts. Elaine was sitting by the window beneath the fan, the *Daily Telegraph* was spread like a picnic rug over the seat beside her. She was reading from a position of comfort: one leg folded beneath her on the chair, the other foot on the floor. The sun from the small, high window cloaked her shoulders. Maurice sat down beside her, took her warm jodhpured knee in his hand, then leaned over and kissed her on the cheek.

Elaine looked up from her paper. 'That was nice. What was it for?'

'I've just had a bust-up with Roy.' Maurice précised the conversation. In the telling of it he came off worse than he remembered.

'That was a bit silly, wasn't it?'

'I don't think so. It had to be said. He's been chipping away at me for weeks.'

'And so have you at him.'

'Yes, but he's a presenter. If you can't bitch about

presenters then the job's not really worth doing.' Maurice rubbed his hands gleefully.

'Would you do it?'

'Talk to myself for a living? No thanks, I get quite enough of that at home thank you very much.'

Elaine sighed and folded her newspaper. 'I asked you to look after Roy today as a favour. You know he can't write if he's in a grump.'

'I know,' Maurice said, lighting up. 'And I don't even care. Curiously liberating it is too. You should try it some time.'

'You're becoming quite bitter. Did you know that?'

'Am I?' Maurice gave the matter a moment's thought. 'Well yes, of course I am. But who isn't bitter round here? I mean it's a climate of bitterness, what do you expect?'

'I'd expect that, just occasionally, you give some thought to how other people are feeling rather than simply yourself.' Elaine shuffled a body's width away from him. 'The fact is that I couldn't face the programme today because Mother kept me up all night. And I particularly didn't want to see Roy because . . . because I didn't. And I thought that you might just once have taken some of this . . . intolerable, intolerable weight from my shoulders.'

'Ah,' Maurice said.

'I'm not super-human, you know. I can't keep taking on everybody's problems all the time. Sometimes, just once in fact, it would be nice to be asked how I was. Just once.'

'Right. And, ah how are . . .'

'Not now, Maurice. Not now . . .'

'Right. Sorry.'

'The point is,' Elaine said more calmly, putting her paper aside, 'that everybody's going through it, this climate of bitterness as you call it. So don't imagine you're on your own.'

'I don't. But on the other subject,' Maurice started, as he mounted a favourite hobby horse. 'These people just don't care, do they? It's all very well having a vision, but there's a danger of them destroying the very thing they're supposed to be preserving. I could tell them that if anybody bothered to ask me.'

'Yes, well . . .' Elaine had been diverted from her point. She was sure she had been leading up to something, now she couldn't remember what it was.

'The way it works is this.' Maurice rolled up his left sleeve, preparing himself to tick off each point on his fingers. But Elaine stood up and walked out before he could start.

FIVE

T HE SHORT TILED path to Polly's front door was coined with the copper of late fallen leaves. Maurice straightened his jacket in the pallid reflection of the door glass, shifted his bottle of Chardonnay from the crook of his right arm to the crook of his left and pressed the bell. The button clicked dully against its backstop. Maurice waited for a moment then knocked on the door. A large blue shape loomed rapidly towards him. The door opened quickly and the blur was revealed as Val: fractious and flushed with a strand of her dyed blonde hair loosely draping her right eye. Val was thick-set, square-faced, habitually angry, and spoke rapidly and ferociously. As a journalist she was regarded as sensitive and caring, her bitterness and passion she saved for her private life. Maurice disliked her for the obvious reasons but found her immensely sexually attractive: he had always been drawn by fuller-figured women. They always seemed to be the ones who wore stockings.

'The sauce is burned, of course,' Val said, blowing the rebel strand of her fringe from her eye. It settled back with the slow trajectory of a falling leaf. She fingernailed it beneath her tortoise-shell hairband as Maurice kissed her cheek and reached a hand round her back, sliding it slyly down so that it lay on her rump.

'Stockings,' Maurice noted. 'I've brought some wine.' Val stepped back to let him in. He led the way to the country kitchen. When Val had replaced him in the marital home, she had imported her taste. Dried flowers hung in inverted bunches from the ceiling, mourning the spring; the pine shelving was cluttered with decommissioned rural artefacts. There was no sign of Will's felt-pen artwork or Polly's Victorian tapestries.

'Polly is bathing William. You'd better sit down. Out of reach. I suppose you're pissed as usual?' Val took up her position at the stove.

'Absolutely.' Maurice sat at the refectory table, laid for three with one midget set of cutlery at the far end. Will's place was underlaid with plastic sheeting.

'I don't understand this woman.' Val peered at the recipe, picked up a wooden spoon, pushed it into the larval sauce and tried to move it round. A smell of burning escaped from the depths of the Le Creuset saucepan. A family of them hung by their handles in an open pine box on the rag-rolled wall. 'I mean she explains things so badly. I bought all the right stuff but it just doesn't seem to be . . . gelling. Is that the word?' She flipped over a torn page of the broken-backed recipe book.

'Do you want me to do something?'

'No. Well you could open the wine.' Val pointed to the fridge. 'I mean you watch her on the television and . . . I don't know, I suppose she has teams of people to do things for her . . . She has terribly ugly hands. Have you seen her hands?'

'I don't know what you're talking about.' Maurice opened the wine, narrowly avoiding severing his right testicle with the corkscrew, and poured them both a glass.

66

'Her hands. Liver spots. Brown shapes; whole continents of them on her hands. Shit!' Scalded, she pulled away from the singed wooden handle of a small pan. Blue flames licked round the base, sooting the blue enamel.

'Turn it down. I'm sure it's not supposed to be up that high.'

'Well isn't it? That's the whole point, you see. The bloody woman doesn't actually say how high the gas has to be. Bring to the boil then simmer. Here . . .' Val picked up the book and scanned a page. 'Yes, here it is: bring to the boil and bloody sim . . . look, nowhere is there any indication of how long it should boil and what simmering actually is. Is there a glossary? Can you see anything about it?' She thrust the book in Maurice's direction. Maurice exchanged it for a glass of wine and made a play of reading it. Much as he was enjoying Val's discomfort he was hungry, so he went over to her and she relinquished her position in front of the stove. Maurice turned the gas down, stirred the sauce, turned off the pasta and drained it. 'I think it's edible. If we just take the sauce from the top.'

'Oh God.' Val was shaking her head like a shock victim. 'Oh God.' She began to cry: fierce tears she fought to hold back. 'Give me a cigarette.'

'Here.' Maurice threw his packet over. 'What's the matter now?'

'I can't bear it.' Val tore the lid as she pulled out a cigarette. 'I'm not usually . . . you see we're trying to make . . .' she sniffed the last of the tears away, brushed her hand across her nose, '. . . there are times when I just want . . . but Polly is so . . . even. Sometimes I can't bear it. I feel like. I don't know, I shouldn't be telling you this.'

Maurice came over and sat next to her. 'I don't see why not. I don't suppose we've got many secrets from each other.'

Val watched him warily. A professional in these matters, she knew that relinquishing the upper hand made her vulnerable. She could control her life only if she controlled all of those she came into contact with. Maurice, though, had never threatened her, even though he of all people perhaps had the most right.

In a bid to change the subject, he said, 'Pol tells me you've been commissioned to do twenty-four pieces a year.'

'Did she? Well that's not supposed to be public knowledge so I'd appreciate it if you didn't spread it around. It's a lot. The stress I could do without.'

'Why should I tell anyone? I'm not in the business of flogging other people's secrets.'

'I'm sorry? Are you insinuating something about me, here?' Val's eyes sparked with anger.

'No. Not just you. Everybody involved in journalism. Right down to newsagents. I wouldn't trust my newsagent as far as I could throw him. They're all hideous porn merchants. Top shelvers. And paperboys: little stool pigeons, poking their noses through people's letterboxes . . .'

'Don't be so sanctimonious. You don't mean it. Pour me another drink.'

Maurice complied. Away from the stove, Val's high colour was now being fuelled by the alcohol. She had never been able to drink more than a glass of wine without it going straight to her head. Nowadays, she couldn't take drink at all, as Maurice could see from the slow-motion blinks of her eye, the slow lag of her movements.

'Well go on, Val. You've started so you might as well finish.'

'No. Oh, I don't know. About me and . . . it's just that living with somebody who's so unutterably good makes me. I don't know. Feel such an ogre. I'm sure I behave much worse than . . . I suppose you were the shit when you were around?'

'No. I wasn't,' Maurice said quickly. 'I'm sure I wasn't. Not at all. I was quite reasonable most of the time. Of course there were occasions, but then that's only human, isn't it?'

'Yes. Exactly. Which makes my darling Polly not quite human. Not human at all.'

'Too humane you mean? Interesting thought. I'd never quite considered it that way. Drink up.'

Val drained another glass and Maurice topped her up. The laziness of her eyes had spread to her mouth as if a slow freeze was proceeding down from her brain to the rest of her body. She took another cigarette and with effort clamped it in the slackened hinge of her jaw. 'I still love her. You see, I still love her, Maurice. She is the very best thing that's ever happened to me.'

'Yes. I'm sure she is.'

'I'm sorry.' Val clamped her hand to her mouth. 'Is that? Yes it is, it's insensitive. Yes. I am sorry.'

'No you're not. But it doesn't matter.' Maurice was sobering at the same rate that Val was getting drunk. He was already feeling maudlin.

'Tell me how you are.' Val leaned towards him. 'How's work?'

'Oh, pretty bloody awful really. Pretty . . . oh, it's boring, I'm bored by it all.'

'Well, go on. I don't mind you boring me about work.' Val laid her hand on his forearm, provoking a spontaneous and unwelcome erection.

'Well, you know Roy, don't you?'

'Roy May? Oh yes. I bump into him round town. Anywhere there's a sniff of free booze . . . weasel. I suppose he's dreadful to work with?'

'Absolute prat. Bloody raving egomaniac. Always throwing his weight round . . . always. I don't know . . .'

'What?'

'I'm amazed they kept that stuff out of the press. I really am.'

'. . . Yes. It was.' In a single beat, the adrenaline in Val's system sobered her. 'The stuff about the . . . I mean I don't know why we didn't print it. I'm surprised nobody . . . was it true?'

'As far as I know. I mean the girl never talked. That's why they couldn't stand it up. I suppose she'd be in her late teens now . . . I did hear he beat her, but then . . .' Hearing the sound of betrayal in his voice, Maurice stopped, liking himself less as the drink worked him over. Another defeat in the day's battle to be a better man.

'But then?'

'Nothing. Nothing. I'm bored by it. By him. By everything. Since Polly left, well, it's been one disaster after another.'

'Oh, dear,' Val said, unable to muster any compassion.

'It's hopeless. Absolutely hopeless: job, life, social life, relationships, health, addictions. Sex drive. Hopeless.'

'Poor, poor Maurice.' Realising that Maurice felt it was now his turn to confide in her, Val decided she couldn't face it. She stood up, blinked her eyes into focus and said, 'Now you have another drink. I'll go and see how Polly's getting on.'

'Do you have to?'

'Won't be long.'

Maurice went back to the stove and lethargically stirred the ruined sauce. Something nagged him: something beyond his usual concerns. When he was drunk he lost his passionate disdain for everyone except himself. Even Roy no longer seemed that bad. At least he was open about his shortcomings, unlike Maurice, who knew he was inherently dishonest. He lived in the quagmire of his own self-esteem. He'd do anything to be accepted, even if it meant betraying the people closest to him. Except for Polly. He would never betray Polly because he loved her. But, more importantly, he believed that she loved him. And he had never, with complete confidence, been able to say that about anybody else. He was even unsure about his mother. She liked him, but she loved his father and Maurice had never believed there was enough love for both of them.

When he thought of his mother it was always in the lounge of the family home. She would be sitting in a chair at the far end of the room, slightly distracted, always formal, her attention on the carpet, a speck of dust on the fireplace, a cobweb on the lampshade; she seemed strangely distant whenever his father was out of the room. It wasn't as though they couldn't communicate. As a child he felt he could talk about anything with her, but it was almost like living with a wise elder sister: one who would ultimately leave him because she had found a more authentic object for her love. He served as the one she practised on. And when his father did return from work the light would come back into her eyes. At the sound of his car on the drive she would stand, straighten her dress, check her hair in the mirror, the seams of her stockings, pat the bouffant into shape, kick off her slippers, put on her heels and meet him at the door with a kiss. It could not have been like that every day, but his memories led him to believe that it was. His mother wore stockings because women then always did. And he became aware of it when he became aware of women.

'Maurice!' His father would emerge from the hall, take his briefcase to the lobby beneath the stairs, hang up his mac, bring out an ashtray, light up his pipe and settle beside the fire. 'Tell me about your day.' The tall, gentle man, with the large hands, the sentimental eyes and steel-grey hair would open his arms and beckon him close. His mother would watch, still standing, and Maurice would shrink down into himself, his mind a blank, searching for something about school, anything. But whatever he managed to bring to mind seemed so ordinary it was almost not worth saying. So he would make something up: a story about a friend, a lesson, an incident in the changing room. And his father would listen and nod sagely, looking for the kernel of some moral he could draw and give Maurice something back from his experience. It was only later that Maurice realised his childhood had been an extended form of amateur psycho-analysis.

Once, when he was nine, Maurice had been playing by the fish pond at his junior school, making small boats out of the reeds and re-enacting the battle of the River Plate. He had rolled up the sleeves of his grey V-necked jumper and laid face down on the slabs that surrounded the pool. He could feel the cold damp of the slabs on his bare knees as he reached into the silt at the bottom of the pool. Scooping up a handful, he threw it at a blond boy called Steven who was watching. Then he found the periscope of a submarine, three inches high: a grey weathered metal spout protruding from the surface of the water. He reached down and tugged it out. The bottom was rusted and muddy. Bubbles rose and carried to the surface the sulphurous stench of a drain. The submarine had dived. Maurice made the sounds of sirens. He chased after the ship with his hand, only to find a vortex of suction where the pipe had been; tugging at his palm, making it an effort to tear it from the floor of the pond. The water level slowly dropped. Maurice watched with horror as the rumoured goldfish, once hidden beneath the filthy water, came up bright and clean as the pond emptied. He dropped the spout into the remaining water and walked quickly away.

The orange-coated dinner lady, to whom he had reported feeling unwell, took him to the medical room where he waited, dangling his legs from a high bed. The room was small and smelt of antiseptic. It was the place where the woman from the health clinic came to look at the school's teeth and the fourth year boys' testicles. He had been taken there when he had wet himself on his first day at school and a secretary had talked kindly to him as she dried him off and found him a clean pair of shorts. He had asked for his mother but she had not come. It was the first time she had betrayed him. He swung his legs and picked at the crust of a dried scab on his knee. He wanted to cry and felt overwhelmingly alone. The headmaster finally came in and sat beside him on the sick bed. As the man talked they both looked at the eye chart on the far wall. Mr Dineen was feared but respected by both staff and pupils. He took his suit jacket off only when he played cricket with the fourth years. He smelt of aftershave and school dinners. Maurice didn't really listen to what Mr Dineen was saying to him, but the headmaster's tone prompted a confession. Maurice was taken back to the head's room and smacked three times on his backside, quite hard. Inconsolable, he was driven home through the streets of the new suburb by the deputy head in her lime-green Vauxhall Viva.

When he got home he jumped out of the car and ran up the drive. The man next door, who was off work with an illness his wife would only mouth at his mother, was cutting his front lawn. Maurice's mother, who had been alerted by the school, came out, smiling at their skeletal, yellow neighbour, to thank the deputy headmistress for bringing him home. Maurice ran past her and went upstairs where, kneeling on the bed and peering from behind the curtains, he watched the two women talk beside the car. His mother seemed to be apologising, then laughing with the woman. Shoulders were shrugged, his misery belittled. The woman was waved off like an old friend, although few friends ever came to his parents' house. When she had gone, Maurice lay on his mother's bed and waited, feeling his heart beat through his jumper.

Some time later, it seemed like hours after the headmistress had dropped him off, his mother came into the room. Maurice sat up on the bed, something prompting him to pull himself together. His mother had brought him up a plate of malted milk biscuits and a glass of cherryade. Though his mouth was still dry from the guilt and shame, Maurice ate the biscuits and drank the cherryade. His mother did not ask him to explain what had happened. Instead they talked as if it was a normal day, both understanding that the explanation and apology would be saved for his father's return from work.

'Poor lad,' was all his father said, administering the bitter punishment of understanding and sympathy. Maurice saved his tears for later, when he was alone in his room.

'Hold me upside down!' Will careered into the room, buffeting off a chair and stumbling into his father's arms. Maurice grasped his son's tiny ankles and swept him from his feet. The boy squealed in delight as Maurice swung his small body like a pendulum, his fair hair brushing the floor, his inverted cheeks moulding over his eyes. Polly came in as Maurice lowered the child to the ground. Will scampered away and Maurice stood, breathless, beside the table.

'Hello.' She slipped her arms under his and kissed him firmly but dryly on the lips. 'You made it then.'

'I was early,' Maurice said proudly.

'I'm not hungry.' Will said, picking up his fork and

immediately dropping it onto the floor. It bounced on the cork tiles and ricocheted under the table. Will tunnelled after it on his elbows.

'I hear you helped out with the pasta.'

'Yes. I . . . ah, you know. Well, just turned it off, really.'

Polly sat down. Will levered his way out from the far side of the table. 'I've given him a bath and washed his hair.'

Will said, 'Do you want to smell it?'

Maurice pulled him close and smelt. 'Lovely. Lemons and apples.'

'I've packed his pyjamas and four sets of clothes. We'll be back on Sunday. All being well.'

'Right. Right.'

They were waiting for Val to come back. Only then could they relax the formality. Val always gave them time to be alone but, resenting that time, behaved badly to both of them if she came in and found them showing any sign of getting on together.

'Sunday, then . . .' Maurice said. Will clambered on his knee.

'Mummy's buying me an aeroplane,' Will said.

'Only if I can get one, darling.'

'Will it be white?'

'Yes. It will be white.'

'Shall I fetch my sword?'

'No, we're going to eat in a minute. Val's just coming.'

'I'm not hungry,' Will said as Val came in. She divined no signs of harmony so she made light of the cooking disaster and served up the meal.

'I'm not hungry,' Will repeated when Val had put his small plastic bowl in front of him.

'Look, Will, for God's sake, just eat it,' Polly said. Will stared at the food. Maurice, thinking it best not to get involved, picked up his fork and tangled three or four strands of ribboned pasta round it. The food was edible but almost tasteless. Polly was watching Will who was prodding at his plateful with his fork. Val was watching Polly.

'Let me . . . You eat,' Val laid down her knife and fork and went to sit next to Will who hunched away from her. Polly began eating.

'Now, come on,' Val cajoled, taking Will's fork, loading it up and forcing it gently between his lips.

'It's too hot!'

'Blow it, then. Here, like this.' Val blew on the pasta, the steam fanned horizontally, then righted itself as she offered the fork to Will. Will blew, blew again, then he allowed Val to feed him. Val tousled his hair, tentatively appropriating him for a while. Will smiled to himself.

Afterwards, Will tooled up for the journey into the city: he slid his sword into his belt and pocketed a robot and a green Power Ranger. Polly kissed her ex-husband and son with similar kisses, then she and Val, their arms linked together, waved them off from the door. Will and Maurice waved back but the door was slammed shut before they had got very far away from the house.

SIX

'Now the thing is,' Maurice said, prompting Will to look up at him. 'We're going on an adventure.'

They were waiting on the Victoria line tube platform for a train to take them to Oxford Circus. The indicator board said 'Correction' and nothing more. The air was thick and metallic and stirred only by the draught of the trains from the southbound platform.

Will adjusted his sword and opened his small satchel. He delved in a grubby hand and fetched out a cling-filmed pack of sandwiches, a packet of crisps and a Penguin biscuit. Then, belatedly, asked, 'Can I have my tea?'

'Well, if you'd eaten all your pasta you wouldn't still be hungry, would you?' Will's eating habits had never conformed to any pattern. He ate a limited menu at irregular times of the day but always looked healthy enough.

'Yes. Can I have my sandwiches?' Will held out his tiny wad of bread and Maurice thought with tenderness of Polly preparing them.

'Go on then.' Maurice lifted him onto a narrow seat. A group of nine or ten people dressed in evening wear were being orchestrated into reading one of the tall posters by a loud, squat and very drunk member of their party. Two youths loitered by a chocolate machine looking dangerous and sullen. A middle-aged woman with ragged hair was standing with her toes to the white line, leaning perilously over the platform edge. Her blue coat was blotted with filth. She wore the resigned expression of the street lunatic. A tiny sooty mouse scampered from the shadows beneath the overhang of the platform, foraging for crumbs. It moved suddenly in short straight lines, twitched its nose, then vanished again.

'I can't open it.' Will held out the twisted pack and Maurice unpeeled the warm bread.

'This adventure,' Maurice said, adopting his genial, fatherly tone and sitting down beside him.

'Will you open my crisps?' Will said, and Maurice complied.

'This adventure,' he tried again.

'Can I take my Power Ranger?'

'Just shut up a minute and listen.'

'All right.'

'We might not be sleeping at the flat,' Maurice said. 'Do you remember the flat?'

After a furrowed-browed pause the child managed, 'There's a pink toilet and I have my bed.'

'That's right. Well, I don't live there at the moment . . .'

'And a lady who sings in the shower.'

'That's right. Anyway . . .'

'And a . . .'

'Look! I'm trying to tell you something.'

'I'm sorry.' Will ducked his head in anticipation of being clouted round the ear.

'That's all right, but . . .'

'I'm sorry. Sorry . . . Sooooorrrry. Sooooooooooooooo.'

'Will! Please.'

The child curtailed his improvised apology but kept his mouth open.

'I was just trying to tell you that we might have to find somewhere else. To stay. Just for tonight. I thought we might . . .'

'Can I take my Power Ranger?'

'Yes, of course you can take your bloody Power Ranger. Look, just finish your sandwich then I'll tell you.' Maurice stamped off a little way down the platform. His son, unperturbed, continued to eat. Maurice watched him as he dropped his packet of crisps onto the floor and the woman in the filthy coat knelt at his feet and began picking them up. She pinched the tiny fragments onto her crusty palm and offered them to the child like birdseed. Will balanced his sandwich on her outstretched hand. Then Maurice saw him wrinkle his nose. He was beside them and thanking the woman for her help before Will had the opportunity to register his disapproval at the rank odour of the woman's clothes. The woman, interested only in the child, moved back to her spot at the platform edge.

'Is that lady poorly?' Will said.

'Yes. I think she's poorly.'

Behind them they heard a battery of thumps as the youths suddenly started kicking the chocolate machine. The party in evening dress moved futher away but kept their respective distance to one another as if they were wired together. The woman in the filthy coat held her palm to her mouth and opened her eyes wide like a mime artist registering horror. When the mashing of metal stopped, Will said, 'That's naughty isn't it?'

'Yes,' Maurice said quietly, not wanting to turn and make eye contact with the youths.

'Will they go to jail?'

'No. Now, look, just get on with your food, will you.'

Maurice broke off a corner of Will's sandwich and forced it into the boy's mouth. But Will's attention was now on the youths emptying the chocolate from the machine. He jumped off the bench, scattering his sandwiches and, before Maurice could grab him, ran up to them. He stood attentively just behind them and drew his sword. This was what he had been waiting for as long as he could remember. There were bad men to be slayed. Cartoon villains never triumphed.

Maurice sprinted after him, grabbed him by the arm and tried to pull him away. 'Will, for God's sake.'

One of the youths turned and offered Will a handful of chocolate bars.

'You'll go to jail, you will,' Will asserted, and Maurice tightened his grip.

The other youth turned round. The one closest to Will had a splayed nose and a pierced eyebrow. His hair was razored to stubble. The taller one, who was still emptying the machine, was effetely dressed in a dated pin-striped suit and a pink neck scarf. A handkerchief of the same silk cascaded from his top pocket. Maurice watched the platform clearing. He heard the distant ring of a tannoy announcement and hoped it was an urgent call for the transport police. He backed off, pulling Will by the shoulders.

'Come on, Will, time to go.' His smile, he knew, was insipid and placatory. Will struck a stance with his sword. The dandyish youth grimaced.

'Come on,' Maurice said, trying to march Will backwards. 'We have to go.' Maurice had so far avoided city violence by adopting certain principles. The cardinal one was never to make eye contact with anybody, particularly lunatics or youths. He knew that the chances of the youths attacking him were slightly reduced because Will was with him; after all, this wasn't New York. However, drugs always seemed to mess up the equation when it came to analysing the rationality of violence, and from the dandyish youth's glazed stare, it looked as if he had taken something that didn't entirely agree with him.

'You wanna control him, you do,' the youth with the splayed nose said.

'Yes,' Maurice said, pulling Will further away.

'Goin' round pointing swords at people an' that.'

'It's plastic,' Maurice said. 'It's a plastic sword.'

'Yes, well. You could put somebody's eye out with that. Couldn't he?' He appealed to the dandyish youth. 'He could put somebody's eye out wiv that.'

'Shut up,' the other youth said. 'Just shut up, Vernon.'

By now Maurice and Will were ten feet away, and edging backwards towards the corridor that led to the escalators.

'Take this chocolate. You wanted it, take it.'

Vernon held his palms together and the other loaded them with chocolate bars.

'He drives me insane,' the tall youth confided to Maurice. 'Insane. His chocolate fetish will be the death of us.'

Maurice had now managed to prise Will's sword from his fist and tuck it into his own belt.

The middle-aged woman, having watched the exchange for a while, walked cagily back towards them. 'To have a bar of chocolate would be very nice,' she said.

'Another one,' the tall youth said, exasperated. 'Well, give her one.' Vernon handed one over.

'Can I have one?' Will whispered to Maurice.

'Give him one as well,' the youth said.

'Well, thanks very much, but he's eaten,' Maurice said. He heard the distant scuffle of steps on the stairs and deduced that the police were on their way.

'Give him one, Vernon.' Vernon gave him one.

'I say!' The wag in evening dress reappeared, leading a

sniggering group of penguins towards them. 'I say, can we have one?'

'What?'

'I said could we have one?'

'He's taking the piss, Vernon,' the dandy said. 'Is he taking the piss?'

Vernon nodded.

'Go and hit him, then.' Vernon handed the chocolates to the dandy and advanced on the man whose smile froze.

'Hit him. Go on,' the youth encouraged. 'In the eye. Poke him sharply in the eye.'

Instead, Vernon hit the man hard in his solar plexus. The man coughed and fell, leaned his weight on his right arm, then lay slowly down on the ground. Two transport policemen careened round the corner of the platform.

'Scram, Vernon. Quick as you like.'

The two youths ran off down the corridor to the southbound platform. The transport policemen skidded on rubber soles round the corner and followed them. Another tannoy barked. The wag in the dinner jacket coughed a gout of bright blood into a handkerchief. The rest of his party stood around watching him without sympathy. The woman in the filthy coat ate her chocolate as if it was the first meal she'd had all day. Then the headlights of a train appeared in the far gloom of the tunnel. The lights rose slowly up the gradient until the alloy tube crashed out into the station. The woman teetered but did not fall into its path. Maurice grabbed Will's hand, made a dash for his satchel, and bundled them into the relative safety of the train.

'This city is insane. Absolutely insane,' Maurice was talking to Elaine an hour after the incident. 'I mean . . . I don't know. We could have been killed. All of us.' They were in the eighth-floor canteen, having dropped Will's bag off in Maurice's office. Will, sitting beside Elaine, was wearily eating a plate of chips. It was 10 p.m. The overnight announcer was eating a dry croissant from a paper plate and reading a copy of the *Sun* propped up against his condiments. A small group of engineers queued at the till to pay for their mounds of toast. A woman was sitting by the door reading a thick novel. It was rumoured that a recent divorce had provoked the onset of agoraphobia, and since then she had taken to living in her office.

'Anyway,' Maurice said, 'what are you still doing here?'

'I'm trying to sort tomorrow out. Warde's still sick and the only thing he seems to have commissioned is a column from a Welshman.' Elaine tousled Will's hair. He pushed her hand irritably away. 'He looks tired. Are you tired, Will?'

'Yes. He is,' Maurice answered, knowing how much his son hated the spinsterly attentions of certain women. 'Phone round the publishers first thing tomorrow, somebody must be out plugging something.'

'I've done that. There's a Chinese dissident who was jailed for years in some Chinese gulag and a blind woman with one leg who climbed Everest.'

'Go for the blind monoped, Roy doesn't know anything about China. Anyway, he likes triumph over adversity stories.'

'I thought I'd get them both on. They must have something in common. I'm sure we'll find something.' Elaine was still watching Will. 'He does look like you, doesn't he?'

'I don't know: I suppose so. He's a pain in the arse at the moment so I suppose he takes after me in that respect.' Maurice helped himself to one of the chips. Will scowled at him, then resignedly laid his head against Elaine's arm and fell asleep.

'God, I wish I could do that,' Elaine said. She pulled the prop of her arm gently away and Will settled down onto her lap. 'He's very beautiful.'

'Mm . . . what's up with Warde, anyway? I mean I only saw him this morning in the café. He looked perfectly all right to me.'

'Oh, I don't know. I can't keep up with him. I imagine it's some woman, or something . . . goodnight Stuart.'

'Goodnight darling,' the announcer said resonantly, then saluted with his newspaper as he pushed through the swing doors to the lift that would take him to the third floor to read the 10.30 bulletin.

'He's a nice man,' Elaine said fondly.

'Stuart?'

'He collects something. Books or rare . . . I think it's watercolours. He was telling me about it last Christmas. At the party. I was terribly plastered. No, I think it's books: first editions.'

'Fascinating.'

'You're terribly grumpy tonight. And I don't think it's very smart to be horrible about Will when he can hear you. Children understand, you know.'

'I know they do. It's just. I don't know . . .'

'What? Tell me what the matter is.'

'No, you'll just accuse me of self-pity again.'

'I won't. I promise,' Elaine said.

'Well, it's just that I'm so bloody tired. And that business on the tube shook me up. And we haven't got anywhere to stay because Dawn chucked me out this morning. I didn't dare tell Pol . . . Are you comfortable there?'

Elaine shifted Will's weight in her lap. 'I could stay like this all night.'

'Well that's why. I'll have to borrow the camp-bed from

Peculiar's office for Will and crash down on the floor myself.'

'You could stay with me if you like.'

'No. Thanks but I don't think Will would forgive me if I woke him up and dragged him off somewhere else.'

They settled into a companionable silence. Maurice sketched a tree on his polystyrene cup with his thumbnail. Elaine stroked Will's hair. She shifted in her seat to look out of the wide window. The lights of Primrose Hill crowned the dark head of Regent's Park. Infant skyscrapers jutted into the night like rocket gantries. The Post Office Tower loomed like a practical joke over the Georgian terraces of Fitzrovia.

Elaine was debating whether to tell Maurice the real reason why she was there so late. Sometimes she had an overwhelming need to confide in him about her relationship with Roy, who had offered to take her out for dinner but had neither turned up, nor called to explain why. She hadn't yet managed to summon up the energy to go home but she wasn't angry any more, just disappointed.

'I like it here at night,' Elaine said.

'The canteen, you mean?'

'Yes. The whole building, really. It feels like the people working here are the ones who matter. Not the managers, or the consultants, or the strategists . . . just us. I suppose it must have felt like this during the war. They turned the concert hall into a dormitory, you know.'

'No. I didn't know.'

'And lots of people were killed when a bomb fell on the place. I suppose they felt that they were doing something that mattered, you know, giving out vital information: keeping people's spirits up.'

Through the far doors Maurice saw Roy come in. He hesitated when he saw the two of them together, then seeing that Maurice had spotted him, motioned that he was fetching a coffee. He was wearing an expensive black single-breasted suit and looked uncomfortable but much younger in it than in his habitual mismatching sports jackets and ill-fitting trousers. Elaine was facing the wrong way to see him.

'I suppose that's what we still do,' Maurice said, watching Roy making a fuss over pouring his coffee from one of the silver urns. 'I mean giving out lots of information; vainly hoping to keep people's spirits up. Perhaps that's why this place sometimes feels like some bloody great heritage park. You know, just reinforcing a quaint notion of what this country used to be when people were all decent, and lived in harmony, and everybody knew their place.'

'I don't know why you don't just leave.'

'Ah, now there's a very good reason for that. This is the one place left where you can still spend all day moaning about it and they won't fire you. There's always been a healthy culture of dissent as well as discontent: without it we wouldn't make the jolly fine programmes we do. Anyway, nobody else would be stupid enough to employ me. Evening, Roy.'

Maurice had watched Roy with the cashier. He had offered a twenty-pound note in the hope she'd refuse it and he'd have an excuse to go with a shrug of his shoulders and without an excuse. Few cashiers in the building ever seemed to have a sufficiently large float in their till to furnish change for any denomination above fifty pence. Unfortunately for Roy, she took it and counted his nineteen pounds and sixty-seven pence change in coins. Nobody dared argue with the night cashiers, so Roy accepted his humiliation meekly. He came over with the pockets of his trousers loaded like those of the tunnel diggers in *The Great Escape*.

'Evening all.' Roy sat carefully, looked at Will sleeping on

Elaine's lap with neither surprise nor interest and said, 'Glad to see somebody's still at it.'

Elaine looked out of the window again.

'And what are you doing here?' Maurice said, more for Elaine's sake than his own. He was not the least interested in what Roy was doing there or where he had been.

'I had to see a man about a dog. But I got detained.' Roy was watching Elaine, trying to hook her attention. She resisted. 'Bloody annoying because I'd booked a table at The Ivy. Champers on ice, the lot . . . Shame to see it go to waste.'

'This man's dog was here, was it?' Maurice said, having belatedly divined the reason for Elaine still being there.

'Round the corner,' Roy said tersely.

'Which corner?'

'None of your bloody business, actually, Maurice.'

'Well thanks for the invitation, but I can't make The Ivy. I suppose you'll have to take Elaine. Won't he, Elaine? How do you fancy dinner at The Ivy?'

Elaine breathed out heavily. 'No thanks, Maurice. I'm tired. I have to get back for Mother.'

'Sorry, Roy,' Maurice relayed. 'She has to get back. For Mother. Another time.'

'Well that's a great shame.' Roy worked a hand into his pocket and jangled his change. His eyes narrowed as he tried to work out whether Elaine meant it.

'I suppose you could take Will,' Maurice said.

'Listen, shit-for-brains.' Roy suddenly leaned forwards. 'Don't think I've forgotten that conversation we had this morning. I bloody warned you to stop taking the piss out of me and I bloody meant it.'

'That's right. You were going to bash me up or something, weren't you?'

'Any time. Any time you like.'

'All right,' Maurice said, patting his jacket down as he stood. 'How about now?'

Roy stood too and drew himself up to his full height which still left him two inches short of Maurice. 'Outside, then.'

'Oh for Christ's sake!' Elaine shouted. Will woke and blinked nervously. 'For Christ's sake why don't you both just bloody grow up.' She eased Will off her lap and stormed out through the swing doors tugging her cardigan round her.

''Night, Elaine,' Maurice called. Roy watched her. Maurice thought he was going to get up and follow, but he seemed to decide against it.

'You're a twat, Maurice,' Roy said.

Maurice shuffled across to take Elaine's place and lifted Will's head onto his lap. The child sniffled but dropped back to sleep.

'It wasn't me who let her down.'

'You see, you don't know anything about women.' Roy leaned forwards into his bar-room lecture pose. 'You think you do. But you don't.'

'Go on then . . .'

'You have to be there for them.'

'Like tonight you mea . . .'

'Shut up, I'm trying to tell you something.'

'Well go on, then.'

'You're never there, boy. I've watched you. You think you are, but you're not. I don't know where you live in that mind of yours, but you're away with the fairies half the time. Now take me. I might not be the most reliable bloke around, and I might not be the most sensitive and all that bollocks but I know how to give a woman a good time. And they respect me for it because I respect them.'

'And Caz respects all this respecting you do of other woman, does she?'

Roy looked at him with a new loathing. 'You have no right to ask that question. No right at all.'

'No, I'm sorry. I really . . .'

'You don't know Caz, and you don't know me. So don't start making assumptions. Get yourself a life. Stop poking your nose into other people's. All right?'

'Sure.'

'You're a fool, Maurice. You're a fool because you don't understand the most basic truth. And that is we can only live together because of the lies we tell each other. Only the fool doesn't realise they're lies.'

Roy walked out and Maurice thought about it as he finished Will's cold chips.

SEVEN

VINCENT EDWARDS WAS listening to the radio in his office when Maurice barged in without knocking. His jacket was draped over the back of his chair and the piece of red tissue paper he'd hung over his desk lamp made the room glow like a Soho grotto. He was listening to a live concert being relayed from the Festival Hall. Maurice didn't know much about what was categorised within the building as 'serious' music, but the dissonant cacophony of metallic clangs issuing from Edwards's loudspeakers immediately took him back to the tube platform and the sound of the chocolate machine being smashed up.

'It seems quaintly outdated when one compares it to Reich,' Edwards said without further elucidation. He carefully laid a small hardback book onto his desk. Maurice, craning his neck, tried to read the title. Edwards turned it face down.

'Sorry to disturb you like this,' Maurice said, though Edwards didn't look the least bit disturbed at the interruption. 'I would have knocked, but I thought you wouldn't be here. I mean I wasn't coming in to riffle through your drawers or anything.'

'I didn't imagine you were.'

'Of course not. I came to borrow the camp-bed, actually.'

'It's over there.' Edwards waved vaguely towards the shadows under the window. 'Help yourself.'

'It's just that. Well,' Maurice sat down, deciding that Edwards, being his boss, probably deserved an explanation. 'Well, you see, Dawn has chucked me out and I'm looking after Will and we haven't actually got anywhere to . . .'

'Maurice, please, no need,' Edwards said, uncapping a half bottle of Bells whisky and pouring a generous measure into a white plastic beaker. He leaned across the desk and handed it to Maurice. 'You see, all day people seem intent on furnishing me with redundant information. My office is cluttered with memos telling me things I already know, or certainly could have worked out given a moment's thought.' Then, more expansively, 'I spend hours and hours sitting in management meetings, liaison meetings, strategy meetings, meetings with resources, meetings with editors, meetings with controllers, watching dull people in ill-fitting suits writing dull things on whiteboards, projecting inane statements onto screens from overhead projectors, listening to young intelligent people or, more often, middle-aged, self-important people patronising me with gobbets of outdated American management speak. I visit and, God help me, even speak on courses to fresh-faced youngsters eager for information – however redundant it is – and now they have begun sending it to me electronically as well. In short, I do not need to know why you wish to borrow my camp-bed.'

'Fine.' Will was asleep wrapped in Maurice's jacket on the floor of his office. Perhaps this was the opportunity Maurice had been waiting for to find out what his boss had in mind for him. 'You seem a bit disillusioned with it all. If you don't mind me saying.'

'I'm sure I do, Maurice.'

'So . . .' Maurice prompted. 'So what's to be done?'

'You tell me.' Edwards seemed to have shaken himself out of his reverie. He fixed his attention on Maurice with an unsettling goggle-eyed smile on his face.

'Well, just leave I suppose. Let them get on with it.'

'You don't mean that, Maurice. You can't leave. You're like me. You need this organisation more than this organisation needs you. Those who complain about the system most vociferously are those who love it the most wholeheartedly. Besides which, you are, I imagine, unemployable elsewhere. So one must put up with the bastards.'

'Is that how you . . . I mean do you really feel like that?'

'Don't you?'

'Yes, but, I thought it was just me. I mean I'm prepared to allow that these changes are for the greater good, etc.'

'And there's the rub. They are. However glorious it was to live under the regime that produced real art, real art comes at a cost. It has to be allowed to ferment among the inertia of creative inactivity. Unfortunately, creative inactivity cannot be costed. And in this brave new world of "efficiencies" and "choice" and "transparency", it *don't* fit.'

Maurice shifted uncomfortably on his seat. He had never seen Edwards like this and, like any child who sees a parent drunk for the first time, didn't like what he saw. 'Are you writing something?' Maurice pointed to the book on the desk.

'Yes. I am as a matter of fact. A few personal thoughts: random jottings.' Edwards gauged Maurice's reaction before he went on. 'I'm writing my autobiography.'

'Fabulous,' Maurice said with genuine enthusiasm. 'I mean it's people like you who need to tell the story of this place. Not the mandarins, the great and the good. Sorry, I don't mean you're, well, I mean, you know what I mean, don't you?'

'I think so.'

'So how does it end?'

'I don't know. I . . . I mean, one imagines the end to be the conclusion of one's career, but I'd rather like it to be more than that.'

'You're leaving aren't you?' Maurice played the hunch he'd had for the past few months. 'I mean, it's none of my business. But you are, aren't you?'

Edwards weighed his answer, then said. 'Yes. Quite soon, but I don't want anyone to know.'

'Of course.'

'I mean it. It's important. Extremely important.'

'You can trust me. I promise.' Maurice tapped the cover of the book. Edwards drew it away from him. 'Am I in there?'

'Possibly. Possibly.' Edwards stood up and went over to close the door. On his way back he opened a grey cupboard and took out a litre bottle of very good single malt whisky. He poured two large measures into substantial glasses and handed one to Maurice. Maurice put his beaker of ordinary whisky aside and took it.

'Do you have a few minutes to spare me?' Edwards stood by the window, silhouetted against the orange lights.

'Yes. Of course I do. Of course.' There was something noble and rather ghostly about the figure at the window. Perhaps Edwards had already gone and a doppelgänger remained to haunt his office.

'Tell me what you think of me.'

'Oh, well . . .' Maurice blustered. 'I mean for heaven's sake. You can't expect me to . . .'

'Simple question. I'll simplify it further. What do you think my achievements have been? Have I done anything that has mattered?'

'Yes. Yes, you have. Quite a lot as a matter of fact.' Maurice just needed time. He liked and respected Edwards, despite his oddness. He was a good man, and there weren't many of them left. 'I've heard . . .'

'No. I'm not asking for chapter and verse. I'm simply wondering whether one's perception of one's own reputation is ever . . . accurate.'

'I think your reputation is safe.' Maurice shifted in his chair. 'But you see it's not just what you've done, it's the way you've done it, and how you've taught others. I mean me, really, how to do it. I've learned an enormous amount . . . well, I don't want to embarrass you, but to get back to your question, yes, that reputation is safe.'

'Thank you. Thank you, Maurice. That does, actually, matter to me.'

'Look. I want to ask you something. You don't have to tell me, and perhaps it's the whisky talking or something. Tell me to mind my own business if you like. But what's going on? What I mean is – this business of making me take leave – you don't really want me to go because you think I need to. So why?'

'Ah.' Edwards emerged from the shadows and came back to the desk, all the time he was watching Maurice.

'So there is something?'

'Yes.'

'And I'm involved in it? I am involved in it, aren't I?'

'I think you'll have to decide that, Maurice. But I would strongly counsel against it.'

'Well go on then.'

Edwards opened a drawer in his desk. He took out a sheaf of A4 paper and passed it to Maurice.

'The White Symphony' Maurice read.

'Open it.'

Maurice turned over the first page. The sheet was blank. As was the second, and the third.

'I don't understand.' Maurice said slowly. 'Is this a script or something?'

'Yes. In a manner of speaking.'

'And you haven't written it yet. Is that it?'

'Oh no. It's quite finished.'

Maurice then remembered one of Edwards's training lectures. He had talked to a small group, quite animatedly, about silence, and the truth began to dawn.

As Elaine let herself into the house, the central heating boiler popped in the kitchen as the gas ignited. The house was otherwise silent. She removed her shoes and trod gently up the stairs. Her mother was asleep in the front room, her bedside lamp still on. Elaine watched the rise and fall of the sheets. The grey face with its mouth half open called silently for breath, then expelled it, contaminated, into the sick room. She went downstairs and into the lounge where she half drew the curtains that she had opened that morning. The cleaner had not been in so the house was exactly how she had left it. She looked out across the front garden. The standard lamp beside the lead-paned window illuminated the cotoneaster bush. The lawn, as far as the light revealed, was white with frost. The roses her father had planted had been cut back in the way he would have done.

Elaine sat on the arm of the sofa and allowed herself a few self-pitying tears. She could never predict when she would miss her father the most, but sometimes she could strongly feel his presence. At times like these, often late in the evenings, she would manipulate this vague sense of him into a belief that he had walked into the room. But she would not destroy it by looking round. Instead she might, perhaps, talk to him; imagine him listening, coming further into the room, taking a chair behind her, but respecting what she was telling him sufficiently not to interrupt her. He was a man who allowed consideration of all matters, however trivial. Even his occasional witticisms were carefully wrought. He had been a draughtsman, and shared an office beside the goods yards at St Pancras Station with others like him. Elaine spent many days with him in her school holidays. He would find her a drawing board and she would sketch beside him as he worked. Occasionally he would look across and she would catch his eye, shyly, not wanting to claim any time from him that he should have been giving to his work. She borrowed his love whenever she could.

He was with her now, and she was grateful for it. He was wearing his gardening trousers, an open-necked shirt, and carrying the ragged gloves that he used for the roses. They had been the first present she had bought for him as a child and, even though they were worn, he had always refused to throw them away. Elaine sensed that he was smiling, he had something that he wanted to share with her. Perhaps something about the garden, or that he had heard on the radio and had just remembered. But Elaine didn't want to talk tonight. She just wanted somebody with her while she cried.

Across the city the others slept, or had begun their rituals of sleep. Roy was cleaning his teeth in a stark hotel bathroom. The flesh beneath his eyes sagged. Reflected in the bathroom mirror he could see the bedroom TV showing a German porn film. A man and a woman were on a red motor scooter, driving through a forest. Her blonde hair was flying loose, revealing its dark roots. His torso was naked as his shirt flapped in the breeze.

Maurice was asleep on the camp-bed in his office, turning fitfully in the hot narrow space. Will, who could find comfort anywhere, had shrugged off Maurice's jacket and was lying on his back in a crucifixion pose beneath Maurice's desk. He was dreaming of rabbits, which he did quite often.

Warde was watching the late film in a small flat in Pimlico which reeked of a doner kebab. The can of lager in his hand was warm. He wanted to go to bed but something was troubling him. He knew he must soon tell Maurice the real reason that Dawn had made him leave but he hadn't yet found the courage.

Dawn, meanwhile, was sleeping a just sleep and dreaming of Brazil. The beach was not a beach she had visited and the small child that squatted and pissed onto the hot sand looked like Maurice. When her dream broke the following day, she would equate it with the abortion she had had on her way to South America. Maurice would never know that the foetus of his second child had been incinerated in a kitchen range in one of the respectable suburbs of Antwerp.

At 1.27 a.m., a casualty consultant in a West London hospital looked at his watch and announced to the small group around him that this was the denoted time of death of the man on his operating table. The man's heart had stopped some four hours before, but, in the ambulance, the paramedics had administered adrenaline which had kicked it back to life. It had then stopped, been restarted, and finally stopped altogether. If the consultant seemed more uncon-cerned than he usually did it was because the corpse was in his late fifties, two stones overweight and was obviously a heavy drinker.

A man called Vernon was playing snooker in an all-night club above a bookie's in Stockwell when the man on the operating table died. He potted a long green, screwed back for a red to the centre pocket, and was chalking up for the black when he became officially designated a murderer. It was a tag he would carry to his death, which would be of a heroin overdose two years later.

In Paris, Val was snoring on top of a green coverlet. She was fully clothed and had lapsed into a drunken sleep. Polly was leaning out of the window. A man and a woman, clinging to each other, walked along the cobbles beneath her. The streetlights threw their shadows ahead of them. Polly, for a reason she did not question, was thinking about the barn on her parents' farm. The connection, had she traced it back, was that, on the night she had left home to marry Maurice, her mother had built a huge bonfire behind the barn. Polly had stood beside her and looked into the flames. Their shadows had been thrown against the barn by the ferocious fire. Although her mother had not told her that she was sorry she was leaving home, she was a woman of few words, and Polly knew her well enough to know that she was.

II

The broadcasters are mostly young men. From the nature of things in the beginning this was, I think, to be expected; in view of the arduous and diverse nature of their labours it is probably fortunate. They are rather shadowy personalities to the average man; they are aloof and mysterious. You will probably not find them at garden parties or social functions; their names may not figure among the distinguished ones present, even if they do go; most likely they are much too busy to spend time in this way. They neither receive, nor do they desire, the attention of the street and market-place.

J.C.W. Reith, op. cit.

ONE

Late on saturday morning, Maurice took Will out to buy a newspaper which he read as they ate lunch in the canteen. The room was quieter and more civilised than during the tray-clattering lunchtimes of the week. Two tables were occupied by sports department staff exuding the naive evangelicalism of those who make a living talking about games. Most of them were wearing logo-embossed jumpers and training shoes: sports territorials, ready to be called up to play at a moment's notice. A small group of emaciated actors in scruffy civvies was competing enthusiastically for each other's attention at a table by the window. A pile of tins of handrolling tobacco was at the centre of the table. They were taking a break from recording a school's radio drama and the young woman producing it was sitting with them, listening intently and nodding vigorously, slightly star-struck. Her nervous attention, however, was fleetingly diverted by the elderly woman in a khaki dress and wearing gold half-rim glasses at a table close by. She was the only actor Maurice recognised, and as she trimmed the fat from her lamb chop, elegantly dissected her duchess potatoes and sipped her claret he replayed the episode of *The Forsyte Saga* he remembered seeing her in. He couldn't work out whether she was sitting alone out of choice or because there had been no room at the others' table. Either way, there was sufficient anxiety in the producer's face to suggest that the afternoon was going to be a tense one.

Will was tired and asked repeatedly when his mother was coming back from France with his model aeroplane. Eventually, as she hadn't appeared, nor was she due to appear in a period of time that was within his comprehension, he transferred his affections to his father. This meant that he told Maurice that he loved him, held his hand at all times and, whenever they stopped anywhere, crawled onto his lap and looked adoringly into his eyes. Maurice, of course, quite liked this attention. Since the separation it always seemed to take at least a day for Will to get used to him. This usually coincided with the time he was due to be handed back. Maurice knew he should take his son to see his father for a couple of days. The old man was leading an active life in his retirement, and seemed to have found a new lease of life since Maurice's mother had died two years before. He was still living in Maurice's childhood home but had recently embarked on a spate of improvements, the results of which were impossible to envisage as none of the rooms were yet finished. The lounge and the dining room looked like building sites and the kitchen had a wall missing. The previous time Maurice had visited there had been a problem with the electricity and they had eaten fish and chips by candlelight. He believed that the old man was still grieving for his wife and the renovations were his way of eradicating both her and his grief from the house.

Maurice had bought a newspaper to find a room to rent. Of the seven numbers he had so far called, only one offered any hope. Three had already been let, another was owned by an old Irishman who wanted a woman to lodge with him. In the fifth, the music was so loud that Maurice couldn't hear what the man on the other end was saying, and the woman who owned the sixth asked too many personal questions, then left embarrassing pauses after his answers. He finally declined her offer of a look round when, in a sudden gush, she told him she felt she ought to mention that she was a vegan, a rabid anti-smoker, loved cats and Jeanette Winterson, and wondered whether he concurred that *Thelma and Louise* was 'just the best film ever made'? His final call was answered by a smoky-voiced woman who sounded as though she had just got out of bed. She told him that she shared the flat with another woman called Grace who was, apparently 'Afro-Caribbean', though this wasn't 'you know, an issue' and who was a smoker. When he said he didn't mind the occasional party and was a relatively good listener, not gay, though this was a different issue, she informed him that Grace would be up at about two o'clock and he should come round for a cup of tea. She gave the address in relation to Barons Court tube station, and rang off.

'So, Will,' Maurice said. 'I wonder what they'll make of you?' Then he realised he hadn't mentioned his son to them.

Polly and Val were, at the same time, walking hand in hand through the Latin Quarter. As a result of her previous night's consumption of red wine, Val was fractious and exhibiting no interest at all in the shops they were passing. Polly was annoyed on the grounds that she didn't go away very often, and felt that Val was insensitive to this because her job often involved overnight stays in hotels. Val was also distracted by a story she was working on, and wouldn't tell Polly what it was. She'd even gone as far as taking her laptop to the hotel bar after breakfast to make some notes. In retribution, Polly had tried to call Maurice but Dawn had answered the phone and explained that he no longer lived there. She then called her mother who demanded to know, in the minutest detail, what she had done, what she intended to do, and whether she was 'looking after herself', whatever that meant.

They hadn't actually argued yet, but Polly's good humour was stretched as far as it would go, and when she stopped to look into the garlanded window of an antiques shop and Val walked on without noticing, she turned and set off in the other direction.

In the face of Polly's rare rages, Val could usually quickly muster a far more effective anger. This would evolve into a self-pitying whine which would resolve into tears and bitter apology – or, occasionally, violence. Polly, therefore, usually managed to keep her emotions in check. But she couldn't bear selfishness, and, as far as she was concerned, Val's mood was utterly selfish. So when Val caught her up she called her a selfish bitch, and Val, caught off guard, reacted as if she had been slapped in the face.

'Well you are,' Polly said, standing her ground though her anger had already burned out. In being able to see the other's point of view on most matters, her own emotional defences were easily disarmed.

'I saw you,' Val said, keeping her distance, but squaring up for a fight.

'What?'

'You know what I mean.' Val sighed heavily and looked into the shop window as if this was what she had intended to do all along.

Polly laughed. 'What are you talking about?'

'You know exactly what I mean,' Val said to her own reflection in the window.

Polly took a step towards her. 'I honestly don't know what you're talking about.' Then, because there was no response, 'Val?'

'The waitress. The pretty little thing. This morning.

Remember?' She annotated the accusation as if she was talking to an imbecile.

'I'm sorry. I'm not. No. This is just. Look. I'm going back. Come back to the hotel when you've made up your mind to enjoy the weekend. OK?' Although she felt she should stay and allow Val a reply, Polly found sufficient strength within herself to walk away. Behind her she heard Val sob and, because she didn't stop, Val shouted after her. It was an appalling obscenity to hear in the stillness of a quiet street and it resounded from the buildings around them. A window shutter opened and clattered against a wall. Polly halved her pace, then quickly regained her composure and speeded up again. Val called something else, but by now Polly was feeling stronger and was almost out of earshot. She would have escaped completely if she hadn't had to stop at the kerb to let a cyclist pass. But as she did she glanced back and saw Val slumped on the pavement like a bonfire guy, her knees up to her chin and weeping authentic tears. Polly stepped out into the road, but she couldn't go on. She walked back to Val, retaining some of her dignity by walking slowly. When she offered her hand to help Val up, it was not taken.

'I am a bitch. You know I am. That is what I am.'

'Come on. Up you come.' Again she offered her hand, but Val, this time, was not acting.

'I've been so awful to you. I can't forgive myself. Really, I can't.'

'It doesn't matter. Let's just go and get a coffee and do something nice. Go to the Louvre. Or on a river boat. Or see Notre Dame. Come on. I want to do something corny . . . come on.'

'I hate myself.'

Polly sighed.

'I do.'

'Don't be silly.'

'I wish it was . . . I wish I could dismiss it as easily as you do.'

'Hate yourself when you go back to work,' Polly said, and sighed again.

'What are you saying?'

'I am saying. I am saying that I am sick and tired of you giving all of this . . . shit to me when you're nice as pie to your, I don't know, your workmates. I'm tired of it. Absolutely tired of your selfish, self-pitying . . .' Polly tried to find exactly the right word but all she could manage was, 'crap'.

'And I suppose Maurice was different?' Val struggled to her feet, the window glass bending as she leaned her weight on it.

'This has got nothing to do with Maurice. Absolutely nothing whatsoever to do with Maurice.'

'I said, simple point, that I suppose he was different. So I am making him part of it.'

'Don't. I'm not interested. I'm not going to be drawn . . . now, I am going back. If you want to come with me then do. If you don't then go and take your shitty little mood out on somebody else.'

'I wonder if you'll ever defend me in the way you always defend him . . . I wonder.'

'I told you, Val. I'm not interested.'

'I wonder . . . I wonder just how far you'd take it.'

Polly looked at her watch. It was two fifteen. They had twenty-four hours then they had to fly back home. 'I wonder how much longer we're going to spend on this. Or are we going to argue for the rest of our time here?'

'You see you think being rational and calm and grown up I'll shut up and start acting like you. Well it doesn't cut any ice, baby. It doesn't work.'

'I'm so tired of this, Val.'

'I bet you are.'

'Please.' Polly offered her hand. Again Val did not take it so Polly walked a step closer to her. Val couldn't bear to look at her. Ashamed, she stared towards the shutters of a shop on the other side of the road. A young woman in mourning black walked quickly past, straight-backed. The gauze hanging from her small hat shielded her expression. Polly took Val's hand, linked their fingers and clenched her palm.

'I'm tired,' Val said. 'I'm just so tired.'

'I know. Let's go and rest . . . Come on, we don't have to go out if you're not up to it.'

Val waited. 'I think I've done something terrible.'

'Terrible? Tell me.'

'I can't. It's too . . . terrible.'

'Come on. I'll forgive you.'

'I can't.' Val pulled her hand away. Where her teeth lay on the cushion of her lower lip a line of blood had formed.

'Tell me,' Polly said, more firmly.

'It's about Maurice.'

'What about Maurice?' Polly took Val's forearm and held it tightly. 'What have you done to Maurice?'

'Nothing yet. Don't worry. Look, don't worry, I think I can get out of it . . . honestly. It's not gone too far yet. I can call it off. Yes, that's what I'll do. I'll call it all off . . .'

Later, Polly began packing her suitcase. It was all she could think to do to take her mind off what Val had told her. Then she unpacked it because they still had a night to spend together in a city which she had come to hate in a way she hated nowhere else.

'So he goes, right? He goes, like: "You think I'm stupid just 'cause I'm a man," right? And I go: "Look, Georgy," 'cause that's what I call him, right? Georgy Porgy cause he's fat, but he's all right about it, but he says this thing and I go: "Look, you are stupid, right? You broke the telly, and the washing machine, and you blocked up the sink, and you use all our toilet paper, now you tell me you're not stupid, right?" And he goes: "Fair enough," and he gets his stuff and just leaves . . . Georgy. That was his name.'

'I see,' Maurice said. 'So George . . .'

'Georgy,' the woman said, dropping the nub of her fourth Marlboro Light into the dregs of her tea. The small living room was cluttered with empty cigarette packets, bottles of Holsten Pils, CDs with no cases, several 12" dance singles, and an assortment of IKEA furniture. A pine table was stacked with newspapers, women's magazines, style magazines, hairdressing magazines, several rental video boxes and a pile of scripts.

'So Georgy left a year ago, and then there was . . . Pete, did you say?'

'Pete!' the woman shrieked. 'Yea, *wild man*. Pete was *mental*.'

Will, sitting on Maurice's lap, was virtually comatose with boredom. He was so bored that he was singing 'One Man Went to Mow' to himself. The tall, thin, loud, energetic, but nevertheless appreciably pretty black woman on the sofa was, as far as he was concerned, a lost cause. She'd given him a cup of Coke and a stale biscuit, he'd been to the toilet twice to relieve his boredom, and now all he wanted to do was to go home. Maurice, however, was intrigued by Grace, not least because, like Will, he found her extremely attractive. Her energy was tidal and fierce, she had given him her life story which had begun in East Anglia and deposited her at the age of eight in London, a city whose culture and attitudes she'd greedily assimilated – the sole daughter of a black airforce captain and a white nurse. Grace was now an actress, cum model, cum dancer, who was, at the moment, waitressing. Maurice was debating with himself whether what he was feeling about her was love or just lust. Grace was knife-thin. Her hair was close-cropped and dyed blonde (something to do with a modelling job), her cheekbones and aquiline nose looked as if they could only have been achieved by plastic surgery, and her eyes were an astonishing cornflower blue.

'So, you own the flat?' Maurice said, looking around it properly for the first time and deciding that he liked the batik prints, was happy at the size of the huge stereo, and could live with a thirty-inch TV. The calendar with a naked man he could live without.

'Well, it's like my dad's flat, right, but he's back home now for another year, at least until next Christmas, and my mum's with him again and I'm like so *excited* about it, and he just lets me live here with who I like so there's Martha and me. Martha and me, me and Martha,' Grace laughed. 'And maybe you. If you want.' For the first time she fell silent and fixed Maurice with an intense stare. 'Let me guess . . .'

'What?'

'Sagittarian, right?'

'Ah . . . yes. Sagittarian.'

'I like Sagittarians.' She lit another cigarette. 'Think of a colour.'

'Ah . . . blue.'

'This is so *spooky*.'

'Is it?'

'No, right, like I go to Martha – I bet Morry chooses blue. *Martha!*'

'What?' Martha called from a bedroom where she was listening to the radio.

'Morry chose *blue* . . .'

'. . . Right,' Martha called back without energy.

'Do you like poetry?'

'Yes,' Maurice managed in the brief pause.

'Martha writes poetry. It's really beautiful. Ask her to read some out loud to you. She won't. But she might. Listen. What do you think of this? This guy in the café, right? Black clothes and roll-neck, everything black. He's sitting there and, like, making notes with a pencil on his newspaper, and I give him his espresso (double, no sugar, cause he's an artist, right? – anyway, that's what he says) and he goes: "Everybody's the same, only in different ways." And I go, "*What?*" and he says it again, and then he goes, "Let me buy you a drink or something," like I don't know what that means and I say, "No way," but nice, because he's a customer, and he goes: "You don't know what you're missing." Anyway, I told Martha about it and she said he was probably a psychoknife killer or something . . . Will?' Grace teased, another, more sober mood washing over her.

Will swivelled his attention towards her.

'Do you think your daddy'll like it here?'

Will looked towards Maurice for a translation. 'You see I might come and live here – for a while, and you can come and visit me. What do you think of that?'

'No thank you,' Will said.

'Will,' Grace said.

'Yes.'

'Do you like French fries?'

'Chips,' Maurice said.

Will nodded.

'Would you like to help me make some?'

Will thought for a moment, then nodded again.

'Come on, then.' Grace stood up, a towering six foot three, and held out her hand. Maurice waited for Will to respond. Without his son's approval he knew he couldn't move in with Grace and Martha which meant that he had to be won over by at least one of them otherwise he'd never come and stay the night. Will clambered off his lap, took Grace's hand and went into the kitchen. As they went through the door Maurice heard Will tell Grace that her hand smelt, and Grace told him she'd better wash it, then.

Maurice stood up and stretched, his back was stiff from the night he had spent on the camp-bed. He yawned and went over to the sash window which he slid open a few inches. The flat backed onto a long shared garden in which a swing had been tied to the bough of a birch tree. The garden was tidy, with a stunted patio, flower beds and sufficient lawn for him and Will to kick a ball around on. Maurice was leaning on the window sill and contemplating why it was impossible to think yourself into summer from the cold of winter, and vice versa, when Martha came in.

'Hello, Maurice.' Grace had met him at the door and this was the first time the woman he had spoken to on the phone had appeared. Her hair was wrapped in a red towel and she was wearing a candy-striped dressing gown. She was a short woman with heavy lidded eyes. Her forehead was grooved with deep lines.

'Hello, Martha.' Maurice quickly pigeonholed Martha with a type of woman he knew well: humourless and troubled, who worried men with their intensity and carried their austere sexuality like an unwelcome burden.

'So are you going to like it here?' Martha pushed a magazine from the seat of a chair onto the floor. She slumped down into it, pulled up her legs beneath her and began plucking the dark hairs from the shoulder of her gown with slow, precise pinches.

From the kitchen Maurice heard Will laugh. 'I think so.' Martha looked at him and nodded slowly.

'Grace tells me you're a poet.'

'If you hurt her I'll kill you.'

'. . . I'm sorry?'

'You heard what I said.'

'Why should I hurt her?'

'Because you're the sort who can.'

'I see . . . and are you going to tell me . . .'

Martha cut him off. 'I want to know whether you understand what I'm saying.'

'I know exactly what you're saying.'

'Then we know where we stand, don't we?'

'Absolutely.'

'. . . You'll do.' Martha stared at him for a little longer, then went back into the bedroom. Maurice took his hands from his lap. He realised he'd involuntarily been clutching his testicles to protect them from a sudden attack.

Maurice and Will spent Saturday night in a bed and breakfast hotel. Will was asleep by seven thirty. Maurice had bought a four-pack of strong lager, but by the time he'd finished one he was asleep in the airless room. He woke before midnight, disorientated and fully dressed, then he saw Will wrapped deep in his bed, snoring shallowly and sucking his thumb. Maurice kissed him on the forehead and brushed the hair out of his eyes. He didn't want to disturb the child, but he wanted him to wake, just for a minute, so they could speak to each other. Maurice was looking for acknowledgement from his son that it was he who was there, caring for him, and nobody else.

On Sunday morning they went to Regent's Park, but by midday the colour had washed from the sky and it had become too cold for them to stay outside. Maurice lifted Will onto his shoulders and they trudged to Oxford Street where they shared a cup of hot chocolate. Will told him about his school, a boy called Charlie who had pushed him into a bush and two boys who had swung him round and dropped him onto his head. Then, like giant flakes grated from the white sky, snow began to fall. The two of them watched in silence as the flakes glided between the stores and melted as they met the warmth of the street.

TWO

MAURICE REID'S LIFE was becoming increasingly isolated from those around him who were 'in relationships'. He lived disconsolately on their margins, picking up the scraps from their more legitimate friendships which tended to be with others who were similarly committed. The lives of these couples were largely unspontaneous: Maurice's life had no form whatsoever. So he was surprised when he delivered Will home to be invited in by Polly without prior arrangement. The reason she gave was that Val was out working, and they (meaning Polly) had bought him a bottle of duty-free whisky that she wanted him to open. So Maurice waited in the living room watching *Songs of Praise* while Polly bathed Will and read him his stories. Outside it had become too cold for the snow and the pavements and roads were icing. A gritting lorry passed the house, its orange warning light sweeping the living-room walls. The urban dragon roared away, blotting out the sound of the television and spitting tiny stones sibilantly against the road surface and the paintwork of parked cars.

When Polly came downstairs, her sleeves still rolled, she was flushed with the heat of the bathroom. The smell of Will's talcum powder clung to her clothes. Maurice shuffled to the end of the settee expecting her to join him, but she went to the chair beside the fire, sat down, and declined a whisky. Maurice turned off the television, and listened as she began an earnest preamble to what she explained was going to be a difficult apology.

'But I don't understand, Pol,' Maurice said, not wanting to spoil the warm glow of domestic intimacy and the warmer glow of the whisky. 'What have you got to apologise about?'

'I'm not apologising for me . . . Look, it's Val. Sorry, do you mind? I've got the most awful headache.' Polly reached up and turned off the standard lamp. The room was now lit by the sparse glow of the coal-effect fire.

'Christ, there's no need to apologise about her, I mean I'm used to . . .'

'Will you just be quiet and listen to me,' Polly said, and Maurice did, silenced by her passion. 'While we were away we had a row.' She stopped, then picked carefully through her words. 'Nothing unusual in that . . . well, except for the fact that I instigated . . . Look, this is not important. The point is that in the course of this row Val told me she'd . . .'

Polly stopped and Maurice, intrigued, prompted her gently to continue.

'She'd done something which I suppose is going to affect you. Your job, I don't know, somehow. Something, anyway. One way or another I think . . . Look, she's gone to try and sort it out but I don't think she . . .'

'Pol. What on earth are you talking about? What has Val gone to sort out?'

'Right.' Then, with greater effort, 'On Friday, when you came round here you mentioned something about Roy May to her . . .?'

'Yes, well that's hardly . . .'

'A girl. You said something about a young girl in a . . .'

'Oh, hell.'

'You see she's been finding it very hard to . . .'

'Shit.'

'. . . come up with ideas for the paper, I mean Val's not malicious . . .'

'Oh, no, of course she's not bloody . . .'

'She's not, not really. It's just that when you told her about . . . well, I'm afraid she called her editor from Paris . . .'

But then, remembering the details of the story, Maurice relaxed a little. 'She'll never stand it up. This was ages ago. Years. Apparently they paid the girl off, she didn't talk. Even if it happened. It was only a rumour, anyway.'

'Yes . . . well, I'm afraid it was rather a widespread rumour, and Anthony, Val's editor, has, apparently, been looking for an excuse to have a go at Roy May for ages. You know what these people are like.'

'It doesn't matter, Pol. Really, it doesn't. For a start they'll never find the girl. And even if they do, it's her word against his. No editor would publish a story like that. Roy would take the paper to the cleaners. He'd have to, if only to salvage his reputation. He's not stupid. Well, he is stupid, but he understands the law well enough to know when he's being libelled. So don't worry.' Maurice smiled, 'Don't worry.'

'There is just one other thing.'

'What?'

'I think they have found the girl.'

'Right.' The odds shortened. There remained sufficient questions to convince Maurice that it would be unlikely that the paper would publish. Even if they did, the chances of it being traced back to him were slight. But Maurice knew it wasn't really about the literal truth. Whatever happened, he'd betrayed Roy May, and however much he hated him, he had to apologise, if only to set his conscience straight.

'So what will you do?' Polly said.

'I'll sort it out.'

'I'm sorry, Maurice.'

'I told you. This isn't your fault.'

'No, but I dragged you into it, didn't I? I mean if I wasn't with Val, well . . .'

'But you are – aren't you?'

As Polly contemplated their separation it rekindled the guilt that had never entirely left her. Touching Maurice, holding him, offering him some of the compassion she still felt for him, helped her to deal with it. She went over to sit beside him, took Maurice's hand and kissed it.

'. . . So, you had a bloody awful time, did you?' he said.

'Not entirely. I mean, we talked, spent some time together. I think we needed to spend that time together . . . just, I mean, just to reassure ourselves. You know?'

Polly had never loved Maurice. She felt something for him which was distinguishable from what she felt about Val. But Maurice was irredeemable, and however much she gave to him, she knew it would never be enough. Val took everything she had. Polly had wanted her in a way that couldn't be contained in a tidy drawer of her life with Maurice. When it all started she had tried for a month, but she began to fear for her sanity. When she knew that she cared less about hurting him than she did for her own happiness she knew the marriage was over.

'Yes,' Maurice said, 'it's necessary, sometimes, spending time together. Otherwise, well . . . I mean I was going to say look what happened with us.'

'Not now, love. Not now.'

Maurice squeezed Polly's hand. 'Hey, listen, I've found a flat.'

'Yes, I tried to call Dawn but she said you'd moved out.'

'That's right. Anyway, it's in Barons Court, and it's owned by this woman, and she's rather . . . unusual, really. Coloured . . . I mean Afro-whatever, I mean can we say black?

Anyway, she's not white. She talks a lot, but Will seems to like her. And there's only one other woman in it, a sort of angsty student type. I think she's suspicious of me, God knows why. But I think it'll do. You should come round when I've moved in . . . Well, you know, if you can get a late pass.'

Maurice slithered along the treacherous pavement towards the underground. He slipped and lurched, each time just managing to stay on his feet. As he reached the end of the street he fell over and landed heavily on his back. He got up quickly to save his embarrassment, but he was badly winded. The back of his coat and trouser legs were cold and damp. His whisky bottle was smashed in its plastic bag. Maurice's shoulder muscles were stretched taut, only by angling his head from one side to the other did the pressure ease. He was muttering to himself. This new trait had recently been brought to his attention by Elaine who had noticed it as she followed him to the Gluepot one evening. She told him (as a friend) that he should try and get a grip on himself because in the young such behaviour was considered to indicate mental illness rather than eccentricity. Although Maurice hadn't been conscious of it, he realised that he had begun to spend a good deal of time talking to himself. Perhaps because it was the only way he could make sense of what he was feeling. The world was conspiring against him and he couldn't understand why. Although Maurice had never had any religious faith, he did hold the belief that life had an inherent set of checks and balances. Nothing was ever unremittingly bad because something good always came along to balance it out. This philosophy he had always applied to external events, but lately had come to understand that he played a greater part in influencing these external events than he had once believed.

Polly leaving him, for example, he would a few years before have categorised as an external event. However, in the hours he had spent analysing their divorce, he had come to accept that it was probably his own fault. If Polly no longer loved him it must be more to do with his behaviour than hers. If he had remained the man she married then, perhaps, she wouldn't have left him. He applied the same analysis to Dawn, which always led to the same cul-de-sac in his mind. He was who he was because that was who he had become. It was too much effort trying to be somebody else. He was more withdrawn than he used to be, but he couldn't help that. The way he was feeling now he knew he could quite happily go and live in a cave and never see anybody again for as long as he lived.

He had told Dr Soames about his wave dream but he hadn't mentioned his daydreams because these confused and frightened him. He often daydreamed that he was walking through a forest and looking up at the trees. He was lost but knew that at the edge of the forest was a wall that was too high for him to climb over. The trees had what he could only call wisdom. He wanted to hug them, but he was repulsed by them. When he fought this repulsion the trees were unyielding, so he went back to staring up at the branches. In this daydream he was a child, no more than six or seven: alone, confused, and frightened.

'What?' It was a youth, waiting by the unlit window of a charity shop, shivering in a sleeveless shirt. Maurice had been talking out loud again.

'I'm sorry?' Maurice said.

'What you goin' on about?'

'Nothing.' Maurice had been walking for twenty minutes and was lost. On reflection, not having anywhere to stay for the night, he decided that he couldn't be lost. So he walked on, northwards, knowing that sooner or later he would come to a place where he would be found.

'Loony!' the youth called.

On the night Maurice's mother died he had been watching television. It was after midnight and Maurice hadn't been able to sleep, which was rare for him. She died just after half past twelve and Maurice knew immediately because he heard her voice very clearly in the room. She told him to 'be good', and the connotations saddened him. As a child he had always tried to be good. He had tried so hard to be good that he soon didn't know how to be anything else.

'Any particular whisky, friend?' the landlord said.

'Bells, a large one.' Maurice sat down by the dark wood partition of the snug bar he had wandered into. A middle-aged woman at the bar stared frankly at him; drunk, bored, and emboldened by drink. Her fur coat was draped over a bar stool, she was wearing a tight red woollen dress and red lipstick, her dark, loosely curled hair spilled over her shoulders. Maurice wasn't interested.

He was, however, interested in the fire which was burning in the iron grate. The landlord came from behind the bar to stoke it up, a portly, untidily bald man in a tatty green cardigan. A pile of logs was on the hearth. The landlord threw one on and kicked it into place with the heel of his boot. He rubbed his hands and smiled at Maurice, but his leering attention never strayed far from the woman at the bar.

'Can't beat an open fire,' the man said. 'You need it on a night like this.'

'Yes. You do.'

''Specially if you don't have no one to keep you warm, eh?' He winked at the woman.

'Shut up, Henry,' the woman said, and Maurice sensed she

was defending him. He looked up from the flames and saw she was watching him.

'You brought me a present?' the woman said, sliding off the bar stool, and flashing the tops of her stockings.

'Present?'

'In the bag?' She stood by the fire, warming her back.

Maurice looked into his plastic bag. Shards of glass swum in the golden whisky. 'It's broken,' he said sadly. 'It was a present . . . and now I've broken it.'

'That's a shame. I like presents.'

'Yes. I like presents.'

'Let me buy you something. To make up for it.'

'No. I couldn't ask you to do that.'

'Bells was it?' She pointed at his glass.

'Yes, Bells.'

'Bells, Henry,' she called, 'large one. And be quick about it. The poor boy's freezing to death. Here.' She sat beside him, closer than Polly had done an hour before, and took his hand in the same way. With her other hand she rubbed his back like a mother trying to wind a baby. '. . . You are cold, and your coat's all wet. Take it off.' The woman peeled it down his back and tugged it off. She brought over a bar stool, put it in front of the fire and folded the coat over it. Almost immediately the cloth began to steam.

'There,' the woman said, 'you'd catch a cold in your kidleys with that on. My dad said that. Kidleys. He was a card, my dad . . . Tell me what's troubling you.'

'Nothing,' Maurice said morosely.

'You say that a lot. I can hear you saying that to people. They say, . . . "What's the matter, darling?" and you say, "Nothing." Like nothing is the matter with you. But it is.'

'Well . . .'

'And I'm asking what it is. And you'd better tell me because I don't just give my time free to anybody . . .' She raised her voice. 'Said, I don't just give my time free to every Tom, Dick and Harry, do I?'

'I'll say you don't,' Henry shouted, and laughed coarsely.

'Wood burns,' Maurice said.

'Yes?'

'I was just thinking. Wood burns. So there is . . . I was thinking about trees. And I suppose I've always considered them to be . . . I don't know, representative of something. But what if they were real? What if it was a real forest? But that doesn't matter, you see. Wood burns. Wood burns. And when it burns it brings comfort. But you have to kill it first. Kill the tree. So she's dead. And I can feel that comfort. Or I could, if I only knew how.'

'Oh dear. What's happened to you?' the woman said. 'You had a fight with your wife or something?'

'No, nothing like that. My fault. It's all self-inflicted.'

'I've had men. Lots of men. And most of them blame themselves. I don't see why they should . . . I mean women never blame themselves.'

'Whisky.' The landlord stood in front of them, holding out Maurice's glass. The woman took it from him. 'You know what you two look like?'

'Don't tell me, Henry.'

'Two foxes, curled round each other. Two foxes. Don't ask me why. I saw a photo once.' Henry wandered back to the bar, shaking his head sagely. The landlord of the Dog Tray was known round the manor as an astute observer of human nature. He had earned this reputation largely through the non sequiturs that peppered his conversation when he was drunk. But women came to him for his fallible advice, and although they rarely acted on it, they always felt better for having someone take an interest. It was rumoured that Henry had a degree from a university in Istanbul. The truth was that he was virtually illiterate, and had never travelled further than Brighton. But he kept a good pub; warm if filthy.

'He doesn't mean anything.'

'What do you want?' Maurice said.

'In the whole wide world?'

'If you like.'

'. . . My boy back.'

'Where is he?'

'Don't set me off. Just don't ask me. I can't talk about him without filling up with tears.'

A log cracked in the grate. The fire shifted and settled lower, blasting the heat towards them, but it could not reach the cold that Maurice felt deep within his bones. Be good, his mother had said. He was a good man. He had a sense of honour, he was decent, he understood people sufficiently well to navigate his way round their sensibilities. Too well, he sometimes believed. But inside he wasn't good at all. He'd bottled the rest of himself up and screwed the lid on tight. God help anybody who opened it up.

'What's that you say, love?'

'Nothing.'

'Anyway, cheer up,' she chided, pulling his arm close. 'Be Christmas soon. Lots of presents then. And turkey and stuffing, roast potatoes. My sister always has me round, Christmas. I think she feels she has to, but the kiddies like me. Yes, they like their auntie all right. If only they knew where the money came from for their toys.'

'It doesn't matter where it comes from. At least you care enough about them to buy them things.'

'I don't think my brother-in-law's keen on me. Mr Hoity Toity, with his new car and double glazing, just because he goes to work in a white shirt . . . "Rene," he says, "I don't know how we managed before we had a dishwasher." I told him how he managed, he managed because my sister did everything round the house. His mother probably never even showed him how to wipe his own behind. It's only a terrace. My sister, she laughs about him when he's not there. I think she's carrying on with somebody but she hasn't said anything yet . . . I don't know what she's told him about me, but I get this horrible cold feeling when we're in a room together. I think he'd like to try it on, Colin. I suppose he thinks I'm easy game or something. I have my standards. I wouldn't do anything to hurt that family. I suppose he will one day.'

Maurice felt the warm mush of the woman's lips on his. He fought a breathless struggle for air as he pushed her away. Saw the hate in her eyes.

'You didn't have to do that,' she said. 'I wasn't going to hurt you. I thought you wanted a bit of company. I'm very choosy about who I spend my time with. I told you about that.' Henry was watching them closely, his hand reaching for the baseball bat under the bar he kept for troublesome customers. 'Is that right, Henry?'

'I'm here,' Henry said.

'I'm sorry.' Maurice watched the landlord, he didn't want any trouble. 'I don't want to offend you, but I don't want . . . this.'

'You think I'm on the game, don't you? You think I'm just a tart.'

'I don't care what you do. I don't give a shit.'

'I'll ask you not to use language like that.' Then she softened. 'I'm an escort. There's a difference. I like my comforts too much to be standing in the cold on street corners. I mean what's the use when you can go out respectable? I'm not saying I don't do the other. I do. And I'm not ashamed of it.' She shouted to Henry. 'We're not ashamed of the other, are we, lover?'

'Not half,' the landlord said, laughing through his yellow

teeth, relaxing his grip on the bat. He had another hanging on a leather strap beneath the hand pumps. Four six-inch nails were driven through it. Sometimes he itched to use it. One day he would and claim he was provoked into it.

Maurice began to wonder whether he would ever meet a woman who really understood him. Sometimes it was like trying to converse with a stranger in a language you barely understood. You were limited to what you could learn about them by the extent of your vocabulary. Maurice had once read that a measure of masculinity was the success with which a man broke away from his mother.

'You are a strange one, all that mother business,' the woman said.

'I'll pay you.'

'I don't want your money.'

'I'll pay you to let me stay the night. I have nowhere to go. I don't know anyone round here. I'm lost.'

Beneath it all was the fear that he looked for women to mother him, because he needed a mother. They screwed him because he needed a whore. The other parts that completed him, which needed companionship, understanding, sympathy, were silenced by these greater needs. He fell in love a hundred times a day. But if he could only discover what love was, then he'd never need to fall in love again.

When the two of them went out together, the landlord stood at the door and watched them walk slowly up the street. The fur on the woman's back was lush and brown, the coat of the man she was with was creased and stained. Her head was on his shoulder, she was whispering something to him. Her arm was round his back; Henry couldn't see an inch of light between them. For the first time in many years, years in which he'd seen her promenade out of the pub with hundreds of punters, he was afraid for the woman. When they turned a corner, the woman's heels clicking on the pavement, Henry closed his door, bolted it, leaned stiffly down and put another log on the fire. Just for him; to warm him while he washed the glasses and emptied the ashtrays.

The smoke in the snug settled to the floor. The decorations hung brown and nicotined from the ceiling. Between them his chamber pot collection dangled from their handles. It was a terrible place, he thought, when the regulars were gone. It was the regulars that made it what it was. Maybe he'd fix up the urinals, splash out for a bit of new flock for the saloon bar. Maybe next year he'd find a woman who would tolerate his temper. Still, soon it would be Christmas and everybody would be happy.

THREE

'SILENCE IS THE fourth colour on the palette of the radio producer. It is the one in most plentiful supply but it is also the most under-used and misunderstood. The others, of course, are speech, music and ambient sound (or wildtrack). The novice producer when, say, being asked to edit an interview for time will inevitably remove the silences first. But to remove the silence is often to remove a significant part of the meaning: the telling pause before an answer; the self-referential beat between a comic anecdote and a self-conscious laugh; the drawing in of breath before and, indeed, between the tears.

'So when I am asked to speak to young producers the first thing I ask them to do is simply – nothing. To pause, to listen, to remain silent and to judge how long we as a group can bear that silence. Rarely a minute passes before one of them spoils the moment with nervous laughter. This provokes the others to do the same, grateful that this terrible imposition is over.

'There is nothing terrible in silence except that it allows us to examine that which we do not wish to confront within ourselves. The noisiest members of our society are often those who have most to fear from silence.'

Vincent Edwards was delivering his well-rehearsed talk to a small group of new producers in an airless building of glass and metal close on Marylebone High Street. Those producers seconded to run the training courses were always grateful for his regular appearances, particularly when the delegates came from overseas broadcasting agencies. They expected to meet figures like Edwards. His was the face they saw when they tuned in to the World Service and listened through the mush of short wave to the voice of London. His was the reassuring voice before the jolting nursery strains of 'Lillibolero': a reassurance that beyond the bloodshed, the coup or the famine, London was speaking and, by inference, listening.

He was confronted by a mixed bunch of individuals at the horseshoe of grey tables that surrounded him. On his right was a neat, literal man in an archaic cloth suit from a South African community station in the Alexandra Township. The man's surname with its surplus consonants had been foreshortened on his name plate. His Christian name was Solomon. It was he who was currently waving his biro in the air and saying, 'Tell me, sir. Do you believe that silence is universal?' He smiled, garnering blank looks from the other course members at the table. It was nearly lunchtime and they were bored and hungry.

'I'd like to offer that question back to you, Solomon. Tell me how you would answer it.' Edwards fingered the knot of his Garrick tie. The tie was a measure of his self-confidence. Few of his fellow members wore their ties unselfconsciously. They knew the cucumber and salmon stripes were an emblem of exclusivity, but nobody dared ridicule or even mention it because then the whole self-conscious edifice would crumble. Today, Edwards's confidence was being tested not only by Solomon but also by an intense, abrupt girl from Belfast.

It was Solomon, however, who was currently dominating the conversation: 'I would suggest first of all, sir, that like my good friend Catherine here, silence is a luxury. I would also conjecture that it is a privilege of the developed world that we can expend our precious time here in considering it.'

'I don't think you understand quite what I'm trying to get across to you.'

'Oh, indeed I do. Yes, indeed I do. I would merely suggest, humbly suggest, that the finesse with which you talk about the beauty, the shape of your wonderful features, the esotericism of your Third Programme talks, is perhaps unnecessary. For me, personally, I should of course add, I come from a country which is learning to use its voice. We have been silent for too long.'

'Yes, Solomon, I'm sorry but . . .'

'Solomon's right, of course,' Catherine cut in. 'When your voice is silenced – or met by silence then, for God's sake, you don't want to waste precious seconds of airtime by saying nothing.' Catherine crossed her arms and stared petulantly. Her hair needed washing: it was a minor criticism, but it was by collating such criticisms that Edwards, in his own mind, subjugated those who challenged him. Unclean hair suggested poor personal hygiene, a slovenly attitude to one's health, an untidy, driven, life. He had already dismissed Solomon on the grounds of his suit and the irritation he provoked in his colleagues. That was enough and he was bored by them both now. 'I can only repeat that neither of you has understood what I've been trying to get across.'

'On the contrary, sir . . .'

'Solomon,' Edwards said. 'You haven't. But I'm willing to accept that as the subject I've been asked to come here and talk about is of no relevance to you . . .'

'I understand what you are saying. Do I express myself

clearly enough? I merely wish to suggest that, as you have indicated, the development of what you choose to call the "art" of radio came after many years of exploring its more fundamental capabilities: a simple tool of mass communication. That your country chose to develop it in the way that you did is indicative of the luxury of a peaceful nation . . .'

'I would hardly call the 1940s peaceful, Solomon.'

'As far as I understand it,' Catherine said, 'your beloved Corporation was instrumental in breaking the General Strike. That's a pretty poor foundation stone for an organisation that prides itself on its impartiality.'

'I think this is another subject. Perhaps we should break for lunch. Does everybody agree?'

Before anybody could answer two people stood up and began collecting their notes. Catherine pushed past them and was out of the room before Edwards could defuse her anger with a few minutes of flattering small talk. He saw these talks not simply as a way of spreading his experience, they were also useful disseminators of his reputation. The short extracts he played to illustrate his lectures consisted largely of his own work, which he never failed self-deprecatingly to mention. Northern Ireland was a hard nut to crack. He'd had more trouble with producers from there than anywhere.

'Thank you for your time, wonderful.' A woman shook his hand and, with each handshake, edged towards the door. She was the course tutor, and wanted to get away. She was meeting a man for lunch, but escaped from Edwards with the excuse that she had to mend the overhead projector for the afternoon session.

Within a minute the room was empty except for Solomon, who was writing in pencil on an A4 pad. Edwards rewound his illustrative tape and, together with his notes, slipped the spool into his briefcase. He watched Solomon for a while, intently writing. As he wrote, he formed the words in his mouth. His handwriting was neat and dense.

'Catching up?' Edwards said, waiting by the door. Down the corridor he could hear Catherine shouting at somebody down the telephone.

'I am writing to my wife.' Solomon laid down his pencil. 'I am explaining to her how odd I am finding this whole experience.'

'You find the course odd?'

'I find London odd. I find your priorities odd.'

'Such as?'

'If you'll forgive me for saying so, I find your concerns rather childish.'

Edwards came back in and sat down, putting his briefcase on his knee. He felt overwhelmingly tired. 'Perhaps you haven't had time to acclimatise yourself to the city. I'm sure you'd find something . . .'

'I am surprised also to be having such conversations with people like yourself.' Solomon was sober now: he was no longer smiling, looking to find favour with his coursemates.

'I don't quite . . .'

'I understood England was a liberal country. I have always admired your stance with regard to the oppression in my country. On the television, I watched Nelson Mandela dance in your streets and I thought it was a place I should come and see for myself. But I find you so cold.'

'We're known for it. I wouldn't take it too personally.'

'I sense a joylessness in you: you have too much and yet you do not seem to know what to do with it. On every street I see children begging for money: standing before shops that have everything. This I am not so surprised about, but I sense that people do not know how to talk to me. I am black. But they treat me with undue politeness: I laugh, I bruise, I feel pain. I am good and bad, and everything that you are. But I am treated with politeness. Everywhere politeness. Will nobody talk to me?' A note of hysteria had crept into Solomon's voice.

'I can't answer for anybody but myself, Solomon. But I can only suggest to you that, perhaps you've only come across . . .'

'You accuse me of not understanding you. You clearly do not understand me. If you'll excuse me I would like to finish my letter.' Solomon waited, not for Edwards's approval, but to see how he would react.

Edwards opened his palms in a conciliatory gesture and stood up again. 'Perhaps we should discuss this at some other time.'

'Perhaps not.' Solomon began rereading his letter.

'. . . Earlier you accused me of equating silence with art. I would, and I can only repeat: that it is more to do with truth. Sometimes truth and art are synonymous; perhaps not sufficiently often. And truth, I would imagine, is a priority of yours, given the context . . .' But Solomon was ignoring him. 'I'll leave you, then. I'm sorry if I've in some way offended you. Goodbye.' As Edwards reached the door he heard Solomon throw down his pencil. It rattled off the table and landed silently on the lush carpet.

'I can no longer write to my wife. You have upset me.' He stared petulantly at the table.

'I'm sorry. I didn't intend to.'

'But you have.'

'Goodbye, Solomon.'

Solomon raised his voice. 'No doubt you are intending to eat with friends?'

'Where I'm eating is absolutely no business of yours.' Edwards felt justified in letting his anger show.

'Am I not good enough to share your table?'

'Of course you are.'

'Then invite me.' By the time the plea had crossed the space between the two men it had become a challenge.

'I have other plans. Another time I would be glad to eat lunch with you.'

'Today. We must do it today. I am leaving in a few days' time.'

'I'm sorry. No.'

'I shall come with you, let me collect my raincoat.'

'No. This is ludicrous.' Edwards walked down the short corridor to the lift. He pressed the call button and waited. He was afraid in a way he couldn't quite understand. Once he had loved a violent man. When he tried to end their affair the man would not let him go. He waited for him at the end of each day and followed him to the train. He telephoned Edwards's wife, once he wrote to his mother. Edwards was afraid the man would never leave him in peace but after two months he did and the calls and letters stopped. Edwards knew that the violent man should have played a greater part in his destiny, and the violent man knew it too, so their bitterness and regret were in many ways the same. In cutting him out of his life he was also cutting off a part of his life: his current relationship with Charles was devoid of violence but not of passion. It was, however, devoid of violent passion.

The lift remained four floors below. As Edwards turned to go down the stairs Solomon, unhurried, came through the door after him. His black raincoat was buttoned and belted tight like a child's.

'I would suggest that we walk down the stairs,' Solomon said, pushing the staircase door open to allow Edwards to go through first.

'I'm sorry. I will not be browbeaten like this.'

'Please, you first.' Solomon pushed Edwards through the door and followed him downstairs. 'I would like to continue the conversation with you,' Solomon put his finger to his lips and whispered, 'outside.'

Edwards followed him out onto the busy street. Solomon led them to the next corner, then they turned into a side road. Solomon immediately stopped and flattened his back against a wall.

'What in God's name is the matter with you, man?' Edwards said. Solomon, eyes prominent and breathing heavily, watched the corner they had just turned. Edwards had no choice but to wait with him. A couple and two women crossed the end of the street. Then Solomon relaxed. 'I believe that we're now safe.'

'Safe?'

'I believe your building to be bugged. Forgive me. This is why I was being so forthright in my condemnation of your ideas.'

'I think you're well off the mark here, Solomon.' Edwards took his arm and tugged him gently back towards the main road. 'Nobody has the slightest interest in what I, or I imagine anybody, has got to say in that building. And I include the students in that.'

'Then we'll have to disagree once again, sir. I know for a fact that my hotel room is bugged, and the taxi that brought me here was bugged also. I am afraid the secret police have an interest in my movements. They will report me to the authorities back home, and if those people who funded my trip feel I have transgressed, they will kill me.'

Edwards was untouched by Solomon's paranoia. He believed it to be another trick to ingratiate himself into sharing his lunch. 'I'm sorry, Solomon. I'm afraid I can't believe a word of it. Surely journalists are not now worthy of that kind of attention.'

'If only that were the case, Mr Edwards. Now, where shall

we eat? I feel like fish, fresh fruit. Or perhaps some bread, or meat. I have not eaten for some considerable time.'

Edwards checked the time. Solomon would have enjoyed lunch at the Garrick but concern over his behaviour prompted another idea. There was one place he knew Solomon would enjoy undivided attention. Edwards strode to the pavement's edge and held out his briefcase at head height. A black cab pulled up immediately.

'Old Compton Street,' Edwards said to the driver, commanding his attention by not raising his voice. He settled onto the back seat. Solomon climbed in beside him and looked out at the city like a fish from a bowl as they turned left towards Soho.

'Mr . . .?'

'Reid. Maurice.'

'Mm.' Dr Soames pulled out Maurice's notes and scanned the last entry. 'You came in last week, didn't you?' He put the notes down on his desk and scrutinised Maurice more intently than he had done during the previous consultation. Most patients could be seen off after a single visit with reassurances and, occasionally, antibiotics. Second visits tended to denote a condition more often psychological than medical.

'I'm . . . I was going to say concerned, but that doesn't quite . . . I'm a bit worried: more than concerned.'

'You do look worried.' Soames had learned this technique during a counselling course. Bouncing a patient's word back to them often prompted an elucidation.

'That's because I am worried, I suppose.'

'Mm.' He was going to have to try harder with this young man, who, despite his notes, Soames only vaguely remembered seeing the week before. He had him down as someone

135

looking for a few weeks off work. Now he was not so sure. 'And what are you worried about?' He picked up the notes again, but still he couldn't read his scribbled diagnosis.

'I'm worried about . . . worried about doing something stupid. No, that's not right.'

'Isn't it?'

'That's what my father, newspapers. The news – doctors – mother – teacher . . . doing something stupid. No that's not it at all.' Maurice shook his head. He knew he sounded like a lunatic but he couldn't stop himself. He wished he could let go and go properly mad. At least then somebody else would have to sort out the appalling mess he'd got himself into. 'I nearly hit somebody. Last night. Quite hard.' He looked at Soames, wide-eyed: watching for the judgement. He wanted it over with.

'You nearly hit somebody?'

'I wanted to. A woman. But I didn't. Look.' Maurice suddenly stood up and walked over to the examination couch. He wrenched off his shoes and lay down. 'This dream I was telling you about.'

'Mm?' Dr Soames had now deciphered a few more words of his notes: 'Sab, coun. suicide? No. Cob lidd oil.' He would have to get some new glasses.

'The dream,' Maurice said, 'about the wave?' He lifted his head from the pillow to see Soames squinting at his notes and rocking backwards and forwards in his seat. 'Are you listening to me?'

'Of course. Please, go on.'

'I told you last time about a dream I had about a wave crashing over me.'

'Ah!' Soames said, remembering at last. 'You're the radio man.'

'Exactly.'

'And how are you?'

'Well . . . that's what I'm trying to tell you.'

'Well, come on then.' Soames dragged his chair across the lino to the consulting table and sat down with his hands in his lap like a tennis line judge.

'I had a dream about . . .'

'Yes, yes, yes. A taxi, wave, sea, all that sort of thing. Usual stuff.' He wafted Maurice's images away like troublesome flies.

'Thank you.'

'Not at all, Mr . . . ah . . . you see we all believe our dreams to be fascinating and different. Rather like our annual holidays. The truth of the matter is that you really have to be there to fully appreciate them. Any fool can have a shot at analysing a dream. And the truth is that we're all correct in our assessment, and equally all, ah, wrong. Psychology is the charlatan's art. Psychiatry the charlatan's science. We understand ourselves better than anybody else. This is the truth.' Soames found himself wagging his finger and put his hand back in his lap. He had got quite excited. Now he was a little light-headed.

'What about daydreams?'

'Exactly the same thing. You have a shot at them. Chances are you'll be as close to the truth as you need to be.'

'Right.' Maurice sat up and swung his legs from the bed. 'You know it always helps talking to you.'

'Thank you.'

'Sometimes I feel as if nobody's really the slightest bit interested in what I've got to say.'

'I'm sure we all experience this feeling of valuelessness every so often.'

'Yes, but it's more than that really. I find people keep living up to my worst expectations of them. All the time. It never used to happen that often. Perhaps I used to know some better people.'

'Or you didn't know them very well.'

'You mean ultimately people always end up disappointing you?'

'That rather depends what you have invested in them.'

Maurice spent a moment in thought. He wanted to confess to Soames about what had happened with the woman the night before. But one of his current difficulties, that he had come to believe that people would only like him if he withheld the truth about himself, held him back. He was fallible – an imperfection he forgave in others – but did not believe that others would forgive in him.

On his way out through the waiting room, Maurice decided to look for somebody else to hear his confession. In the meantime the prescription for anti-depressants should, the old man had said, help him through the next few weeks. He was going to need something. He could tell.

Edwards, meanwhile, paid the driver through the cab window as the taxi idled in the narrow street. Solomon was already transfixed by the black and red rubberwear in the window of the shop next door to the pub. He went to get a closer look and stood with his hands in his pockets, his waist a little bent, peering at the display. Edwards tapped his shoulder and ushered him into the dim and din of the pub. It took a moment for their eyes to become accustomed to the light, their ears to the noise. When they had, Solomon stared and Edwards took a quick inventory of the collection of men who were in there. Next to them at the bar stood a flaccid book reviewer with a goatee beard and a red felt jacket who looked as if he'd wandered off from his maiden aunt during a Christmas shopping trip to the West End. Dangerous moustached leather queens sharked the room with pectorals chiselled from marble. There were furtive older men in macs drinking straight doubles and pretending to read the previous day's *Evening Standard*; muscular feral boys with shaved heads, button-fly Levis and packs of Marlboro sculpting the short sleeves of their pristine white, fine cotton T-shirts; vile fat sissies, screaming the details of their sex lives over the deafening thud of club music.

Deals were transacted by the flash of an eye or the nod of a head: everybody was bidding, everybody an auctioneer. Jackets were slung quickly on; arrivals, departures, all noticed, all silently applauded. *Look behind you* at the pantomime of gay life on Old Compton Street.

'Drink.' Edwards pointed at the bottle of American lager he'd put between Solomon's knuckles on the bar. Solomon nodded, cocked his head back and took a long draught. The barman watched his Adam's apple bob, then looked at Edwards with approval.

'She's thirsty, Vincent,' the man said. 'What have you two been up to?'

Edwards raised his glass of Scotch in a toast to Solomon. The day may not have been wasted, after all.

FOUR

SOMETHING WASN'T COMING together. On most days Roy May could write the script for the programme in a couple of hours. This provided him with enough time to phone Caz, a few of his cronies and his bookie, catch up with Elaine, chat to Peculiar, speak to his agent, read his mail and buy a sandwich before taking the lift down to the studio for the programme. Sometimes he even went as far as reading his interview briefs. Roy preferred the instinctive approach to broadcasting: he could usually manage to manipulate his guests into talking about something personal whatever they imagined themselves to have been booked to discuss. If the worst came to the worst and they wouldn't be swayed, Roy always had seven or eight questions written out for him. The result of this was that his producers were occasionally frustrated by Roy's approach and frequently embarrassed when they had to escort their bemused guests back to reception for their cab home. But Roy seemed to have a talent for asking the right personal question at the right moment which meant his programmes were never dull or predictable and in some quarters (universities, medical schools, and amongst a surprising number of home potters) Roy May was something of a cult. The greatest accolade, however, was that journalists often phoned the programme to request the contact numbers of the contributors. The irony was that these guests had usually been pirated from the newspapers in the first place – occasionally even from the paper phoning up for the number.

But, as the producers often commiserated with each other, there is no such thing as a new idea – particularly in magazine programmes. Hence a form of shorthand was used when they were trying to sell ideas to Edwards at the weekly editorial meeting. A 'follow-up' was a story the producer discovered had been done by another producer the week before – but with different guests. An 'exploration' of a subject was one in which the two or three guests all knew and felt exactly the same about the item in question: they would then have a 'discursive' discussion which was short-hand for meandering, consensual, and usually boring. An 'author interview' was a plug for a book. A 'polemic' or 'polarised' discussion was one in which two people shouted at each other for six or seven minutes (the format, of course, much favoured by news producers). A 'character' interview was usually a mentally deficient person with a regional accent. A 'human interest' interview (the hardest to find, but Roy's preferred format) was one in which the interviewee was a victim of something – a rare disease, child abuse, alien abduction, a cult, the police or criminal fraternity, HIV, CJD, racism, sexism (most isms, in fact) or, occasionally, their own success. 'Outside Broadcasts' were hybrids of 'character' interviews, 'explorations', and 'location features' (a 'location feature' being a six- or seven-minute taped item set somewhere that wasn't in London and in which three or four 'characters' talked tediously about something that had happened in their locality – Shrove Tuesday football matches, village feuds, lighthouses, anything to do with hedges, angling, vicars, vegetables or fruit, town criers, the death of the village shop/community, all fell within this category).

Today, however, he just couldn't get started. Roy's script usually opened with a personal anecdote, a piece of music, a letter or complaint from a listener and round this he would construct an elaborate, homey introduction to the programme. Sometimes this lasted for rather a long time and, on these occasions, the studio producer was carpeted by Peculiar in the post-mortem for letting him go on about himself for too long. This was preferable to provoking Roy's greater wrath (born of his belief that the programme team considered him to be semi-literate) by having attempted to change a word of his script. So unless it was hopelessly factually inaccurate, libellous, or genuinely excruciatingly bad, few producers bothered.

But today Roy wasn't happy and the evidence of his writer's block was now papering the floor of his small office. It wasn't so much the items that were causing him trouble (there were no academics or tedious abstract discussions for him to deal with) it was the answerphone message he'd picked up when he arrived that morning. The message was from a nineteen-year-old girl who Roy was very fond of. He felt a warm glow in his neck and shoulders whenever he thought of her and he hadn't seen her for almost three months. The girl had asked him to call her back 'as soon as you can'. It was those five words that worried him and, because he was worried, because he didn't want to hear the worst, he couldn't bring himself to do it. So he tore another sheet from his pad, shook his fountain pen, drew breath, tried to clear his head of the dread that was weighing him down and started again. But then the phone rang and Roy, knowing he couldn't put it off any longer, answered it.

* * *

'Oh,' Val said as she opened the door. She blushed, then quickly regained her composure and invited Maurice in. 'I don't suppose you were expecting to find me here. I suppose you've come to see Polly for one of your heart to hearts.' Her face without the benefit of make-up was bereft of its *trompe l'oeil* cheekbones and artfully shadowed cavities.

'You'll do. It was you I wanted to talk about anyway.'

'I'm off work through stress you know. I won't have you being horrible to me in my own house.'

Walking past the living room in which the TV was showing an old British film, she led Maurice into the kitchen. Seeing the magazines and papers on the living-room floor, the empty teacup and the packet of biscuits, all distractions now thrown aside, Maurice felt sorry for Val. There was no comfort in that scene; nothing in the room was substantial enough to fully distract her from the way she felt about herself. Small children and people like Val, he knew, should never be left on their own for long.

But Maurice's sympathy was short-lived. 'Then why not go back and live in your own house and get the hell out of mine?'

Val switched on the kettle. 'I hope you're not intending to get violent.'

'Don't be ridiculous,' Maurice said, sitting at the table.

'I suppose you want to talk about this Roy May thing.'

'Yes. This Roy May "thing". That I mentioned to you in confidence. And you decided to write up in your evening rag.'

'You should know never to trust a journalist,' Val said, vainly trying to turn it into a joke. Turning 'things into jokes' was one of the clichés her editor was always picking her up on.

'I wasn't talking to a journalist. I was talking to the

step-spare mother of my son: the wife of my wife, the woman who's living in my house.'

'Yes, well it's not just men who occasionally bring their identities home with them.'

'Is that the best you can do?'

'Didn't Polly tell you I was sorry?' Val said. 'And that I tried to get them to pull it?'

'Yes. But *you* didn't. I was waiting for you to tell me. I thought you might at least have the guts to apologise to me in person.'

Val turned away from him and found some tea bags in the breakfast cereal cupboard. She threw one into each cup and poured the water over them. The kettle hadn't quite boiled but she wasn't really paying attention. The bags bled red into the lukewarm water and the smell of strawberries lifted from the cups. 'You don't mind fruit tea?' Val said.

'Anything.'

'Look . . .' Val brought the cups to the table and sat down opposite Maurice. 'I am sorry. I know you think I haven't got any morals. But I have. And I honestly did try to get them to spike the story.'

'I don't see how they can spike it before it's written.'

'You know what I mean. Anyway, I refused to write it. I thought . . . I thought that gesture might have been enough for my editor . . .'

'And you're surprised that it wasn't?'

'I really have been terribly stressed about it. I have a rash all over my shoulders . . .' She half-turned her back on him to illustrate her point but her silk shirt comprehensively covered the problem area. 'All over here,' Val lamely gesticulated.

'And what's that supposed to tell me?'

'That I'm sorry. I really am sorry. And if you knew how difficult it was for me to say . . .'

'God, you're more messed up than I am. Look.' Maurice took out his new bottle of pills, shook them, held the bottle up to the light, then put them on the table. Val picked them up and, squinting, scrutinised the label.

'I had these.'

'Really? Any good?'

'Not really. Not unless you take them in quantity.'

'Mm.'

'Anyway, getting back to this other thing . . .'

'Yes?'

'You said you hated him. You told me that he was boring, so why aren't you pleased to see him exposed as a child molester or whatever? At least you won't have to work with him any more.'

'It's more complicated than that.'

'People always say that when they don't want to face the simple truth.'

'Do they? What an astute observer of human behaviour you are.'

'Why don't you just go. I'm really not in the mood for this.' Val sniffed, then sipped her lukewarm tea. She didn't really want Maurice to go, a good row always cheered her up and she could never have a decent argument with Polly.

'The reason it's complicated is that Roy doesn't deserve to get shit-bagged this way. Whatever happened is all in the past, I'm sure he's paid for it, and I can't see that anybody can possibly benefit from it being dragged up again. Except, of course, your editor. And the other reason is that . . . it just feels so disloyal. I know I told you I didn't like the bloke. But I work with him and you just don't shaft the people you work with . . . Anyway, I've decided to come clean.'

'You'll tell him?'

'I have to. If nothing else at least it'll clear my conscience.'

'How nice that must be. I don't think I could ever clear mine.'

'Really?'

'No way, Maurice.' Val looked at him slyly. 'You won't get anything out of me.'

'God, you really do have an appallingly jaded view of humanity, don't you?'

'No. Not in the least. I know who I can trust and I know I have no reason to trust you. It's quite simple.'

'I suppose I'm not allowed to smoke in here, am I?'

'Yes you can. You always do. I'll find you an ashtray.'

Maurice lit up. Since he had given up giving up, cigarettes tasted better. He took particular delight in lighting up in the houses of non or part-time smokers: polluting pure air was more gratifying than adding to the already fugged atmosphere of a pub. Val slid a saucer across the table.

'I'll trade you, then,' Maurice said, briefly buoyed, as he always was with the nicotine.

'Trade me what?'

'I'll trade my conscience for yours.'

'. . . Why?'

'Because . . . because, believe it or not I'd value your opinion on something. And I know you'd never dare betray me again. And also, and this again may sound rather hard to believe, I don't have a huge number of people I can talk to about . . . well, sensitive issues.'

'How do I know . . .?'

'Look,' Maurice said with some force. 'You don't *know* anything. There are no guarantees. Now try and put aside your paranoia, stop yourself from wondering what you're going to get out of it and just for a change, try trusting somebody.'

Val looked away for a second. Her focus was more intense when she fixed it back on Maurice. 'I wish my mother was dead,' she said, watching closely to see how he would react. '. . . Is that too terrible even to comprehend? Is it too big a thing . . . sometimes I just can't . . . I can't forgive myself for that sort of thought. But there it is. That's it.'

'It's not so terrible.'

'You're just being kind.'

'. . . You don't intend to kill her, I assume?'

'Of course not.'

'Have you ever examined why you feel like that?'

'I try not to think about it, let alone consider it.'

'Well what's the second thought that comes into your mind when you imagine her dead?'

Val gave the question some thought, then said. 'This sounds really stupid.'

'Go on.'

'I'm in bed. With Polly. And the curtains are open . . . and when we look through the window it's a shop window and we're being watched by hundreds of people . . . and we just laugh. It's so . . . liberating!'

'Well there you are then,' Maurice said. Val looked puzzled. 'When my mother died. I mean she died two years ago. When she died I didn't cry. I felt . . . I felt like I hadn't lost a mother. It was so . . . strange. But it was only when she died that I really started to examine what she meant to me . . . and I realised . . . like it was as though we were together in something . . . complicit. Her and me, and then there was my father, on the outside. But we were tied together. Just me and her. So when she died it was almost as though half of her hadn't died because . . . because I was still alive.'

'You're saying? I'm sorry, I'm a little . . . I thought we were talking about me, my . . .'

'I'm saying they never die. They're with you. All the time. For ever. They just don't happen to be here any more, and they're not in some other town you never visit. They come and stand at your shoulder. That's how I felt.'

'How awful.'

'It's not that awful.'

'No. I suppose it's not . . . I could quite like you.' Val made it sound like an offer she was only prepared to consider if Maurice gave her something in return.

'I'm supposed to be grateful or something, am I?' Maurice said, and immediately regretted it. Val was too easy to hurt. This time, rather than striking back, she rode it with a breathing exercise her yoga instructor had taught her.

'Your turn,' she said.

'I went home with a prostitute. Last night. I went home with a woman and paid her.'

'That's not so shocking, Maurice,' Val said fondly as she wrote the story up in her head.

'Isn't it?'

'Well I suppose . . . Why did you do it?'

'Because I was lonely. Because Pol told me about your story and I felt guilty. Because I was in a pub and she started talking to me. Because, I suppose, it was easy. And because . . .' Maurice felt a catch in his throat, he swallowed, he sniffed, he felt profoundly sad. 'Because my mother is dead.'

'Yes.' And Maurice liked Val a great deal for not saying any more.

'So there we are.'

Maurice walked back to the tube station, his pills rattling in his pocket, thinking about the purple nylon sheets of the woman he had slept with the night before. There was something more profoundly shocking about the white of a naked body on dark-coloured sheets. Pallid flesh on pale cotton softened the impact. He had stared at the black mound of hair between her legs, the way she hunched herself up onto her elbows to watch him as he touched her there.

But he felt no desire and when he had touched her he pulled the sheet up from their feet and tugged it up to his shoulders. With her but completely alone. Then he laid his head on her breasts and slept. When he woke up the next morning he hadn't moved and neither had she. Her eyes were closed, her eyelids making minute flickers. Her eye-shadow was creased like the lead lines of a coin rubbing. She breathed evenly and deeply and looked serene in her vampire sleep. Then he felt guilty about scrutinising her this way so he picked up his clothes and went to dress in the bathroom. Above the bath was a shelf of powders, oils, ointments and balms; bright colours in clear, glass-stoppered bottles. He lifted the lids and sniffed each one, dropping the stoppers back from a small height so that glass grit ground on glass. When he had finished he felt absurdly as though his nose had played the xylophone of her scents. He felt an intimacy with her more profound than if they had made love, or whatever would have passed for it between them.

When he crept out of the small house into the frigid, freezing dawn he believed for a moment that he loved the woman. But, not quite knowing what love would mean in these circumstances, he dismissed the feeling. Even so, he carried the image of her face with him through the morning. It was the talisman of her care that later led him back to see Dr Soames because for the first time in as long as he could remember he had a reason not to be sad.

When he reached the tube station it was still shut for the night. A metal grille curtained the ticket hall. Two men were talking inside beyond the barriers, exhibiting the shift worker's lack of urgency. Maurice found a newsagent's shop in the next street. He bought a *Guardian* and had a brief conversation with the Indian woman serving him. She wanted him to go, nervous of early strangers. She'd just despatched the last of her paperboys and all she wanted to do was to read her magazine, hunched close to the fan heater pumping out a narrow radius of warmth which evaporated as soon as it hit the cold of the shop. Maurice was inebriated with life. He wanted to dance; to tell somebody about the woman. Anybody would have done.

Maurice arrived at work at 12.30 and immediately went to see Roy May. He knew that if he put it off, he'd lose his nerve. Roy was on his own in his small, smoked-glass-fronted office and was writing his script longhand. A young, nervous PA waited by his door. It was her responsibility to type the script up before the programme and Roy had never left it this late before. Warde was on the rota to produce that day's programme, but he, as usual, had disappeared. Elaine was in a meeting. So when Maurice arrived, the PA was glad of a friendly face and asked him to ask Roy whether he had anything for her. Maurice walked into Roy's room without knocking.

'Afternoon, Roy,' he said. Roy didn't look up and tried to dismiss him with a cold, 'It'll have to wait.'

'It can't wait.'

Roy wearily put down his pen. 'Can't it?'

'No, you see I have . . .'

'Well?'

'I mean I need. No, the point is that I have an apology to make.' Maurice knew that he didn't really need to say any more. The incredulous look on Roy's face said it all. 'You?'

'Are we talking about the same thing here, Roy? Only, I would . . .'

'You sold me to the papers. You. It was you? Was it you?'

'I'm afraid I think it . . .'

'Of course it was,' he shook his head. 'I mean I've been trying to work out . . . it all falls into place. Jesus buggering . . .'

150

'I'm sorry, Roy . . .'

But Roy moved so quickly that Maurice didn't have a chance to get out of the door before he had leaped up and pushed him against it. The PA hurried off to fetch help.

'Why?' Roy said.

'It wasn't how,' Maurice said, 'it wasn't how you imagine . . .'

'Why did you do it? I cannot understand why anybody should want to peddle that old trash to the papers. Do you bloody hate me so much that you . . .?'

'No, of course I . . .'

'Then there must be some other reason. I mean did they pay you? I just can't work it out. Tell me.' Roy was puce with rage.

'Let go of me and I will.'

'No.' Roy, who had been holding Maurice's lapels, slid his hands up to Maurice's throat and pressed his thumbs to his Adam's apple. 'Talk. Fast.'

'I was talking to . . . I know a woman who works for . . . Look, I didn't sell the story, Roy. It just came out. I mean I was drunk. We were talking and I was . . . I mean she asked how I was and I suppose I was pissed off with you about . . . anyway. Look, I didn't give her the story. I don't know the story. I only. All I heard were the rumours, I just assumed. I mean you assume everybody knows the same rumours . . .'

'No, Maurice. No, they don't. Everybody knows different rumours. They only know the same truths.'

'Yes . . . well. I was stupid. It was stupid. And if it means anything to you I knew I shouldn't have said it. Even if it was true. Which I'm sure, ah, incidentally, that it isn't.'

Roy let Maurice go. Maurice relaxed. 'Thanks. I'm . . .' but the rest of it caught in his throat as Roy smashed his fist into Maurice's face. Maurice heard something crunch in his skull. He tasted warm blood. Then, after the numbness of the shock, he felt the delayed agony of a huge hot needle thrust into the bridge of his nose. Fog fell on the rest of his thoughts. His hands reached to assess the damage. His nose felt as though it had already blown up to three or four times its size.

'Bastard,' Roy said. Tersely and conclusively. Maurice swayed a little, and when he focused, saw Roy was back at his desk. The door supported Maurice's weight. He rocked forwards and found his centre of gravity.

'Thank you. You had every right . . .' Maurice began.

'Get out of my sight,' Roy said. He was writing feverishly now. Inflicting punishment on Maurice had released the lock on his thoughts. There was only one way he could start the programme. He would do it as he always had. He would begin with an anecdote and there was only one thing of significance that had happened to him in the previous twenty-four hours. He would just have to tell the truth.

'Maurice,' he shouted. Maurice's face appeared tentatively round the door frame. 'Call the newsroom. Tell them they might want to listen to the top of the programme. And call the press office. Tell them I'll do one telly, one radio and one national paper interview. Then the story's over. Well, go on.'

Many of the newspapers on the following day reported Roy's confession verbatim. One of the tabloids headlined their front page with 'Hello, my name is Roy May, and I have a confession to make.' It displaced the new crime figures from the lead in the heavyweights, and the tabloid sections of the serious papers allocated four or five pages to recapitulating the highs and lows of Roy May's career. But the tone of the coverage was fond and, for the British press, remarkably supportive. Only one paper took the trouble of finding the mother of the child in the hotel room. She turned out to be an actress – but she wouldn't talk. For many years, Roy had preserved her anonymity. As he said later to Edwards, it was perhaps the only decent thing that he had done in his life and he genuinely didn't want anybody to know about it. But his hand had been forced. Anyway, the girl was now of an age to understand. He loved her. And that was all that mattered.

This is how Roy started the programme:

'Hello, my name is Roy May and I have a confession to make. It sounds awful, that, doesn't it? It sounds like I've done something terrible. Well, in a way I have. But to explain it all I have to take you back a few years to when I was on the telly. Remember? *Roy's People*, six twenty, Saturday nights.'

Here, the theme to *Roy's People* was played.

'I know the clever papers sneered at the programme. I know it was just a bit of fun. But it was harmless fun, and I'm all in favour of a bit of harmless fun.' Roy would have winked and paused here if he'd had a live audience.

'And then it all finished. The story went round that the programme had been axed after two very successful series. And nothing more was said. Well. I'm going to tell you what happened. Why it happened. But you'll have to bear with me, and you'll have to wait a few minutes until you meet my other guests today.'

Here, he grudgingly mentioned the other people who were on the programme.

'Well, and this is the difficult bit. I was discovered in a hotel room with a fourteen-year-old girl. Sounds terrible doesn't it? They took her picture as she went out. I don't know who tipped them off but this profession is full of people who'd stab you in the back as soon as smile in your face. I could name names. But I won't. And then the paper came after me. Said I had to confess to an illicit relationship with a young girl because either way they were going to publish the facts. Even though the girl wouldn't talk. And they tried to make her. But she still wouldn't. Her name's Rachel, by the way. But the truth was that they'd got it wrong. Completely wrong. And I tried to tell them but they wouldn't believe me. And because I didn't tell them what they wanted to hear they went on and on and on . . . and I got so mad with it all that I left. I just couldn't be doing with it. I resigned from my telly show and went to live with my wife in Northumberland. There were other reasons, but that was the main one. And they lost interest. But they never printed the picture because in the back of their minds they knew they just might have got it wrong. And they knew that if they had it would have cost them a lot of money.

'But. This place runs on rumours and the story was put round that Roy May had been . . . well, you can imagine the worst. And stories like that never die. They get repeated at clever parties and you start to know the look on people's faces when they're telling them to each other. And I suppose I knew that sooner or later some newspaper would drag it up again, and this morning Rachel phoned me and said a reporter had been after her and wanted to talk. And I said, listen, love, this has to stop. The truth has to come out.'

'He's good, isn't he?' Elaine said.

Maurice, who was holding a tissue to his streaming nose, just nodded. Roy's confession continued to spill from the office speakers.

Eleven floors below, Warde was watching Roy intently through the studio glass. Edwards had slipped into the cubicle shortly after the programme had gone on air but he had stayed by the door, nodded to Warde, and adopted a stance that suggested support without interference. Everybody sat up a little straighter. Then the phone light flashed on the panel above the studio clock. It was answered in a terse whisper and put down again. All eyes in the studio were on Roy who had now put his script down and was improvising. He was telling the story to Warde, looking directly at him, and Warde, who was a good radio producer, was listening and responding in the way he knew Roy needed. Nothing broke the contact between them, neither man moved. Roy went on, and the needles on the desk registered his voice and through cables and lines, from tall masts and satellites, Roy's confession was carried like the rumour of war across the nation.

III

Occasionally some of the broadcasters will cast their reticence aside and emerge from their obscurity in the guise of uncles to countless children, with whom they swiftly become intimate in voice, beloved and real, unseen but not unknown. This is one of their little relaxations, and, properly handled, one of their most important functions.

J.C.W. Reith, op. cit.

ONE

AFTER THE PROGRAMME, for the first time in his career, Roy May left the studio and went immediately to his office without putting his head round the cubicle door and thanking everybody for their efforts. Warde collected the tapes in silence. The studio managers unplugged the jackfield and threw away the gash tape. Beryl sorted the paperwork and tidied the surplus copies of the script into the bin: all of the team exhibiting an intense and unnecessary concentration on their tasks. Edwards looked at his watch and slipped out of the room having allowed sufficient time for Roy to get to the lift alone.

Upstairs, Maurice and Elaine were already devouring the implications of Roy's confession. When Warde came in and dropped the programme box onto his cluttered desk they fell silent out of respect for the bizarre tragedy of the event. Then Elaine went over to Warde, who was slumped into his chair, legs astride, and began massaging his shoulders as if in some way she could manipulate the significance of it all out of him.

'Is he all right?' she said.

'Seems OK,' Warde said.

'She was his daughter, then,' Maurice reflected. 'Unless, of course, it was some sort of elaborate lie.'

'Don't even think it,' Elaine said.

'No,' Warde said, 'it was the truth. I don't think I've ever seen so much truth. It was like . . . tears. But for his daughter. As though he was announcing her birth to the world or something . . . I don't know. I don't know how people feel when they have kids but . . .'

'What I don't understand,' Maurice said, going to the door and pushing it shut, 'was why he allowed the press to hound him out like that. I mean if the girl was his daughter by this woman then surely, knowing Roy as we do, he'd have put his career before preserving her anonymity. Wouldn't he?'

'Except in doing that, he would also have revealed to them who his daughter was,' Warde argued. 'And they wouldn't have left her alone. And that's where he drew the line. Which is intriguing, I have to admit. The notion of Roy having any scruples, or indeed morals, is weird.'

'You don't know him,' Elaine said. 'You see . . . you just don't know him.' She let her hands drop from Warde's shoulders. But it was too late. Like Maurice a week or so before, a simple statement was sufficient for Warde to divine the truth. Elaine went to her desk and shuffled some papers. A smile insinuated itself on Warde's face. He looked at Maurice who made an almost imperceptible nod of his head.

'Well,' Warde said brightly, springing to his feet. 'Moral support time. What do you think?'

'Yes,' said Elaine. 'Let's get him out of here. The press office can wait.'

'Maurice. Stiffener?'

'Yes . . . yes. Except, I suppose there's something I'd better tell you first.'

'About your nose?' Warde said. 'I was, of course, going to ask.'

'Indirectly, yes.'

Elaine was delegated to go into Roy's office while Maurice and Warde stationed themselves outside the door. Roy was laying the telephone receiver gently onto its rest. Elaine waited to see how he would react to her. She couldn't yet know how the rest of his life would be changed by what had happened. Roy smiled and motioned for her to come in and close the door. She walked over to him and stood close. Roy held her waist and pulled her closer still. They stood like that for a while until the telephone rang. They waited in silence until it stopped.

'We've formed an escape committee,' Elaine said. 'We're taking you for a drink before you have to face the jackals.'

'Don't talk,' Roy said. They clung onto each other for a while longer. Then he said, 'Everything feels mucked up. I didn't want her to get dragged into this.' He pulled back far enough away to see Elaine's face. 'Do you understand?'

'Of course.'

'Because . . . what it comes down to is that everything is shit. The rest of it. All of it. This. That. Talk, talk, talk, all nonsense. But not her. And now I've dragged her into it. Into this.'

'You had no choice.'

'I know. I know I didn't. And it makes me so sick to my stomach, I'll tell you that for free. It makes me feel so . . . anyway, it's over and done with and we'll just have to make the best fist of it we can. At the end of the day that's all you can do.'

Elaine pulled gently away. 'Caz knew?'

'Of course she knew.'

'Has she always known?'

'Right from the start.'

'But you didn't tell me.'

'Like I said, it has nothing to do with this. With here.' Roy waved at the room.

'I see. And you see me as just a part of this, do you?' Elaine mimicked his wave.

'Please, love. Not now.'

'No,' said Elaine, more angry than she had been for as long as she could remember. 'Not now. Not ever.'

'You deserve better than me.'

'Don't insult me, Roy. Please don't insult me like that.'

'So . . .' Roy said, as if they had only just begun the conversation. 'What a day.'

'Who was she?' Elaine said with bitterness. 'The mother of your love-child.'

'I suppose it'll come out soon enough.' Roy shrugged, demeaning her again; relegating her to the position she felt she had always held in his estimation. To him, she was one of many: to her, he was everything. Only when they were apart did she allow herself the luxury of believing he really cared about her. Elaine had always been sustained through the cheap reality of her relationships by the glossy fictions she constructed when she was alone.

'Tell me.'

Roy named an actress who had recently converted to Catholicism. A beautiful tyrant who, with age, had become known as a harridan. Elaine knew Roy wouldn't have been able to stand up to her, just as he wouldn't be able to stand up to their daughter.

'You did very well for yourself, didn't you?' Elaine said.

'I thought there was more to it. But there wasn't. Look . . . I thought you mentioned something about getting out of this place.'

'Right.'

'How's Maurice?' Roy said.

'Bruised. And apologetic.'

'I should think so. Let's go then.'

Roy pulled his tweed cap out of his macintosh pocket and put it on. Elaine went to link her arm in his then, thinking better of it, pulled it away. Roy followed her out of the room. Maurice offered his hand in apology. Roy waited sufficiently long before taking it to diminish the gesture. They left the building by the side entrance. The commission-aire saluted as they went out and told Roy that there was already a group of reporters at the front desk. Roy winked and slipped a ten-pound note into the man's top pocket. The automatic doors slid open and the December cold advanced over the threshold of the building. Four abreast they set off into the dark of the late afternoon feeling a sense of solidarity. For once, they all knew what they were doing and why they were doing it together. They were looking after a comrade who had been wounded in the battle.

Later, in a locked office, Elaine pulled off Roy's shirt, grabbing handfuls of the material and dragging it up his back and over his head. She could smell his anti-perspirant, the beer on his breath, small pockets of other sudden odours. He was tearing at the belt of her jeans. She helped him by unlatching them and slipping them off. He looked at her white legs and, for once, she was unashamed of them. This was the only pause in their frantic race towards consumma-tion.

But until that moment the evening had been dull and all four of them had drunk too much. They knew each other well enough for there to be no embarrassing pauses in the conversation and too well for the conversation to take any unexpected turns into new revelation. Roy and Elaine wanted to be alone together. Maurice was maudlin and just wanted to be on his own, and Warde was bored with them all. They wanted to talk about Roy's daughter, but Roy did not.

Maurice arrived at the house where he was staying shortly before midnight. The cab driver helped him up the path, got his key in the door for him and gently pushed him inside. He was comprehensively drunk. His motor co-ordination had deserted him two hours previously. He had a precarious hold over the contents of his bladder and his stomach, but he was extremely hungry. Maurice found the kitchen and stood by the fridge door swaying backwards and forwards. Then he reached forward and with great concentration wrenched the door open. A milk bottle fell out and shattered on the floor. As he leaned down to pick it up the floor lurched out of focus and he fell onto his knees, cutting himself on the glass. He pulled himself up using the kitchen cabinets for support, holding the flap of his torn trousers across the cut on his knee. The blood seeped through his fingers and speckled the milk on the floor. Maurice rested his weight against the oven and breathed in deeply three times. But the oxygen was too rich for him and he leaned against the sink and resignedly prepared himself for the appalling inevitability of throwing up.

Maurice had always made a meal of vomiting. He had developed a technique. As the food rushed up his throat he would take a huge intake of breath. This he would expel with a bark as the half-digested food and alcohol reached his mouth. The extra impetus this provided to the contents of his stomach had the effect of projecting it over a huge distance. This had happened twice and he was limbering up for his third bout when an old lady in a dressing gown walked into the kitchen. She looked at the shattered glass, milk and blood puddled on the floor, then at Maurice, who managed to smile at her before averting his face and shouting, 'Whoooooooooarghhhh,' at the kitchen window. There wasn't much left in his stomach, but his stomach didn't know it and spasmed again, throwing a cupful of bile into his mouth. Maurice spat this into the sink.

The woman backed off a little. She looked at him as if she couldn't make up her mind whether he was real or just another of her hallucinations. She was, Maurice reckoned when he found himself able to look her over, at least eighty years old.

'Very, very, pleased to meet you,' Maurice said after the next and final wave of nausea had subsided. He held out his hand.

'I'm sure.' The woman seemed to say.

'I'm a friend of your daughter. She said I could stay for the night. She said I was to make myself at home.' Maurice surveyed the vomit-splashed window, the glass, milk and blood on the floor, sniffed and was assaulted by the appalling stench. 'I hope that's all right.'

The woman continued to stare at him. The painkillers made her feel as if she was in a tunnel. For an hour after she had taken them all she could hear was a sound like the rush of heavy traffic past her. Words were merely echoes. Faces were foreshortened like those she remembered seeing when she was a child in the hall of mirrors on Worthing Pier. Night and day were meaningless. She tried to ask whether the young man had come to look after her but her mouth was dry and her jaw and tongue lagged behind her thoughts. The young man answered, his words crumpling his kind and rather doleful face. She saw him wash his hands in the sink and dash the drops from his fingers onto the floor because he couldn't find the tea towel. She knew where the towel was. It was on the back of the door where she always left it. She found it and handed it to him. He said something she couldn't understand, then, *very kind*. They were the only two words that emerged from the swimming-pool echo. The man waited for her to move. She wasn't sure where he expected her to move to. He came towards her and took her gently by the elbow and she let him lead her upstairs, pull back the sheets and help her into bed.

As the man switched off the bedside lamp, she stared into the awful dark and cried out and somehow the young man knew that he wanted her to turn it on again. She was glad to see his face when he did. He sat down on the bed and straightened the sheets like a scarf at her neck. She pulled her arm out of the warmth of her covers so she could touch his soft hand with her papery skin. He smiled at her and she wondered for a moment whether she did know him. As soon as she wondered she fell asleep, even though she felt him pulling his hand gently away from hers and his weight lifting from the bed. But night was no longer night. Sleep was no longer sleep. It was simply a different kind of oblivion to the medicated somnolence of her days.

Maurice went downstairs and cleaned up the kitchen. He took a glass of water into the living room and sat in the darkness. He had not seen his mother in the days before her death. Helping the woman to bed felt like an act of contrition. With the peculiar logic of drunkenness this led him into thinking about his job and the people he worked with. It was a line of logic that led directly back to his mother. The only way he could make sense of this confusion was that it was at his mother's knee (quite literally) that, each lunchtime, he had listened to the radio. And he had listened to it in the same way that he listened to his mother.

When Elaine came in she found Maurice asleep on the sofa. She went upstairs to check on her mother, then came back down and gently shook him awake.

'What time is it?' he said.

'Two fifteen. You'll freeze down here. Why don't you go up to bed.' Elaine looked tired. She was trying to be convivial but couldn't quite manage the deceit.

'Thanks.' Maurice sat up stiffly and stretched. 'Everything all right?'

'Yes, fine.'

'Roy all right?'

'I imagine so.'

'I'm sorry. I just wondered.' Elaine's temper sobered Maurice into wakefulness. He sensed the need to keep his wits about him.

'Why shouldn't he be all right?'

'I don't know.' Maurice rubbed his eyes to try and clear the fog away from them.

'Well he is.'

'Good.'

'Why do you ask?' Elaine wouldn't let it rest. She was still standing beside the settee and Maurice felt as though it was he who was being interrogated.

'I just wondered. That's all.'

'Why did you wonder?'

'Elaine, I don't know. I just did.'

'I wish I could trust you.' Elaine went over to the window and ran her finger along the sill. She inspected the grey dust and made a mental note to fire the new cleaner. She was the third in as many months. A sour woman whose sighs were cries for help that, if answered, provoked a litany of misery. Elaine didn't like any of her cleaners. None of them liked her. The second one had called her a stuck-up cow. Elaine cried when she had gone. When she gave her mother her evening powdered drink she found herself being short with her. Elaine could contend with her life only if nothing upset the rigid routines of home, mother and work.

'Why can't you trust me?' Maurice said.

'I don't know. I just can't.'

'. . . Elaine.'

'Yes?'

'Thanks for putting me up. I appreciate it.'

'Get some sleep.'

'Yes . . .' Maurice struggled off the sofa then, again, said, 'Why can't you trust me?'

'I don't know.'

'Goodnight, then.'

'Goodnight.'

When he got to the door, Maurice stopped. Elaine was looking out at the garden wondering which jobs she needed to get done on the outside of the house. The guttering over the porchway leaked and there was now a damp patch on the hallway wall.

'You can you know,' Maurice said.

'Can I?'

'I've never betrayed a secret. Not on purpose. Only when I didn't know it was a secret. Or when it was a rumour. And everybody does that. Secrets are safe with me. I'm probably the only person I know who wouldn't let anybody down in that respect.'

'Are you? Why?'

'Because I don't have anybody to share them with. Nobody I could tell them to that I'd trust not to tell.'

'And that's your definition of keeping a secret is it?'

'Sort of.'

'I slept with Roy tonight,' Elaine said without looking round. She straightened her back a little as if she was anticipating a knife between her shoulder blades.

'Right.'

'And if you tell anyone . . .'

'I wouldn't.'

'Say something then.'

'What?'

'Laugh, or tell me that I'm stupid, or that he's just using me.'

'Is that what you think?'

'No . . . well, yes. Yes, I suppose it is, but the fact is that I don't care. I fancy him. I don't see what's wrong with that.'

'Nothing.'

'I wanted him. He wanted me.'

'And now?'

'I want him more, I imagine. And I expect he wants me less. You see that's what always happens. When I say always, I'm talking about a relatively few occasions. So perhaps I'm setting myself up for . . . I suppose that's what you'd say to me.'

'What?'

'That I look for men who'll do that . . . Shall I tell you something?'

'Yes.'

'Nobody has held me without wanting to screw me for almost ten years. No man. I mean I don't have many women friends who . . .'

'That's very sad.' Maurice went to Elaine and held her, and was surprised to discover he did not want the same as the other men.

'Tenderness. That's all. That's what I miss, living alone.'

'. . . So what will you do?'

'About Roy?'

'Yes.'

'Nothing, I expect. We'll go on. He'll get bored or frightened that I'm getting too dependent on him. We'll finish. I'm not an adolescent. I know what I'm taking on.'

Maurice said, 'Do you think it's possible to love somebody after just one night?'

'Of course I do.'

'Even if you've never really understood what it means?'

'It's not to be understood. It can't be.'

'Right. Thanks. Goodnight then.'

'Goodnight, Maurice.'

In the night, Maurice woke with a cry. He had dreamed of the lift carrying him down into the basement of the building. When the doors opened he had stepped out. They closed behind him, marooning him in the darkness. He had reached for the wall and felt his way along it until he found a door handle which he turned. The door opened into a garden. It was spring. The trees were laden with blossom. A woman in a full white dress was swinging on a seat suspended from a bough. When she saw Maurice she jumped from the swing and ran towards him. The swing twisted and thrashed and then settled back to stillness. Maurice took the woman's arm and they walked down the garden. They crossed over a stile and came onto a narrow track of dry mud that ran beside a river. A rowing boat was moored at a jetty. It was old. It had been green but the paint was all but gone. There was a pool of dirty water inside it. Maurice stepped in and pushed it into the flow. He turned to help the woman in, but the mooring rope snapped and he was borne away. The charging water carried him faster and faster. He knelt in the bow and grasped both sides of the boat to prevent himself from falling out. He bumped down a shallow weir and careered beneath a stone bridge, faster, faster. A man was fishing from the central span. He was smoking a pipe. He lifted his bowler hat. The boat raced on, past a town. The river widened and darkened. The countryside flattened into a plain. As the sun went in, Maurice found himself in the open sea. When the tide had carried him far away from the coast, the sea threw up a huge tower of water. It teetered, fell and engulfed him. He cried out, grabbing at the boat to hold onto something.

He felt a hand in his. He opened his eyes to see the ashen face of the old lady smiling at him. She pulled up the sheets to his chin. Though age had caricatured her beauty, Maurice knew that she was the woman on the swing.

'I suppose you haven't told him?' Dawn said. Warde was undressing in the dark. He had watched a film then an American cop drama through to the end at which point an energetic voice had urged him to stay tuned through the night. He had gone into the bedroom at 3.15. Not because he was tired, because he rarely was, but because he felt he ought to sleep. Warde's needs were minimal: he ate out of a sense of duty rather than hunger. He drank out of an obligation to join in rather than because he was thirsty. He slept because if he didn't, he looked dreadful, his lungs ached and he came out in boils. He took a variety of drugs because these presented him with alternate versions of his needs: different hungers. If he took them often enough they provoked a genuine need in him: a physical dependence. Even these he dealt with with short and very painful periods of withdrawal. He was living with Dawn without guilt, because he enjoyed seeing her naked. He couldn't quite understand why Dawn was still so concerned about Maurice's feelings. He would get round to telling him sooner or later. Or perhaps he and Dawn would just fizzle out and it wouldn't be necessary.

Warde was bored almost all of the time. People saw him as being cold. He wasn't, he had just never had the necessary conditioning to feel. His father was an antiques dealer. His mother had inherited her family's wealth and he was brought up in his mother's family home: an elegant Georgian mansion on the edge of an overgrown village in Derbyshire. He had been enrolled at the local grammar school because his father did not want him to have a private education. This was out of spite to Warde's mother whose wealth subsidised the relative failure of his business. Warde's brother, Tristram, who was three years older, went to medical school. Once he brought home a penis in a shoe box. When they went to the local pub, Tristram sewed the penis onto the fly of his jeans. When he removed his long army greatcoat, he took a scalpel out of his pocket and cut off the severed penis. A woman fainted. Tristram dropped out of medical school and went to India in a van. Warde's father put sugar in the carburettor to stop the van from leaving. He found it difficult to articulate why he didn't want to lose his son. Warde had not heard from Tristram for five years.

Warde was used to profanity and to having to cater for his own needs because his parents could barely service their own. He could cook by the age of six. He shopped for his own food and clothes from the age of twelve. He lived on money stolen from his mother's purse and often stalked imperiously round the cold house dressed in black like a raven with clipped wings. He skipped the bridge between childhood and adulthood and missed out on the bruising teenage trashing of his ego. When his mother's drinking worsened he left home, incomplete. He joined the Corporation when he was eighteen by lying on an application form for a training scheme. He read the papers. He knew what they wanted him to be, and he impressed them with his maturity. He had, much to his own surprise, been there ever since. Each day, however, he imagined would be the last. He was convinced that his life was leading somewhere and he was just passing time until it became clear to him where that place was. He was not unhappy. He had a sense that he was growing and changing, and that one day he would be quite a good man.

'I'll tell him tomorrow,' Warde said, running his hands

over Dawn's body. He took a pornographer's delight in female flesh.

'Does he ever ask about me?' Dawn asked, then answered, 'No, why should he? He doesn't know you're here.'

'I don't think Reid's currently interested in anybody but himself. He's in danger of disappearing up his own fundament. I think he's spent too much time on his own.'

'Well why don't you go out with him? Perhaps he needs a friend.'

'He needs more than that.'

Vincent Edwards regretted having abandoned Solomon in the Old Compton Street bar, but it had, at least, solved the problem of how he was going to get rid of him. He knew what he had done was unforgivable, but Solomon deserved it for ruining his lunch. Edwards knew that the time was coming when he would have to leave the Corporation. He considered the proposition as he walked back to his office from the canteen. He had gone there to fetch a coffee to prolong his day. Another half an hour and he would be just in time for the last train home.

Edwards had listened to Roy's confession with a growing sense of unease. Since then he had passed the time ruminating over his loss of control over the programme. It concerned him less than it should have done. He knew that intelligent creative people when not working to their fullest potential use their surplus creativity to cut corners. If this tendency is not checked, more and more creativity is channelled into creating a situation where less and less is done. Ultimately, all of their energy is harnessed in this way.

What Edwards could no longer judge was just how many of his staff were now suffering from the effects of under-achievement. Elaine would never succumb because she was a habitual hard worker. Most of his junior staff were reasonably productive. Warde was in danger of it but he knew where to draw the line. Edwards knew he would soon come to terms with his ambition: he was presently in denial of the condition. Maurice Reid, however, was well on the way to a complete seizure. It was this, as much as anything, that made Edwards's mind up for him. He was intending to produce his 'White Symphony' before Christmas, which gave him just two weeks. His intention was to mire the network in an hour of silence: unannounced, unexplained. His swansong. He had already begun to put his affairs in order. He had spoken to Charles who said he was ready to leave at the earliest opportunity. He had spoken to his mother who, though she was approaching her ninetieth birthday, encouraged him to go. He had also spoken to the personnel officer to find out exactly where one stood with one's pension if one had been forced to leave the Corporation through dishonourable conduct. Now he was just waiting to tell his wife.

Edwards paused by a noticeboard. A bulletin sheet, defaced by a crude pencil sketch of a man fellating a donkey, disseminated the glad tidings that another of his contemporaries had reached the inner circle of top management. Edwards had never particularly aspired beyond editorship. He could not understand why the people he knew and respected were sold on power. It wasn't something they had been trained for or most were particularly good at. He knew of few people who were equipped to wield power effectively; who could subjugate their self-interest beneath the greater good of those they controlled (though this, he accepted, was an old-fashioned definition of leadership). This was why the Corporation was often in such a hideous mess. But since he had taken the decision to leave, he told people that he no longer cared what the Corporation had become.

In truth, he cared a great deal. Leaving the country was as much to do with removing himself from the temptation of listening to, and passing judgement on, his beloved Corporation as getting away from his wife.

As he approached his office, he saw that the door was open. The room was not due to be cleaned until the morning and he wasn't expecting any visitors. The corridor was empty. A lift bell rang behind him and a robot voice announced the floor, but nobody emerged. As he got closer he heard music coming from his office. It was Bartok: the solemn beauty of *Bluebeard's Castle*. With the shock he dropped the coffee he was holding. The polystyrene cup struck the floor at an angle, the lid sprang off and the coffee spilled out and was immediately blotted into the carpet. Edwards watched it seep away. The music was not loud. Perhaps he had left it on when he went up to the canteen. But the significance of it could surely be no coincidence. It was the music of the violent man, the soundtrack to many moments of passion and pain. Edwards began to edge away, back towards the lift. Then he stopped. He had run away from his destiny once before, if such a thing is feasible. And what was there to fear? The man would have had to bluff his way past security and would, therefore have been noticed. He would have to be faced.

Edwards walked slowly towards the door. The stark beauty of the music filled the air like perfume. He waded through it towards his room. He stopped at the threshold. Somebody was at his desk. He could hear the rhythmic tapping of a pen. Then the sound of his drawer being pulled open. It was the top drawer, because that was the one which stuck and had to be forced. The act of forcing it sent the contents rattling around and percussing to the back. It was the drawer that contained his script.

He pushed the door open. It swung on a slow and steady

arc to reveal the striped shadow of the blinds on the left wall. Then the edge of his drinks cabinet, the side of his desk, a lamp, the back of his computer monitor, grey cables, a man's hand tapping a pen, the cheap cloth of a suit, the bad cut of a jacket, a tie loose at the neck and the full face staring at him. Bloodshot eyes. A clumsy lion's shake of the head, the loose skin lagging. A slurred accusation. Not the violent man. Just Solomon.

'Get out of my office immediately or I'll call security.' Edwards switched on the light and Solomon was robbed of his *noir* menace.

'I should like an explanation,' Solomon said, picking through his words with the caution of a drunk.

'An explanation for what?'

'I should like an explanation from you as to why you took me to that place.'

'You deserve no explanation, Solomon. You asked me to take to you somewhere where you would be accepted.'

'I would suggest,' Solomon waved a finger. 'That as an act of racial aggression it is perhaps the worst I have ever encountered.'

'I'm sure everything can be analysed on the grounds of race if one chooses to do so. I took you there not because I don't like the colour of your skin, but because I don't like you. Please don't diminish my dislike of you by ascribing it to brute prejudice.'

In the impasse that followed Solomon eventually smiled. He opened the manuscript which Edwards now saw was on his desk, partly obscured by his computer keyboard.

'The White Symphony,' Solomon said and flicked through the pages. 'Blank pages. Pages all blank. I ask myself the question whether this is indeed a great work of art which is still to be written, or one which is indeed complete.'

'Give it to me.'

'Then it is finished.'

Edwards picked up the phone.

'My father was a writer. A poet. He instilled in me something of the awe he had for language.' Solomon clenched his palm and looked at his fist as if he held the words in it. 'For the nuances of language. He wrote many beautiful poems: profound poems. He taught me to revere the blank page. He told me that on a blank page everything is profound; the most fundamental truths are already inscribed. With each word he writes, the writer is charged with not diminishing that profundity.' Solomon smiled; a reverential acknowledgement of beauty beyond analysis or comprehension.

'And what happened to your father?'

'He was arrested as a member of the ANC. He served five years in prison. When he came out he did not write again. His legacy,' Solomon continued, 'is a poem in which he associated the struggle of my country with a page of white paper being punched by the keys of a typewriter: each blow significant, each symbol adding to the last.'

Edwards waited.

'My father did not believe in violence. Violence,' Solomon said, 'embeds itself into the language. It becomes another tool of subjugation. My father did not like what his organisation became . . .'

'Solomon, what are you trying to tell me?'

'I came here to learn. And you leave me in a room filled with strangers.'

'The two are not connected.'

'Why do you hate?'

'Go.'

'Why do you hate?'

'I don't hate, Solomon. Not in the sense that you mean.'

'I sincerely hope that when you have need for friends, you will find them.'

'I have all the friends I need.'

'I very much doubt that to be true.' Solomon stood, unsteadily. 'I find it interesting that you choose to leave me – a person you profess to despise – in a place where you argue I will be accepted. I can only take from this that you see this place as some form of punishment. You argue that your dislike of me is not rooted in race. Therefore one could argue that you are consigning a part of yourself to such a fate.'

'Absolutely not.'

'I ask you again. Why do you hate?'

Vincent Edwards could not answer.

TWO

ALTHOUGH GRACE HAD given Maurice a key for the Barons Court flat, when he arrived with his luggage on the following day, out of politeness he rang the bell. Nobody answered the door so he let himself in. The hallway floor was covered with a fresh fall of take-away flyers. Behind the door was a deep compacted drift of free newspapers. The flat smelt of stale cigarette smoke and talcum powder. From the direction of the living room a reedy transistor radio was pumping out the high frequencies of a woman's voice. Maurice left his bags in the hall and went into the kitchen, taking his overcoat off and hanging it on a cluttered peg as he passed. It settled against a fake leopard skin with the cautious proximity of strangers in a crowded underground train. In the kitchen, Maurice wearily encountered the inevitable communal clutter of shared flat living. The drainer was stacked with a mixture of clean and dirty mugs, egg- and sauce-soiled plates, the cornflake-scabbed bowls of that morning's breakfast. With some trepidation he opened the fridge. At eye level, a half-eaten can of baked beans with a treacherously serrated lid was lodged on a slab of rock-hard pizza. In the door was a carton of fresh milk and a half carton of semi-skimmed which was sour. On the shelf below were a plastic tub of low fat margarine, a shallow plastic tub of low fat cheese, a heavy polythene slab of mature Cheddar, a lettuce which was liquefying in a swamplike drawer, and a saucer which looked as though it was growing a laboratory sample of bacteria. He prepared himself to face the carnage of the bathroom but the door was locked and a woman whose voice he didn't recognise called out that she was having a bath. This was the source of the radio. She didn't sound the least bit surprised that he was there. Maurice fetched his cases and plastic bags and took them through to his room.

The bedroom, at the north side of the south-facing house, afforded an oblique view of the garden. The previous tenant had left a poster print of *Guernica* Blu-tacked to the wall, slightly out of true. The mattress sagged and was blotted ochre with the forensic evidence of a long sexual history. The melamine chest of drawers contained a sports sock and a pair of blue nylon Y-fronts. The wardrobe offered five rusty coat hangers that jangled long after he had opened the ill-fitting door and a paisley tie. The carpet was dusty; there was a malodorous towel on the radiator. Maurice was consoled by the fact that at least the radiator was working and that he wasn't living within twenty feet of a suburban railway viaduct which is where he had spent the first weeks of his life post Polly.

He sat on the bed, bowed his head and contemplated his feet. He laced together his fingers, turned his hands over and cracked his knuckles. He made a steeple with his first fingers and rehearsed a childhood rhyme. He found himself thinking about Will, and when this provoked the usual aching loneliness, turned away from the pain and thought instead of the woman he had met in the pub. His heartbeat settled to a more even rhythm and his anxiety soaked away.

'Morry,' Grace said, towelling her hair at the door. Her

energy was on a lower setting than when they had first met. She was wearing a short, carelessly tied bathrobe.

'Oh, it *was* you. I thought it was someone else.'

'No, it is me.'

'Hello.' Maurice stood up and went to shake Grace's hand. She smiled at the formality. Embarrassed, he sat back down again.

Grace looked him over, checking the version that had arrived against her memory of the one she had chosen a few days before. They seemed to coincide and she relaxed. 'Like the room?'

'It's fine. Fine. I thought I might, you know . . .' For no good reason Maurice mimed painting the walls. It seemed too conventional a suggestion to make to someone like Grace.

'Pete was going to paint the walls deep purple. And get all sort of moody lights and everything. And then get them wired up to his stereo so they came on with the rhythms.'

'Yes?'

'But he put the poster up instead.'

'*Guernica.*'

'Picasso.'

'Of course.'

'You see, Pete liked to think about things before he did anything.' Grace floated off into reminiscence. 'Everything, really. Even getting up. Like some days he'd just consider it and not do it. And he had a girlfriend once and he wanted to buy her some flowers but he spent all day in the shop because he just couldn't choose. It was kind of beautiful but also kind of weird. He was like that.'

'Fascinating,' Maurice fought the nagging realisation that Grace was not who he remembered her to be. He remembered her beauty, and her beauty had distracted him from her *naiveté.* He feared it wouldn't work out with Grace.

She'd irritate him to a point beyond politeness. They wouldn't argue, but when the time came for him to leave they'd both look back on their time together with a puzzling free-floating unease: as though they had argued viciously over something trivial when the real dispute lay between their disparate personal histories.

'What's the matter, Morry?' Grace tangled the towel round her hair, let it go and somehow it had become a turban.

'I'm not sure whether it's going to work out, you know, me being here.' Maurice looked resignedly at her as he reached for a lie. 'You see I'm not very good company at the moment . . .'

'Don't be silly.'

'I'm afraid I might not have been totally honest with you before . . . I mean you asked if I was a, a what? A "fun loving guy", was that it? I think it was and I assured you that I was . . . but I'm not. Not at the moment, anyway . . .' Gravity having slowly bowed his head, Maurice looked up again. During the speech, Grace had come into the room, passed before him, then stood watching him from beside the window. Now she sat down beside him on the bed.

'Morry. Do you believe that we've been here before?'

'Here. In this flat?'

'On this earth?'

'Not particularly. I mean it's not something I waste much time considering. Perhaps we have. It's irrelevant, though. You play the hand you're dealt whoever deals it.'

'No you don't. Well you do, but the way you play your hand is, like, decided for you by whoever deals it.'

'Why do you ask?'

'I was listening to this woman on the radio and she said that you have to deal with all your past lives before you can deal with this one. She puts people – pop stars mainly – into trances and gets them to remember their other lives. I think I'd like to do that. As a job, I mean. I thought I might try and ring her and see how she got into it in the first place. Do you think she'd help me? Or I might train to be a vet.'

'I don't know. I really can't be bothered with this reincarnation claptrap, Grace. I mean it's all about people feeling guilty over not giving enough to charity. This whole bloody "more wounded than you" culture. I get sick of it.' He allowed his impatience to crowd the dismissal. 'Look. I suppose I'd better just go. You really wouldn't want me here.'

'I don't mind, Morry,' Grace cajoled. 'You do what you like. I think you look like you need somewhere to stay, that's all. Martha said we should . . . well, she like thinks you should stay. Anyway, at least stay for a ciggy and a cup of tea. All right, babe?' Grace took his hand and squeezed it. 'All right?'

'All right.' Maurice allowed Grace to lead him through to the kitchen.

That cemented the arrangement. Polly often accused him of having no staying power. If she had already written the phone number in her address book then he certainly was not going to give her the satisfaction of knowing he'd run away from somewhere else.

'Everybody I know's in a mess,' Grace said soberly, when they returned to Maurice's predicament. 'I don't think it's my imagination.'

'Really? I mean, you don't think . . .'

'Men mainly. But not just . . .' She didn't seem to be able to shake off her morning vagueness.

'Well what do you put it down to? I mean . . .'

'I put it down to the people who say they aren't in a mess, like those people who reckon they've really got themselves together.'

'I'm not . . .'

'You see, I think, right, most people spend most of their lives confused: yeah?'

'Yes.'

'And they sort of accept it because there's no alternative. I was talking to Martha about this last night. And we decided, right, that because loads of people are seeing counsellors and stuff, they're starting to wonder whether what they feel is any different, I'm not explaining this very well.'

'No, go on.'

'Well, it's like seeing a colour: like that teapot. Now I say it's red. And you say it's red, but I don't know whether we mean the same thing by that. Same with emotions. I say happy, you say happy, but they might not mean the same thing. Same with messed up. Suddenly what I might think is, like, my normal state, right, you might think is completely messed up.'

'And the people who suddenly feel better because they're seeing shrinks . . .'

'Might just be feeling the normal things now, rather than any better. It's all relative.'

'But some people are happy.'

'You're happy, Morry. You're just too miserable to see it.'

Maurice drank three cups of camomile tea and smoked four of Grace's cigarettes. The spiritual void in Maurice's life was often filled this way. Sharing time with someone who wanted to believe in something meant he could travel some of the journey with them. When their paths ultimately diverged, it didn't matter. He had, at least, moved some distance from the point at which he had begun. By these small increments he assimilated belief.

When Grace went to get ready for work, he telephoned Polly.

'Hello, Pol. I've moved in,' Maurice said proudly. The

hollow echo of the hallway made his voice sound disembod-
ied at the other end of the line.

'Good. I'm glad. You need somewhere to settle down.'

'What's up?'

'It's Val.'

'What now?'

'Wait a minute.'

Maurice heard the receiver being put on the table,
pictured her walking across the room, heard the living-room
door being closed and saw her walking back. She would be
frowning: a look she always wore when she thought nobody
was watching her.

'Hello?' Polly said, as if she was afraid Maurice had been
cut off. Now she would be sitting on the settee, her legs
hunched up beneath her, her shoes off.

'What's wrong with Val?'

'She's terribly, terribly depressed. I can't get her out of
bed. I don't know what to do.'

'Leave a bottle of paracetamol and a half bottle of Scotch
by her bed and go out for a few hours . . . Pol?' But Maurice
was talking to the dialling tone.

He dialled the number three times before Polly eventually
picked up the receiver.

'Thank you, Maurice,' she said before he had announced
who he was. 'This is all your fault anyway.'

'What is? I mean for Christ's sake, what have I done now?'

'You know what you've done.'

'Pol. Please. I really haven't got a clue.'

Grace came out of her room and went into the bathroom.
She winked encouragingly. When she came back out again
she was naked. 'Jesus,' Maurice said, but Polly was explaining
about Val and didn't hear him. '. . . And then, apparently her
editor accused her of telling you that he was intending to run
the story on Roy May which you then told . . .'

'What? I'm sorry. Can we just go back a bit. Are you saying Val is pissed off with me for apologising to Roy that it was me who told her . . .?'

'She says you sold her out. That you promised not to say anything to him. That you'd worked it all out between yourselves when you came round. She says you were apologetic . . .'

'Now just wait a . . .'

'Anyway, she blames you for spoiling her story. I just don't know what to do.'

'Well don't do anything. Val is lying. She knows that. I know that. It doesn't matter. She's just angry at herself for being such an appalling human being. She'll get over it.'

'This isn't helping.'

'Well . . . look, I think you've got to work out exactly what is it that you need to do. I mean are you suggesting that I should apologise to her? Or are you wondering what to do because she's depressed?'

'Everything. But of course I'm not telling you to apologise. I know what she's like. And I also know that she can't help it. It's not her fault. I don't think she lies on purpose. I feel so terribly sorry for her. I know it's not a constructive thing to feel. It doesn't help her. What she needs is, I don't know, some sort of help I suppose.'

'Probably. But then who doesn't? I mean Soames was trying to get me to go and see some amateur trick cyclist. I told him I would but I don't think I'll bother. I was just talking to Grace about it . . .'

'Grace? Your new flatmate?'

'Landlady, I suppose.'

'And you were discussing your personal stuff with her? I mean you've only met the woman once before, haven't you?'

'Yes. So?'

'Well, you know . . .'

'What?'

'It's just . . . I don't know, a very personal thing . . .'

'Yes. And?'

'You know what I'm saying.'

'It's personal so I should only be discussing it with you. Is that it?'

'Not at all.'

'I think it is.'

'Now look, Maurice, I'm only trying to protect you, that's all. I know how easily you get . . .'

'Well go on.'

'No, I really have to go . . .' Polly hadn't the energy to sustain two arguments. 'It is good to talk to you. You can't blame me for being . . . for caring.'

'It's the only thing that keeps me afloat . . . It's good to talk to you.'

'I just had to, you know, share it, the stuff about Val, I suppose.'

'How's Will?'

'Oh he's very bright at the moment. I think he's got a girlfriend.'

'Is it serious?'

'Oh yes, she's very pretty. He had her to tea yesterday. They stared at each other over their fish fingers.'

'I fell in love when I was five. She had a blue tricycle. I remember cycling up and down her drive with her. She had incredibly blonde hair and blue eyes. And she was always smiling. I think it was real love . . . I really think it was.'

'I hope you find it soon, Maurice. I really hope you do.'

'Again?'

'Yes.'

'I . . . well . . . look.' Maurice's voice broke. 'I'll call tonight. See how you are. Speak to Will before he goes to bed.'

Maurice didn't like the pause that followed. He heard Polly say something. Then somebody shouted. A door slammed.

'. . . Pol?'

'She's up. I must go.'

'Call me if you need to. Try and get away for an hour. I'd like to talk to you about something. Ask your advice.'

'Yes,' she said, no longer listening. 'Got to go. Oh, by the way, Vincent Edwards called. He said if we spoke that you should telephone him. He hasn't got your new number.'

'Thanks Pol. I'll . . .' But she'd already cut the line.

'What's up, Morry?' Grace came out of her bedroom dressed in the pencil skirt and red shirt of her waitress uniform. Maurice could tell from her tone that she'd been listening to the conversation. She kicked her feet into the sandals that lay beneath the coat hooks, knelt down and strapped them. 'Morry?'

'Oh, just. I don't know. Polly. My wife. Something. It doesn't matter.'

'You're very close to her, aren't you?'

'I was.'

'Ask her round. We'll have a party to welcome you. Ask her round then.'

'I don't think so.'

'No, it's tradition. We always do it. I'm going to work. Back at seven.'

'Right.'

'Make yourself at home.'

'Thanks.'

'Cheer up. It might never happen. TTFN.' Grace waved, blew a kiss, pulled her leopard-skin coat from beneath Maurice's mac, then, tugging it round her shoulders, left the flat like a starlet hurrying from a limousine.

188

'See you,' Maurice said as the door slammed.

When he had fetched his diary from the bedroom, Maurice called Vincent Edwards. Loud music was playing in his office. Edwards tried to talk over it, then he gave up and went to turn it down. 'That's better,' he said jovially when he came back on the line. 'And how are you, Maurice?'

'Fine. Absolutely fine. Never felt better.'

Edwards sprung the trap. 'Then is there another reason for your not being in the building?'

'Well . . . what time is it? Oh, 12.15.'

'You say you're not ill?'

'Yes, well I was just getting ready.' As an afterthought he added. 'I was in yesterday.' Then, 'Moving leave?'

'You've moved again?'

'To Barons Court. I thought I was allowed two days.'

'Yes. I think that's restricted to one move a year. It's also discretionary. With the prior agreement of your editor. I seem to recall that you've already availed yourself of this allocation twice this year.'

'Sorry. It's not good enough, I know. I don't really know what's happened. I think I've become part-time by mistake.'

'I'd like you in as soon as you can get here. Elaine is feeling a little under the weather. Mr Warde has a hospital appointment which means I'd like you to come in and oversee the programme.'

'Fine.'

'If you can manage that. And I'd also welcome the opportunity of discussing that other matter with you.'

'Yes. I'll call in later.'

'I would appreciate it. Goodbye.'

'Would you like some soup?' Polly said. Val was sitting in the living room staring hard at the blank television screen.

189

'No I would not like some soup.'

'Can I get you anything else?'

'A new life?'

Val's initial outburst had not resulted in the usual hysterics. After shouting at Polly for the disloyalty of discussing her over the phone with Maurice, she had stamped upstairs and dressed herself from the pile of clothes she had discarded the previous night. She had then come down and taken a phone call from her editor, during which, Polly had diplomatically gone upstairs to allow her the privacy that Val had not granted to her. When she came down again, Val was in position in front of the television. After the opening shots the conversation died.

Polly prompted it back to life. 'Well, is everything all right at work?'

Val laughed mirthlessly. 'Why shouldn't it be all right?'

Polly struggled to maintain her patience. She knew she should leave Val to calm down alone, but instinct told her that something had been discussed over the phone that she needed to know about.

'Well is it or isn't it?' Polly tried again.

'As I said, why shouldn't it be?' Val looked at her petulantly.

'Oh, piss off then.'

Polly ran upstairs. She slammed the bedroom door behind her and picked up the alarm clock. Without premeditation she threw it against the wall. It smashed and fell satisfyingly to pieces. The brass bell rolled beneath the bed. Liberated by this, she picked up a hand mirror and sent it the same way. The plastic handle fractured. The glass split into three even pieces. The wallpaper was scarred with a thick black weal. Polly caught sight of the postman watching her from the street. She waved. He waved back. She knelt down, out of sight of the window, and picked up a shoe horn. This she aimed at the framed print on the wall. It caught the centre of the glass and crazed it. She cheered silently, then heard Val's footsteps on the stairs. They approached the door and stopped. Polly looked round for something else to destroy. The first thing she saw was Val's typewriter, a Remington, which she kept loaded with paper and carbon for moments of night-time inspiration. Polly picked up the machine, her thumbs pressing the keys. The hammers lifted weakly, poised to strike the roller. She held it above her head and was surprised at how light it felt. Even now there was a distance between her anger and her abstract interest in what she was feeling. This is why she had never completely lost her temper. Nothing had ever seemed sufficiently important to warrant it.

Val pushed open the door. Polly saw her in the mirror: a large, heavy-jowled woman, giving in to middle age, and dressed carelessly like a mental patient on a secure ward. When Val saw the shattered glass, the careless devastation, she backed out into the corridor, holding onto the door-knob. She turned to go downstairs but stopped herself, her indecision caught in the mirror. Polly put the typewriter back down onto the desk. The postman whistled his way from another front door. Polly went to the window and smiled. He looked behind him, thinking she was smiling at somebody else. He blushed and made a show of concentrating his attention on the wad of mail in his hand.

'Has the mail arrived?' Polly called.

'The mail?' Val was just in sight. She answered Polly as though someone had called her from downstairs.

'The postman's across the road.'

'I don't think so,' Val said cautiously. She didn't know the rules of this new game.

Polly knelt down and pulled out the wastepaper basket from beneath the desk, she picked up the larger shards of glass and laid them in the basket.

'I'll fetch the Hoover,' Val said, watching her cautiously from the door.

'Thank you.'

When Val had carried the machine upstairs, Polly took it from her and vacuumed the powdered glass from the bedroom carpet. She unhooked the print from the wall, looked at it from arm's length. Then laid it on the bed.

'I don't know what to say,' Val said. Something fundamental had changed between them.

'What was all that about on the phone?' Polly said.

'Oh, well . . . you see, it was Anthony.' Val focused her explanation on the print.

'Yes.'

'He was quite sweet really . . .' Val smiled. 'He said he knew I'd been having a tough time and everything . . . You see, I think he does care. I'm sure he likes me, otherwise I don't suppose he'd have employed me in the first place. Except for my father, well, he's always said that he never . . . but Anthony said he thinks I need a break. A change.'

'Good.'

'He wants me to go to New York. For six months. With a view to extending it if we're both happy . . . just to do the Friday column, and whatever features I can come up with. I mean, as he said, all you have to do is to watch the TV all day and . . . well, that's what he said.'

'New York?'

'There's a company flat. In Manhattan. Rent-free . . . expenses. I mean we could rent this place out for twice what we have to pay for the mortgage . . .'

'You want me to go with you?'

'Of course I do. Of course.'

'And Will? And Maurice?'

'I suppose that's the only sticking point, isn't it?'

THREE

IN THE EARLY hours of the previous morning Elaine had given up trying to sleep and gone downstairs. Her mind would not rest. She had adequately justified to Maurice why she had done what she had done with Roy May, and for a while had been happy to believe that justification. But what kept her awake was that she had regretted it as soon as she had done it. It wasn't her pride or her conscience that troubled her, she had neither in significant quantities. It was the fact that Roy had disappointed her, and no man she had wanted as much as she wanted him had any right to do that. He left her feeling empty, not used or any of the other things she had heard other women say when men let them down. She reasoned that her needs must have changed since the three months and twelve days she had spent with her last man, an investment banker called Matthew. But he fell short in many other ways. Roy had always promised to be something else. That was why she had defended him to Maurice and Warde. It was also why she had stood up for him at editorial meetings when everybody else was tearing him apart. He had allowed her to see something that, it seemed, he hadn't shown to anybody else. He was honest and he was original and you couldn't say that about many presenters nowadays.

Unfortunately, having sex with him revealed his needs: his clumsy, pawing hands, his lack of finesse, the delight in his eyes when he came. She could have been anybody. Elaine would have compromised in many areas, but she needed a grown-up lover. She already had her mother to mother.

She arrived at work late having overslept and missed seeing Maurice before he left. Tiredness ambushed her on the stairs, causing her to regret not taking the lift up to her office. Walking up the sixteen flights was her sole concession to keeping fit, but she gave up at the second-floor landing and collected a coffee at the tea bar before she got into the crowded but silent lift. Although she had showered twice that morning, on the bus she could still smell Roy on her. She had doused herself in Opium and breathed deeply until she was light-headed but could smell nothing else. When she had unlocked her office, switched on her computer and picked up the messages from her voicemail in case the agency nurse had called, she considered how she was going to approach him. It was too late to catch him before the editorial meeting, so she decided to wait downstairs and talk to him before he started on his script. Perhaps they could go to the canteen together for some privacy.

Elaine took out her gold compact – an archaic ritual that always provoked nudges and sneers from the younger women in the office – and checked her lipstick. She smudged off a clot with the nail of her little finger, then angled the mirror so that she could see her eyes. Her mascara was unfashionably heavy but that was how she liked it. Her eyes were smiling at her. She smiled back with her mouth, provoking a deepening of the shallow wrinkles that crowded the top of her cheeks. Her face often surprised her. It rarely looked the way she expected it would. Her expression was more resolute and her light-heartedness nowadays no longer registered on it at all. She was still smiling into her mirror when Roy came in. She knew it was him from the lazy drag of his soft soles over the carpet. She glimpsed her eyes dulling as she snapped shut the compact and dropped it into her large bag. Roy stood in front of her desk holding out a large bunch of roses. His left hand, unemployed, hovered over his pocket. Elaine admired the flowers but did not take them. Roy laid the bunch on her desk, his expression an acknowledgement of worst fears confirmed. He walked out before she had the chance to say anything to him.

A card was lodged in the foliage. With her fingers, Elaine scissored it from behind the cellophane and opened the miniature envelope. It said: 'You made yesterday bareable.' She wasn't sure whether the neologism was accidental and was still looking at it, having turned it round 360 degrees, looked at the back and smelt it, when Warde telephoned. He told her in his habitual, off-hand way that he'd been trying to reach Edwards to explain that he wouldn't be in until later because he had a doctor's appointment. He clearly imagined the statement had sufficient momentum for Elaine to translate it into a request which she would then immediately grant.

'Can't you come up with a better excuse than that?'

'It's not an excuse,' Warde protested. 'If it was an excuse I'd have told you it was an excuse.'

'So what's the matter with you?' Elaine found herself in the mood to talk. She was not usually strong enough to deal with Warde until late in the morning.

'That's none of your business.'

'I see.' Elaine hooked the receiver under her ear, opened her desk drawer and took out a razor blade to slit the cellophane. She liked the image this suggested to her; a carefree woman with time on her hands. Not the other woman who worked twelve hours a day just to keep up then went home exhausted to deal with the demands of a dying woman.

'See you later, then,' Warde said.

'How's Dawn?' This was how friends talked. Breaching confidences seemed to draw them closer together.

'Dawn?'

'Yes, how is she?'

'. . . She's fine.'

'Good. I suppose Maurice doesn't know yet. I mean he hasn't mentioned it to me . . .' Elaine pushed on, but already she knew she'd made the second biggest mistake of the year. She knew about Dawn because they had spoken on the phone at a time when Dawn had needed somebody to confide in.

'Is this any of your business?'

'No.' She shrank inside. 'Look, of course it isn't.' Now, a cold, sharp transfusion of regret. Was she mad? Had she any right to judge? None. Even though she knew they judged her every day of her life. Nobody, however, judged her more harshly than she judged herself.

'Right, then let's leave it, shall we, Elaine?' Warde used her name to bludgeon the friendship to death.

'I hope everything is all right. At the doctor's I mean.' Shrinking now, smaller and smaller. Fading to the eloquent scream of silence.

'Yes. So do I.'

When Vincent Edwards came into the office five minutes later – a knock, a tentative push of the door, a pause, then his face peering round – Elaine was still staring at the flowers. Her telephone receiver was lying on its side on the desk. A robotic voice repeatedly invited her to replace the handset. The roses were matt crimson. The gloss of the foliage smelt sharp and clean. Elaine had touched her thumb to a thorn, testing its edge from the acute angle at which the base met the stem, all the way along the short, rising distance to the point. Time was pocketed in moments like these, when the pendulum slowed as it did in the minutes before sleep and she was forced to contemplate the weight of the moment she was caught in. She pressed hard at the point of the thorn and, feeling the pain, pulled her thumb away. Blood burst to the surface. She smudged it onto the petals of the largest rose. The colour was indistinguishable from that of the flower. She sucked her thumb, the salt treacle of the blood cut through the sour coffee that cloyed her tongue. Blood and men, the two tasted the same. She wanted to hurt Warde but she couldn't. He was better at hurting than she was because he took up all of the space inside his skin. Elaine felt as though she just took up a little; a small warm chamber round her heart. There was more room for her to shrink into. The pendulum swung again. Thank God. Just the ordinary sum of life to deal with again, not the timeless diversions that, themselves, lasted lifetimes.

'Elaine?' Edwards soothed. Once Elaine had even loved him. Like the men who adored Marilyn, she loved a gay man believing not just that he wanted to be saved, but also that she was the one who could save him.

'Elaine?'

Elaine looked up: a communicant waiting for the wafer. 'I think I'll have to have a lie down.' Elaine tried to stand and achieved it by clutching the edge of her desk. 'And Warde's not coming in, he called. A doctor's . . .'

'Shall I call the nurse?'

'No. I'll be . . . I'll manage.' Elaine saw his relief. As she stood, he had taken a step back so that if she had fallen he wouldn't have had to catch her.

Maurice knocked on Edwards's door.

'Come!'

He walked in. Edwards waved him towards a chair and followed it through by brushing his hair from the crown to the nape of his neck. He was talking on the telephone. The call, Maurice could see from his exaggerated expressions, was causing him a great deal of distress. Edwards's terse trademark smile of empathy had transmuted into broad gurning. His finely wrought laugh escaped as a loud bray. Somebody he knew, but was earnestly protesting he didn't know very well, had been taken into hospital and Edwards was trying to absolve himself of any responsibility.

'No, he was not a student of mine.' He raised his eyebrows at Maurice then shook his head very quickly. 'No, he was not . . . I am sure that's what he is saying to you but, as I think you've adequately attested, the man is unwell . . . possibly schizophrenic. Now I suggest that you . . . no . . . yes . . . no, I cannot spell his surname. You'll have to call the number I've already provided . . . yes . . . goodbye. Thank you. Goodbye.' Edwards put the phone down, took out a handkerchief and wiped his forehead with it. The cotton smudged with orange, confirming a long-held rumour that Edwards wore make-up. He folded and pocketed it.

'If you ever choose to exhibit schizophrenic tendencies, Maurice, I recommend you give your GP adequate notice and that you make sure your next-of-kin knows where you are so they can come and deal with the unholy mess.'

'Somebody here, is it?'

'Oh, some fellow on a training course. Over from South Africa.'

'Long way from home, then,' Maurice prompted. He had already worked out that Edwards was, in some way, implicated.

'Apparently . . .'

'So, what . . . I mean if you don't have to breach any confidences, what happened?'

'Well,' Edwards tented his hands and rested his chin on them, 'apparently the poor fellow had been here for a week and his money had . . . well, there had been a mix-up and he hadn't eaten . . . you see he was too proud to ask. That was it, you see, he was too proud to, in as many words, ask . . .'

'Christ.'

'Yes. Yes, well one can only assume the man had these tendencies before . . . and . . .'

'What happened to him?'

'He destroyed his hotel room claiming that he was looking for hidden microphones. Secret microphones. Secret police. That sort of thing.' Then, as if it had only just sunk in, 'Absolutely bloody.'

'Terrible, yes, but you can't blame yourself. You mustn't.'

'One feels that one should have done more. I should really visit him. Yes, I shall.'

Having helped him towards this course of action, Edwards now seemed to be waiting for Maurice to leave which prompted Maurice to remind him that he had been asked to drop by and see him.

'Yes, of course. Of course.' Edwards still seemed to be weighing something up. 'This, ah, this other thing,' he said.

Maurice scratched his ear and looked blank.

'In the cold light of day. With the perspective of a little reflection. I wonder. I wonder.'

'You were talking about . . .'

'I was talking about what I've chosen rather pretentiously to call "The White Symphony". A symphony of silence. Did I explain this to you? You're no doubt aware of the avant-garde piece using the same conceit?'

'Yes. John Cage or somebody, isn't it?'

'I think there is more to be said.'

'Or less.'

'Indeed. Indeed.'

As Maurice listened to Edwards talk and watched him pace the office, it didn't seem such a bizarre project as he had first imagined. An hour of silence explained as, 'Not simply an absence of sound. No, one could achieve that by simply not fading up the microphones. But an active piece of radio comprising a collage, a symphony of the most beautiful silences that we can find. Taped, live, near, far, reflective, joyous: sacred, profane; silences of awe, pain, envy. Everything should be represented.' Edwards was conducting now, waving an imaginary baton in the air. Maurice watched, half convinced by him, half certain that they had put the wrong man in hospital.

'All right, Roy?' In his capacity as editor-of-the-day, Maurice, carrying his editor-of-the-day's clipboard, popped in to check up on Roy. Roy nodded but did not look up from his script. 'See you in the studio, then.' Maurice continued along the corridor and, at the point where it broadened out into the large open-plan production office, slowed to a managerial saunter. The office had been built into the eaves of the back roof which meant that the room was triangular and the windows were too high for anybody to see out. A number of tall plants in white plastic buckets were dotted around the room to cosy it up and compensate for the lack of any view. They looked out of place and served only to trip people up. A white vertical tube had appeared outside one of the offices when they arrived one Monday morning. It was about two feet in diameter, punctured by thousands of small holes, and stretched from the floor to the ceiling. Sometimes it vented warm air into the room. Various theories had been proposed to explain its function: the exhaust from the local Turkish restaurant, a very large bugging device, the air inlet for the smoking room, but it was eventually revealed to be a device for improving the humidity in the office. Warde claimed that the staff were medical guinea pigs and the Science Unit were trying to cultivate mould on exposed areas of human flesh.

Hardiman was hunched close to the vent at a tape machine editing on headphones. Maurice could smell his armpits from the moment he walked into the room. Telephones rang and were quickly answered. A fax spewed hot paper into a tray. A photocopier tirelessly dealt sheets of A4 into neat piles. Occasionally there was a shout or a laugh from one of the ten or eleven people in the room. Somebody was saying into a telephone, 'A child abuse "survivor", and that is, exactly?' A young woman was playing a violin phrase again and again, and saying to somebody who was hidden behind a pillar, 'There, did you hear it? There. Again. There.' But they hadn't so she re-cued it and it all started again. Maurice saw Beryl peering over the top of her glasses at her computer screen, touch-typing. Her cardigan cloaked her shoulders. He smiled as he passed her, she smiled back. In the dark hutch of a senior's office, a man in a denim shirt was talking on the telephone with his feet up on the desk. With his other hand he was playing a computer game called Anal Golf. In the next office a hunched figure was trying to download a picture of a naked woman from the Internet.

Maurice felt the warm fireside glow of home. Everything was as it should be. Everybody knew what they were doing or were at least busy with the pretence of looking busy and there was absolutely nothing for him to do. Responsibility without responsibilities, his favourite condition. He knocked on Elaine's door and walked in. She was drinking coffee from a polystyrene cup and staring out of the window at the rain straining through the grey net of the sky. There was a large cellophane-wrapped bunch of roses on her desk. Maurice took a quick reading of the evidence, decided that it stacked up pretty badly, and settled himself into a chair prepared to offer sympathy.

'You should go home. If you're not feeling up to it,' Maurice offered.

Elaine continued to stare out of the window. 'I'm not a bad person, you know. Not really. I do try my best to be good.'

'Elaine, you're the best person I know. What's all this about?'

'Do you really think so?' she said, as if his opinion didn't really count.

'Yes I do,' Maurice said. Elaine's mood was now threatening them both.

'So what else do you have to be? What counts?'

'With who?'

'With those who matter.'

'Elaine, you're beginning to sound like *The Prisoner*. Tell me what's happened?'

Elaine came back to her seat and sat down. 'I think I've offended Warde, and Roy, and traumatised Peculiar all in one morning. Roy thinks I'm, well . . . Warde thinks I'm a nosy interfering cow, and Peculiar thinks I'm pre-menstrual or, possibly, menopausal.'

'Full house, then.' He embarked on a laugh, but stalled it when he saw the effect it had on Elaine. 'I'm sorry,' he added for good measure. 'All I mean is that they probably all deserved exactly what they got.' This seemed to help. Elaine's expression softened. 'And it's not as though you go round throwing your weight about. Is it?'

'It's not Peculiar. Not really. I can deal with him. Or Warde, except, well, that's something else. It's Roy, really. He bought me these.' She took the roses and cradled them, looking maternally at the flowers. 'But I don't think I can. I mean I think I have to finish it with him. Perhaps I already have.'

Maurice shrugged. 'Have you?'

'When he gave them to me I didn't say anything. I just . . .'

'What?'

'Took them.'

'And what did you want to say. Mean to say?'

'Goodbye. It's over. I don't love you. I was mistaken. You're a fool, just like the rest . . .'

The door burst open and Roy walked in. He looked at Maurice, said, 'Hello, Maurice', reached over Elaine's desk for her hand and, when he had it tight, pulled her to her feet. He tugged her out of the room, pausing only to say, 'I'll be back for the programme. Script's in the office. Change a word and I'll smash your teeth in.'

Then they were gone and Maurice wondered whether he'd dreamed it all.

Over the following week Maurice felt as though he was standing in the eye of a storm. He was calm enough himself. In fact the tablets that Dr Soames had given him seemed to be having a beneficial effect on his state of mind. He wasn't sleeping particularly well, alcohol tasted like urine and his muscles occasionally spasmed causing him to drop plates or cups of coffee, stumble or, on one occasion, fall over in the street. But despite the freezing weather, the slow, inevitable approach of the nightmare of Christmas and his failure to find the courage to visit the woman he had met in the pub, he experienced a number of warm surges of optimism. Everybody else, however, seemed to be in torment. Polly was never in when he telephoned, though this meant he had regularly spoken to Will. Val was either off-hand or over-friendly. She had a new job and was dying to tell him about it, but for some reason she couldn't – just yet. Warde was at home with a mystery virus and never answered his phone. Elaine and Roy were cloistered in the canteen at every opportunity, having intense conversations, the contents of which neither would reveal to him, and Edwards kept being called to the fifth floor for long meetings. The rest of his time he seemed to spend visiting the man from South Africa in hospital. No more mention had been made of his 'White Symphony'.

The highlight of Maurice's week was the arrival, on Wednesday, of a man with a light bulb which fitted, was the correct wattage and, when he turned it on, lit up. Maurice felt absurdly happy about this. It seemed to be a metaphor for something, but like all metaphors, caused him to cringe slightly in embarrassment when he thought about it.

His new digs were working out. He had re-revised his opinion about Grace, and had begun to warm to her *naiveté*. It was a relatively sophisticated *naiveté*; one which was wise to the alternatives and for good reasons had dismissed them. He rarely agreed with her, but he enjoyed her company and he suspected that she was fond of him. One night, they had talked long after midnight and, when he admitted defeat and told her he really did have to go to bed, she stood up too and took his hand. She led him to her bedroom door and let him go. Then she threw her arms round his neck, leaned down and kissed him hard on the lips. When they broke apart she pushed her bedroom door open. Maurice didn't take up the invitation and Grace wasn't offended. They had reached an understanding which meant neither had to justify their actions to the other. This survived and would survive for as long as they didn't sleep together. Maurice took Martha's threat seriously. Martha wanted Grace for herself. She camouflaged this need with the pretence of caring. But it was the desperate clinging of the terminally lonely. If Martha lost Grace she would lose everything. She spent most nights in her room reading and listening to popular classics on her transistor radio.

Maurice had conceded defeat over Grace's party idea. It was planned for the weekend before Christmas and, so far, everybody he had asked had agreed to come. Office parties were few and far between due to the fact that few people seemed to want a celebration that had anything to do with work. A Christmas party at someone's flat which included a number of people from work was a different matter. The day following it he'd organised to have Will. This he had done for the previous two years, celebrating their Christmas together early so that Polly and Val could have use of a child on the day itself.

FOUR

Vincent Edwards had been busy on two fronts: the heart-rending duty of visiting Solomon in hospital, and taking part in a series of informal chats in the Controller's office. The Controller had never before shown much interest in Edwards. He had listened politely at review board, made sure he spoke to him at the Christmas party and indulged his vanity by sending him occasional e-mails to praise his programmes. But, beyond that, Edwards believed himself to be consigned to the ranks of the never-beens: the workaday editors who kept the place afloat, the libels at bay and the quality sufficiently even to avoid attention: positive or negative. Now, he was being asked to join groups on strategy, asked about his views as to how more 'young people' could be attracted to the network, and quizzed as to his career aspirations. Edwards realised, with a mixture of dread and joy, that he was going to be invited to the fifth floor on a permanent basis. He would have to buy a fashionable suit and a few of those shirts that didn't seem to require ties.

He visited Solomon on the evening that he had spoken to Maurice about him. The hospital was a long tube journey out of the West End then a fifteen-minute walk along a busy dual-carriageway. Solomon was in a first-floor ward, lying nearly comatose, huge and doped across the tangled sheets of a bed. He was wearing a nightshirt. His suit was crumpled across a chair. His lips were white and dry, his eyes fixed on some private horror that was being projected onto the wall. Edwards cried. It was the only response he could make to Solomon's condition. He drew up a chair and sat beside the bed until, after ten minutes, a warder with a pony-tail, a white coat and a name badge that said 'Terry', told him he shouldn't be there. No visitors were allowed until Solomon had calmed down sufficiently for them to reduce the medication. Edwards asked for a coat hanger, hung up Solomon's suit, and left.

Three days later he visited again. This time he found Solomon in the television lounge. He was watching a quiz show with a disturbed, elderly woman with skin like papyrus and a youth who kept trying to wipe an imaginary insect from his sleeve. Behind them, sitting alone against the back wall, was a smartly dressed man in a black three-piece suit, a red tie and highly polished shoes. He regularly looked at his watch and tutted. The imagined bus was late.

'Hello, Solomon.' Edwards gently touched Solomon's shoulder and sat down beside him. Solomon looked at him without any recognition then went back to watching the television. It wasn't until the next visit that they talked, and the one after that that they managed a coherent conversation. Edwards tried to tell Solomon how sorry he was, not just about his predicament, but because he hadn't listened when he was being asked for help. Solomon graciously forgave him. When Edwards visited the following day Solomon was gone. Terry said that he'd recovered sufficiently well to travel, and Edwards went back to work feeling as he often did: that there was more he could, or should, have done.

Vincent Edwards had always been regarded as a good

manager. He was unsympathetic towards members of staff who professed to be ill, but he would do anything he could for those who genuinely needed his help. Over the last three or four years, however, he had changed. He had become more intolerant, more impatient, more self-obsessed. Everybody he knew was turning inwards. Many of his colleagues argued that it was the only way they could protect themselves from the changes that were going on. Edwards had never lacked self-belief, but he wasn't entirely self-sufficient. Ultimately he respected the people he served and although he would never admit it, he was pleased to receive notes of praise from the people above him. It was the way the Corporation had always worked: a pyramid of respect with the greatest respect being reserved for the pyramid itself. But now there were those who had appointed themselves curators of the pyramid. The fabric was crumbling, the climate was destroying it. The curators argued they needed to act quickly to preserve it. And so they had, but in order to act they had had to assimilate more power than any curator had previously held.

While Edwards held with the pyramid theory, Maurice, being further down the pyramid, was a member of the baby-out-with-the-bathwater club. This group held that it was impossible to say how the Corporation worked: it just did. There was a shared but unspoken understanding of what everybody was doing and how they were doing it. It wasn't necessary to turn it into mission statements and project it onto screens. One of the worst days of Maurice's career came when he, along with a hundred or so colleagues, was invited to attend a day of 'focus groups' in a conference centre. The idea, it seemed, was to come up with a consensus view of the values the Corporation was supposed to embody. Within a few minutes it was clear that the only ones who were unclear about those values were the consultants who had been brought in to 'facilitate' the focus groups.

When 'transparency' supplanted 'choice' as the new watchword and the curators tried to analyse how the structure worked, people sat down with pencils and pieces of paper, rulers and Venn diagrams, and explained it to them. The point was that a lorryload of money was delivered to the front door each year and this paid for everything that came out of the transmitters. Of course, a few extra pounds were earned by selling the programmes abroad and a few pence came from the books that were advertised after the cookery and travel programmes, but ultimately it was a straightforward equation. Making money was frowned upon, it drew attention to the commercial potential of the Corporation and that was dangerous territory. The logical step from that was to take advertising, and although this was acceptable for the Corporation's own products, it wasn't really done to advertise anybody else's. The fact that three of the radio networks promoted the music industry all day and every day, even going so far as to recommend one brand over another and then, each week, trumpeting the relative sales figures of these products, nobody seemed to notice.

This lack of transparency was decreed unsuitable. The way to operate was the way the curators had when they worked in the independent sector. So they pulled everything apart and stuck it back together in a way they understood and was therefore transparent to them – if nobody else. In the process, departments became business centres, colleagues became competitors and, overnight, everybody was charging everybody else for services that, previously, they had naively considered to be free. However much Maurice protested about the new system, in his heart he knew it was necessary. What he regretted was what had been lost, and that was unquantifiable. It would certainly never show on a spreadsheet. It stemmed from the fact that everything he now did had become a commercial transaction. He employed engineers to put out his programmes, he bought the services of the man who came to replace his light bulb, he sold his programmes via Edwards to one of the curators. If he didn't buy his technical services from the engineers they went bankrupt and were fired. If he wanted them to work fifteen hours without a break they no longer had a choice. The effect of this shift in relationships was multiplied a thousandfold when it was applied to the whole organisation. It was inevitable that the spirit had to change. Something had been lost, and even Maurice was hard pushed to define what it was. He just knew; when he walked into the canteen he felt it. What had happened was that Maurice had become a commodity too and he didn't yet realise it. The only ones who were safe were the curators, because they effectively bought their own services from themselves. To achieve this they had had to assimilate more power than any curator had previously held – and power is never given up lightly.

It was, therefore, with certain misgivings that Edwards contemplated seeing out his days on the fifth floor. It would mean that his life with Charles would have to wait and that he would have to continue to live in Tattenham Corner. But neither of these things really seemed to matter. His protests that he didn't want more power had always been hollow. He wanted it very much, but had never been offered it. In time he would forget Solomon, just as he would forget what he and the Corporation had been, and soon the folk memory would fade. The way the Corporation used to work would be discussed with the same fond condescension that sound engineers reserve for the wax cylinders that were once used to record the human voice. The engineers of the new digital age apply the same condescension to audio tape and razor blades. But Solomon's fate had been avoidable, Edwards knew it wouldn't have happened five years before. He would have listened to what he was being told, and, more importantly, he would have acted on it. The days of 'The White Symphony' were over.

For a week, Polly had refused to answer the telephone. When it rang, as it was doing now, she watched it and waited beside it until it stopped. She had come to hate the instrument: a squat shrill impostor that screamed until it was held and childishly insisted on being the centre of attention whenever it woke. She and Val had talked about America and nothing else for almost a week, but when Val had first mentioned it Polly had known that there was no decision to make. America offered her the opportunity for the new life she had always wanted. She would use Val's contract to get her over there and then decide what she was going to do next. Smashing up the bedroom had liberated her in many ways. As far as she was concerned, Val could now look after herself.

'Shall I get it?' Val said, drawn from the kitchen by the unanswered phone.

'If you like.' Polly sat on the sofa and tugged a cushion to her chest.

'Maurice,' Val said and looked at Polly who shook her head. 'No, I'm afraid she's not . . . Yes, I gave her the message. Yes. I did . . . no I'm not still angry . . . no, not at all . . . yes, I know . . .'

Polly scrawled something on the phone pad and held it up. Val read and relayed the message. 'Why don't you come round for supper tomorrow, about seven . . . no, I'm sure Polly will be . . . yes, I guarantee it . . . yes, I'm so pleased about that . . . yes . . . are you? . . . seven o'clock . . . yes, goodbye, Maurice.' Val put the phone down. 'Do you want me there?' she said.

'I don't know,' Polly said solemnly. She was already rehearsing the conversation in her head.

'I could go out. I mean we could eat together then I could invent a meeting or something . . . I don't mind.'

'Do what you want.'

'I'm only trying to help.'

'Look. I'm not interested in whether . . . look, just . . . do what you want.' Polly walked out.

Val followed her to the kitchen. 'I told you. I'm only trying to help.'

'Then help.'

'Well what would you like me to do?' Val laughed, offering Polly the chance to join in. 'I mean give me some help here.'

Polly opened the fridge and took out a bottle of freshly squeezed orange juice. She didn't want a drink. She wanted something to occupy her hands to stop them lashing out at Val's face.

'I wonder if you ever listen to yourself,' Polly said calmly.

'Not this again, please.'

'No, I just wonder if you do, that's all.'

Polly took the juice to the sink, poured herself a glass and went back into the lounge. Val had learned enough in the last tempestuous week not to follow her. She waited in the kitchen and when she could bear it no longer, went up to the bedroom where she lay on the bed and cried into the pillow. She felt very lonely.

That night, buoyed up by the unexpected supper invitation, Maurice summoned up the courage to take the tube to Brixton and ask around until he found the Dog Tray. He got there shortly after seven and stood at the bar of the snug tapping a coin on the counter until, eventually, Henry heard him and came round from the public bar to serve him. He had been watching American football on the Sports Channel.

'What can I get you, sir?' The landlord was wearing the same shabby cardigan as he had on Maurice's previous visit.

'Bells. Large one.' Henry turned his back and notched two measures into a glass. He touched the rim to the optic to release the final stubborn drop. 'Have one for yourself, Henry.'

'I'll take a half pint of Best Bitter with you, sir. Very kind of you. Compliments of the season, sir.' Recognition flickered in his eyes.

Maurice handed over a five-pound note. Henry keyed the sum into the mechanism of the ancient till. As he handed over the change he said, 'I got you now . . . it's ah . . .?'

'Maurice. But I don't think we were introduced.'

'That's right. You, ah . . . yes, I got you now. Well I haven't seen her for a couple of weeks if that's why you're here.'

'No?'

'It's not like Rene. Not like her at all.' Henry waited to see whether Maurice knew something he didn't.

'You know her better than me, Henry.'

'I was worried. I called round. No answer.' He shrugged.

There was nothing else to be said but Maurice was happy to join Henry in speculating as to what might have happened to Rene. If nothing else, it shed light on the landlord's gothic imagination. Maurice bought another Scotch and Henry joined him. They talked about Maurice's job, the weather and Christmas. Henry sold him a book of tickets for the meat raffle. Later, the landlord came out to build up the fire. Once or twice he shuttled between the snug and the public bar to serve. An elderly man came in, bought a pint and took it to the furthest corner of the small room. He took a folded puzzle book out of his pocket and, hunched beneath the Bass mirror, applied himself to it. An hour passed. Somebody in the public bar put money in the jukebox. The voice of Slim Whitman soured the mood into melancholy. Maurice was drunk and melancholia was not a bad thing to feel.

'I think,' Maurice said, 'that I'm going to come here regular . . . ly. It's a fine pub, Henry. You should be applauded.'

'I've had Peers of the Realm in here, you know. And I'll tell you something else.' Henry's fat finger beckoned him closer, Maurice leaned forwards. 'They get the same service from me. I treat everybody with equal respect. In my book everybody deserves it. And they get it until proved otherwise.'

'That's a good. A good philosophy, Henry. A sound philosophy.'

Henry gave sober consideration to this, then he said. 'I should like to ask you a question.'

'Anything.' Maurice threw out his right arm and knocked the blind box onto the floor. As he knelt down to pick it up the last mouthful of Scotch sluiced back into his mouth. It still tasted of whisky rather than vomit so he swallowed it again.

'You don't have to answer.'

'Henry,' Maurice slurred, 'you can ask me anything you like, mate. Anything you bloody well like.'

'Well, you're not a bad looking gent . . .'

'Thank you.' Maurice fumbled some change out of his pocket into the slot in the charity box.

'So why did you go home with Rene?'

Maurice swayed and steadied himself by holding onto the bar. 'Because . . . because, Henry, I love her. I do. Well, I really think I do.'

Henry shrugged. Nothing surprised him any more. 'The bloke that does the snooker,' he said, 'he's a twat isn't he?'

'I don't know,' Maurice said. 'I don't work on the telly. Probably.'

'Women,' Henry started on another tack.

'Women?'

Somebody called for service from the public bar. 'With you in a moment, sir,' Henry called. 'Women. You see. I don't think they like blokes.'

'Don't you?'

'No. I don't think they think we're clever enough for them.'

'And are we?'

'Well, you see . . .' Henry was distracted by somebody ringing the bell in the other bar. 'Hold your bloody horses in there!' He shook his head and leaned on the bar. 'I don't think men and women should live together. Not all the time. I think they should come together, occasionally. You know what I mean? Just for a bit of company. But not live together. Problem is, though, that if that happened there'd be war. Forget your religious persecution, your race wars, there'd be nuclear sex war if that occurred.'

'Three cheers it hasn't then.' Maurice raised his glass. Henry sauntered round the corner to serve the scrum that was waiting for him there. Maurice had one more drink then shook Henry's hand, wished him a Merry Christmas, shook the hand of the man doing the puzzle book and staggered outside. The fierce chill sobered him. His vague memory of where the woman lived led him to turn left then left again, away from the well-lit main street and into a narrow terrace of small houses. The road was lined on both sides by cars. He stopped to take a fix on his bearings. For a moment the houses continued to move, then they drew to a halt. The smell of frying floated from a window. Grey smoke shunted from a chimney. The street was sanctified by the night. Maurice felt no fear walking down it though he chose to stay in the middle of the road to avoid walking in the shadows.

He recognised the house by the violet door and the plastic 'one pint today' collar hung round the neck of an empty milk bottle. The bottle was spotlessly clean. Maurice looked up the soot-black wall towards the first-floor window. The curtain was shut but there was a light on in the room. The hallway light, too, showed through the coloured glass above the front door. He knocked and waited. A woman walked quickly along the pavement behind him. Maurice watched her go down the street. She was wearing training shoes and carrying a plastic bag of bottles. The smoke of a cigarette trailed over her shoulder like a steam train. Twenty yards further on she turned into a doorway and called, 'Get those plates out the oven,' as she went inside. Maurice felt a pang of profound envy. When he and Polly parted, after the initial shock, what he missed most about their life together was the domestic routines. He could not have predicted how important the mundanities of life were until they were gone. He knocked again, this time with the conviction his knock would be answered. He heard a door open, deep within the house.

'Who is it?' Rene's voice, from behind the door, was thick with a cold.

'It's me. Maurice.'

'Maurice who?'

'I met you in the Dog Tray . . . remember?'

'You'll have to do better than that, love. Anyway I'm not seeing anybody at the moment. I'm not very well . . . Come back in a couple of weeks.'

'I've bought you a present.'

After a brief pause the door opened on the chain and the woman looked out. She said, 'Yes, I thought it was you.'

Then she looked down at Maurice's bag. 'What you got there then?'

'Just a bottle. I should have thought about it earlier and bought you something nice, but I came on the spur of the moment. Can I come in?'

'I've not been well, love. You'll have to excuse the mess.' She pulled her hand through her hair.

'I don't mind. I just wanted to see you.'

'Come in, then.' The door swung shut and Maurice heard the chain rattling off. Then it opened again and Maurice stepped into the dim corridor of the hallway. None of it was familiar. The woman looked him up and down before shutting the door behind him. 'I don't want any funny business,' she said, then led him into the front room.

Maurice took off his coat and sat down on the sofa. The fire was lit and the television was on. A chorus-line of men in tails was high-stepping slightly out of synchronisation as a woman in a swimsuit was carried past them, held horizontally by three other men. Rene picked up the pink tissues that were scattered over the carpet and threw them into the fire. They flared and died. One took flight up the chimney. Maurice relaxed, laid his head on the cushioned back of the settee and crossed his legs at the ankles. The rich heat from the fire played over his forehead and cheeks. He felt it lap against the slow pulse in his neck. The woman sat beside him, hunched her legs up beneath her and looked him over again, this time more closely. She licked her finger and brushed it across his eyebrow. 'Sticking up,' she said. Then she gave a sigh and laid her head against his shoulder. Maurice put his arm round her and they watched the television in silence for a while.

'I like him, he's cheeky,' the woman said when a baby-faced comic came on.

'Henry's worried about you,' Maurice said.

'No he's not.'

Five minutes later Maurice said. 'I don't know why I came. I just wanted to see you again.'

'That's all right, love. You don't have to explain.'

'Thanks.' Maurice said. He was happier when they didn't talk. Living alone, it was rare to enjoy both silence and companionship. In fact he was happier now than he could remember being for a long time. And when he was happy he always thought about his son. 'I've got a boy. Called Will,' he said. 'He's four. He's a good kid.'

'Who does he look like?'

'He used to remind me of Ilya Kuriakin from *The Man From Uncle*. Now I think he looks like Pol. My wife. Ex-wife. Anyway . . . anyway I was just thinking about him. I'm sorry.'

'Don't be sorry for being happy.' After another pause Rene said, 'Have you had anything to eat?'

'Yes. I had something earlier.'

'I'll get us a drink. When this is finished.'

'He's not frightened, Will I mean. The world doesn't intimidate him. Sometimes I envy him because he knows who he is . . . what he's for.' Then Maurice remembered the conversation he'd had with Rene about her absent child the last time they met. He said, 'Shit. I'm sorry.'

'I told you. Stop being sorry.'

They watched the programme through to the end and Maurice was immensely disappointed when it had finished. The compère seemed to have been talking directly to them, as if they were the only ones who were watching.

'I'll fetch us that drink now.' Rene stood then caught the arm of a chair to steady herself. 'I can't shake this cold off, Maurice. I'm all light-headed with it.'

'Let me get it.'

'I won't say no.'

Maurice went out into the kitchen. There was no central heating in the house and the windows were freezing up on the inside. He took the bottle of wine out of the fridge and found an opener in a drawer that was cluttered with Co-op stamps, string and brown tape. The glasses were in a cupboard beneath the drainer. The wall inside it was damp and mould was creeping up from the skirting towards the shelf. He went back into the lounge. Rene smiled as he handed her a glass. She held it up and he filled it from the bottle.

'I thought you might come back,' she said. 'Are you watching this?' The news had started.

'No.'

Rene switched off the set with a remote.

'I did think about you. Shall I tell you why?'

'Yes.' Maurice sat down beside her again. She walked her fingers up his arm and ran a nail over the stubble on his cheek.

'Because I watched you in the bathroom, that morning before you left. You thought I was asleep, but I wasn't. I followed you out in case you took anything, but you just opened all my bottles didn't you?' It was a gentle admonishment.

'Yes.'

'Why did you do that?'

'Because I wanted to get to know you better.'

'You could have got to know me much better. You had your chance.'

'Not that way. I didn't want to know you that way.' Maurice smiled, embarrassed.

'You didn't. Or you don't?'

'I didn't, and now I don't know.' Rene put her glass on the floor and pushed the hair back from Maurice's forehead, her fingers traced the furrows on his brow, the perfume he could smell on her wrist was familiar. She took his wrist and laid his hand against her breast.

218

'Why the perfume?' she said.

'I don't know.'

'Because the perfume isn't me, is it? The perfume's not me at all.'

'It's what you choose to be.'

'It's what I choose because it's what I expect men . . . expect me to be.' Rene sighed; something had clouded her mood; she shrugged off Maurice's hand. 'Once I read a story in a magazine. It was about a woman who let a man talk his way into her motel room in America, it was an American magazine, and he attacked her with a knife and she was nearly killed, but they saved her life. Anyway, she was saying why she let him in, and what they talked about . . . and I thought, God I've talked to men like that. They talk like they need something from me, and I can't give it because . . . because it just doesn't come from talking. And in his article the man got cross because she didn't understand. But he didn't understand it either. She didn't talk about this bit. I worked it out for myself . . . Anyway, and then you read about these teachers in the homes who can't, you know, hug the children, because they're frightened they'll get had up for abuse or something . . . but you see it's all the kids need. And then I saw this thing about the American President and it said his mum never held him and I read about all these women he goes after. You see, some things can't be talked about. It's just about somebody holding you.'

They made love beneath the sheets and the eiderdown, tunnelling down into the darkness. Maurice saw colours and shapes, cells blurring and multiplying. The colours changed, he saw summer and sun as he felt her hot shallow breath on his chest. She held his head in her hands, bringing him back to her and the room and the winter night, and when she saw he was back she forced his mouth hard against hers. Their teeth clashed together. She took his lip in her teeth and bit hard. The tension built in his back, the muscles in his legs tightened until with a cry it was all released and the colours lurched and lurched and flowed away. He lay beached by a calm blue sea. The sun was warm on his stomach, the breeze cool on his back. A boy was tipping watery sand from a red bucket. He was wearing a wide-brimmed sun-hat. Maurice had to squint against the sun to see him clearly. The edge of the tide foamed over his pink toes. The boy watched as his feet emerged from the clear water, it looked as though the water was pouring out from his body through his toes.

Rene saw him off early the following morning while the street still slept. The milk had been left on the step. It was frozen and had forced up the silver top. In the night a fall of snow had blanketed and blurred the lines of the city. A breeze whipped up eddies of fine powder from the pavements. Maurice stepped out into a cold that felt clean and pure only because of the warmth he felt inside. He was not tired even though he had had little sleep. The weight of weariness he had been carrying seemed to have diminished. He had been taking Dr Soames's tablets sufficiently long for them to be influencing his mood, but it was a profound optimism he felt, he doubted whether chemicals could have induced it.

'You take care of yourself, Maurice,' Rene said, kissing him on the cheek as she pulled her dressing gown tight around her.

'I'll come back soon.' Maurice said, holding her shoulders, then pulling her close and embracing her.

'No you won't, darling.'

Darling. The word was rusty with misuse. All day it rang in Maurice's head until the greater din of Polly's news drowned it out.

FIVE

FIVE CENTIMETRES OF snow had paralysed the transport systems of the capital. Elaine's bus arrived late and as soon as it pulled away from the kerb it joined a half-mile queue of traffic waiting to cross the river. She would have undertaken the twenty-minute walk to the tube station but the radio traffic reports from Scotland Yard were warning of a massive power failure on the underground. The man in the Travelcopter with the high-energy voice announced that the Westway was tailed back for five miles. The Hangar Lane gyratory system was not gyrating and Hyde Park Corner was gridlocked. On the trains, frozen points were making life hell for the suburban traveller. Transport officials faced the barrage of rage with weary politeness. It wasn't their fault, it never was.

Elaine looked out from the upper deck of the bus across the park. Nobody was walking through the avenues of leaning trees, the gates were still chained. The coating of unblemished snow made the bowling green look like a huge linen-covered table waiting to be set. The snow on the stone folly softened the austerity of the building. For the first time Elaine saw it as laconic rather than menacing: no longer a crime scene, just a place for lovers to meet and kiss. To

Elaine, parks had always served as poignant reminders of her childhood: Sunday greenhouse visits, the smell of earth and lime, the collar-moistening warmth of the hothouse, ice cream, her parents arm-in-arm, Sunday formal, she attached firmly to the hand of one of them, never swung between them like other children. One, two, three, UP we go! Gentle; firm; no impropriety: good parents, serious-minded, but always serious. Sunday: the day of broken promises; the day on which she was taught how she would feel when her working life was over.

She was thinking of her parents because it helped her not to think about Roy May who had announced that he wanted to leave home for her. She knew her mother would have been 'shocked', her father 'speechless'. Being her parents' creation she had been both shocked and speechless when Roy told her. He was waiting for her response before he told Caz. Elaine didn't know the answer. She would only know it afterwards, when it would be too late. Roy loved her. He had said so on more than one occasion, and love was not a word that came easily to the lips of a man like him. He had told Elaine that when he spent time with her he felt like the man he had been before he had left home to earn a living by his glib wit. The youth who had climbed the town's Victoria memorial to declare his love for a girl called Sally.

'I can't decide for you.' Elaine had said. She and Roy were in the canteen. The conversation could have taken place on any day the previous week, the agenda was always the same.

'You can help me decide.'

'If you want to leave Caz then leave her. If you're so unhappy . . .'

'I'm not unhappy.'

'Then stay with her.'

'But I'm not happy.'

'Then leave. I don't know . . . I can't decide for you.'

Elaine's confusion was heightened because she had already decided that she didn't want anything else to do with Roy. Fundamentally she felt no differently from the way she had the morning after they had made love. But when she tested her feelings about him against the litmus of her other relationships she began to wonder if she had the capacity to feel differently. Perhaps her lack of commitment was a defence against being deserted. Perhaps she needed to commit herself to find out what that really felt like. But she had lived by herself for too long, her independence was valuable to her. Soon her mother would be dead. She would inherit the house, sufficient money and investments to enable her to give up work. But what did she really want? She had, if she was lucky, perhaps thirty years of good health ahead of her. Roy had fewer.

The bus lurched forwards and picked up speed. When the conductor came for the fare, Elaine didn't hear her. She was trying to picture herself in ten years' time, walking arm-in-arm round the park with Roy. Whatever she dressed him in, the image of the two of them together didn't look right.

'The party. Saturday. I'm doing a head count. How about it?' Maurice said, catching Elaine an hour later as she came out of the Ladies lavatory.

'I don't know, Maurice.' Elaine hated bumping into men outside the toilets. She walked through the swing doors, hoping that Maurice wouldn't follow her.

He did. 'Bring a bottle. Wine, beer, anything . . .'

Sometimes Elaine preferred Maurice when he was depressed. At least then he didn't bound round the building getting under everybody's feet. He looked drunk, though it was only eleven o'clock and she couldn't smell anything on his breath.

'I'll try and come. It depends on Mother.'

'Fab. Well then . . . see you there.' Maurice put his arm round Elaine's shoulders and hugged her. She shrugged him off.

'What?' Maurice said.

'It doesn't matter. Leave it.' Elaine said.

'Leave what?' Maurice stepped back and stood as far away from her as the corridor would allow.

'It. Leave it.'

'What's the matter?'

'Nothing's the matter.' Elaine tried to walk away, Maurice took her arm.

'Will you stop pawing me!' Elaine pulled away.

'I'm sorry. If there's anything . . .'

'Maurice. There isn't anything. Just leave me. Alone.'

Maurice watched her walk off down the corridor. Her arms were crossed, her chin was down. When she disappeared through the swing doors at the far end Maurice couldn't tear himself away from the spot. A moment later Warde was walking towards him.

'Well, where the hell have you been?' Maurice said.

'Off.' Warde said and walked straight past him.

'I'm having a party. Saturday. I put an invite in your pigeon hole. Bring a bottle . . . wine, beer . . .'

'Sure.' Warde said, without turning round.

'Well don't put yourself out or anything,' Maurice said lamely, but the corridor was empty again.

Maurice spent the morning filling in expense claims forms then went downstairs to the reference library to read the tabloids and skim the Sundays. When he returned to his office just before lunch he found an e-mail waiting for him. It had been circulated to the whole department and was the announcement that, with immediate effect, Vincent Edwards was to take up a new position within the 'commissioning structure' on the fifth floor. His job was to be advertised externally (i.e. in the outside world) and, until a new appointment had been made, David Warde had agreed to 'act up' into his post.

'Well bloody hell,' Maurice said to himself. 'Bloody bloody hell.' He wasn't sure whether he felt more betrayed by Peculiar taking the promotion or Warde being asked to take his place. Either way, neither of them had consulted him, and nobody had approached him to see whether he wanted to have a bash at the job himself.

He telephoned Elaine, 'Have you heard?'

'Heard what?'

'About Peculiar and Warde?'

'Of course I have. It's been common knowledge for a week.'

'Well not with me it hasn't.'

'Well perhaps if you ever left your office . . .' Elaine put the phone down. Maurice decided to write the day off and go home. That way he could have a shower, watch *Countdown*, and enjoy a few tins of industrial-strength lager before setting off for supper with Polly and Val. At least he still had that to look forward to.

Until she decided not to, Elaine felt guilty about the way she had treated Maurice. Once she had, the guilt diminished sufficiently for her not to see his pathetic hangdog expression each time she allowed herself a moment's thought. Warde was also in the office, sitting at his desk and staring at his computer screen. Intermittently he would lazily nudge a key and, like a habitual nose picker, examine whatever it was that his finger had summoned. Elaine knew he was pretending to work only to avoid having to talk to her. Since he had come back from sick leave they had maintained a cool distance. Elaine had decided she didn't really like Warde any more. Perhaps she had never really liked him, but as everybody else did she had never contemplated feeling any differently. Warde seemed to sense this and for a while had tried his best to win her round. When she didn't smile at his puerile jokes and didn't even answer his witty e-mails he gave up and sulked. Now they communicated by a series of grunts and gestures, but because they had shared an office for five years nothing was lost in their transactions.

'Maurice?' Warde said when Elaine put the phone down.

'What?'

Warde was forced into reformulating the grunt into a question. 'Was that Maurice? On the telling bone? Speaking?'

'Mm.' Elaine feigned distraction by sucking the end of a pencil and looking pensively out of the window. She remembered Lauren Bacall or some other icon of cool doing the same. Unfortunately the pencil tasted as though it had been dipped into dog excrement so she took it quickly out again, stripping off some of the paint on her top set of teeth.

After a pause, Warde said, 'Dawn thinks I should be worried about Maurice. I told her that he's beyond help.'

'Did you?'

'Mm.'

This time Elaine broke the silence. 'Why did she think you should be worried?'

'What?'

'I said why did she think you should be worried?'

'Oh, I don't know. She feels responsible for him. Christ knows why.'

'You mean she cares about him? As a friend.'

'Exactly. Exactly.' He settled back, the point made.

'Mm.'

When Warde lost his nerve and looked over at Elaine, he saw her looking directly back at him. 'Well, are you worried?'

'Not worried, exactly,' Elaine said.

'What then?'

'I don't know. It's just a feeling.'

'Elaine. Can I ask you a question?' Warde swivelled his swivel chair round to face her.

'You can try.'

'I mean, if it's too personal don't feel you have to answer it.'

'Go on.'

Warde vaulted his feet onto the desk. 'Are you having regular sex or something?'

'Yes,' she lied. 'Why do you ask?'

'You look . . . I don't know . . . sort of . . . sated.'

'Sated?'

'Mm.' Warde made a globe shape with his hands, 'Sort of sexy and . . .' he made another, 'I don't know . . . whole.'

'Good.'

'Anybody we know?'

'Somebody I know, yes.'

'Good . . . good.'

'Anyway, I thought we were discussing Maurice.'

'Yes, he's having a party,' Warde said.

'I know.'

'Are you going?'

'I don't know.'

Warde's phone rang. He glanced down at the small window above the keypad announcing the number, swung his legs off the desk and answered it. Somebody important, Warde was unctuous, switched on.

'Well?' Elaine said when the conversation was over.

'They want me to start after Christmas. I'll have Peculiar's office. He's moving his stuff out this week.'

'Will you still talk to me when you're important?'

'Only when I have to.'

'So this party . . .'

'Yes. I'll go. We'll go.'

'But you'll tell him first. About you and Dawn?'

'I'll try.'

Maurice hadn't intended to get drunk but after the first can of lager he lost any will not to. By the time *Countdown* was over, four empty tins were stacked neatly on the kitchen drainer. Maintaining some order amidst the chaos of inebriation allowed him to pretend he wasn't as drunk as he felt. After all, if he was drunk, he wouldn't care where he threw his cans. He rehearsed both sides of the argument as he stood beneath the shower. As the water sobered him, tiredness filled the void. He wrapped one of Martha's towels round him, went into the bedroom, lay foetally on the bed and fell into a deep sleep. Grace woke him at seven thirty and handed him the cordless telephone. He felt wretched, cold and sober. Polly told him with deadly politeness that he was late for supper. He apologised and handed the phone back to Grace who was still waiting by the bed.

'Everything all right, Morry?'

'Not really, no.'

Grace sat down beside him. 'I telephoned that radio station and got the number for that woman.'

'Did you?' Maurice looked around the room for his clothes, then remembered he'd left them in the bathroom. 'The trance woman?'

'She said she wasn't looking for anybody to help her. Never mind, worth a try.'

'Of course it was.' Maurice wasn't really listening. Polly had said something about his being late making 'it easier for her to say what she had to say'. He didn't like the sound of it. Already the night he had spent with Rene felt like a dream.

'Still,' Grace lit up and stood up. '*Party time*! Saturday. Are you excited, Morry?'

'Yes. Exceptionally.'

'I'm going to buy a new dress and some new knickers,' Grace said, dialling a number on the cordless phone as she walked out of the room.

Maurice thought for a moment about Grace naked except for a pair of black lace knickers. He stopped himself just in time from animating the image into a sweaty, X-rated movie. Already Bridget Bardot was edging into the frame wearing a black basque and suspenders. He channelled his attention into choosing what to dress in. He had three good suits but rarely put them on. If he wore them at work Warde ridiculed him. If he wore a suit to the pub he usually spilled beer down it and, by the end of the evening, the waistband of the trousers had folded in half under his paunch. But tonight he wanted to dress for Polly.

As he waited at her door he adjusted his tie. He was carrying a bunch of flowers and a bottle of good claret which felt like a Christmassy drink. He could already smell the meal which meant that Polly and not Val had cooked it. Through the door glass he saw Polly come into the hallway, pause by the long mirror, flatten her dress then stride towards the door, her arm reaching out prematurely to open it. Only when she had opened it and the heat of the house spilled out did Maurice realise how cold he was. Polly kissed him on the cheek, took the flowers and the wine, and led him in. In the kitchen he unbelted his coat, shook down his suit sleeves and readjusted his tie.

'You do look nice. Are you going on somewhere special?'

Polly looked him over as she put on an apron. She was wearing a short black dress and dark tights. Possibly stockings. She had a black velvet Alice-band in her hair.

'Well,' Maurice said. 'Yes, I'm, ah, going to a . . . leaving do. Later. Maybe.'

'You're not, are you?' Polly said tentatively.

'Well . . .'

'You put it on for me.'

'. . . Yes.' Maurice tried to loosen the knot of his tie. All of his shirts were too small to be fully buttoned at the neck and he was now having difficulty swallowing.

'Sorry.' Polly turned away so she wouldn't have to face him. 'Look, sit down.' She went to the stove. Maurice waited by the sink. He didn't want to drink or smoke or sit down, he just wanted to hold Polly. He went and stood behind her and took her in his arms.

'It's really good to see you,' he said, feeling that some explanation was necessary for the unprompted embrace.

'Mm. And you.' Polly reached up and took his right hand which was sliding up towards her breast.

'Where's Val?'

'Oh she's out. Some work thing.'

'Excellent.'

'Yes, I said you'd be sorry to miss her.'

'Will asleep?'

'Yes. He stayed up for you but . . .'

'I was late.'

Maurice let Polly go. 'Shall I?' He held up the bottle of wine.

'If you like, there's some in the fridge if you'd rather.'

Maurice opened the fridge. There were two full bottles of white wine in the door and one laying down on the shelf. 'We'll have one of these, shall we?' Maurice took it out and looked at the label. 'Any good?' He held out the bottle for Polly to see.

'Yes. It's lovely. You'll like it.'

Maurice opened the bottle, as usual, his sole contribution to supper. The cork broke in half as he tried to draw it out of the bottle.

Polly watched him as he shoved the corkscrew back in. She said, 'I'll do it.'

'No, I can manage.' He extracted the rest and held the bottle up in one hand and the half cork, proudly, in the other.

'Well done.'

'Shall I . . .?' Maurice gestured towards the huge, pristine wine glasses beside the candlesticks on the kitchen table.

'Yes. Light the candles if you like.'

Maurice poured the wine and lit the candles. Then he went to turn out the overhead light. The candles burnt through the windows of wine, barrelled by the bow of the glass. Maurice looked over the tableau of the table, then at Polly, standing over a steaming pan, lit by the white downglow from the air extractor. She didn't seem to be doing much beyond watching the saucepan's rattling lid.

'Did you get the invite?' Maurice handed Polly her glass. She took a delicate sip, Maurice took a substantial draught.

'Yes. Saturday is it?'

'Mm. Bring a bottle, wine, beer, nothing formal. Grace wanted to do a fancy dress party: ghosts of Christmas Past, that sort of thing. I said nobody I knew would dress up so we decided it would be optional . . . Do you think people like dressing up?'

'I think it depends on whose party it is. Some people you just can't, you know, be bothered for.' Polly took another loosening sip. 'Val likes dressing up.'

'I'm sure she does: brass breast-plate, something Wagnerian.'

'She'll make an effort. She does try to join in.'

'Everybody used to have vicars and tarts parties didn't they? It was a sort of eighties thing. Pathetic really, just a bunch of sad wankers wanting their girlfriends to dress up in suspenders but being afraid to ask.'

'We had one, didn't we?'

'Two, I think. Have you still got those black . . .?'

'Somewhere.' Polly sat at the table. Maurice stayed by the sink, he liked to look at her from a distance.

'You really are astonishingly beautiful, you know,' he said.

Polly sighed. 'Don't say that . . . I mean, thank you, but . . . look, just tell me how you're getting on with Grace and the other woman.'

'Martha.'

'She's a student, isn't she?'

'Media studies. I told her that didn't count as study. It's just an excuse to watch *Coronation Street* and write ironic essays about it. Do you ever use the term "Post-Modern?"'

'No.'

'I don't either. She does. You see I was thinking about this when I was watching *Countdown*. I think people who use words like that and "Zeitgeist" don't have a clue what they mean. It's just a substitute for learning – an excuse to get away with knowing nothing about three or four hundred years of culture. You say "post-modern" and they go "Ya, terribly" and nobody knows what the hell anybody's talking about . . . I don't even know what it means, do you?'

'No. I suppose Val does, I'll ask her.' Polly took another sip of her wine. 'Anyway, how's work?'

'Difficult to tell really. Peculiar's got a new job. Which is OK. Lucky, really, because I think he was trying to fire me or something. Warde's taking over for a while.'

'Not you?'

'No. I suppose they assumed I wouldn't be interested.'

'And would you?'

Maurice thought about it for a moment. His ambition briefly flared into life, but the flame was quickly extinguished. He had become a career under-achiever. 'No. I wouldn't,' he said.

'So what are you doing?'

'Nothing. Peculiar thinks I'm working in the Features and Dead Poets department and the Dead Poets think I'm working for Topical Dailies. I just walk about purposefully a couple of times each day, leave a jacket on the back of my chair and never turn up for meetings.'

'Well somebody's bound to find out sooner or later.'

'Of course they are. But when they do I'll just plead special projects or audience research or drivel on about focus groups for the disabled or something.'

'Well I'm sure you know what you're doing.'

The conversation faltered again. Maurice said, 'It's not like Val to miss out on spoiling an evening for us.'

'Val? No, it isn't. She's gone to see a friend I think.'

Maurice came to the table and sat down. 'You said she was at a work do.'

'Did I?' Polly drained her glass. 'Pour me another.' Maurice filled her up.

'So were you fibbing or don't you know where she is? Or, indeed, have you kicked her out and this meal is an attempt to cajole me into moving back in? Or none of the above?'

'Look. There's something we need to talk about. We can eat afterwards, if you still want to.' Polly stood up, went to the stove and turned everything off.

'Well?' Maurice said when she sat down again.

Polly nodded, trying to get her bearings. 'Look . . . look, this isn't going to be easy.'

'God, this is really very serious, isn't it?' Maurice undid the top button of his shirt.

'Quite serious. It depends how you take it, really.' Polly took her head in her hands. 'Look. Something's . . . no. I mean Val's been . . .'

'Yes, I thought it wouldn't be long before her name . . .'

'Please.'

'Sorry.'

'Val's been offered a chance to go to New York for a while.'

'I thought you said this was bad news.'

'Maurice, shut up.' But Maurice couldn't stop himself from smiling. Bad news often had this effect on him. He had laughed when his parents told him their next-door neighbour had finally succumbed to cancer. Unfortunately, the man's wife was drinking brandy in the Reids' kitchen at the time, having just got back from the hospital. She was a nice woman and passed it off as teenage insensitivity.

Polly wanted to wipe the smile off his face. Her tolerance with everybody had run out. 'I'm going with her. And I'm taking Will with me.' Then she regretted her brutal tone and said softly, 'I'm sorry.'

'You're joking,' Maurice said, but he knew Polly wasn't. He just didn't know what else to say.

'I'm sorry. It's selfish. But I'm going. It's something I have to do.'

'No.' Maurice stood up, took a step away from the table, turned back and said, 'I won't allow it. I won't allow you to take him. I'll . . . I'll get a solicitor and stop you.'

'You could do that, I know. But I don't think you will. Not when you've thought about it for a while. I mean he can come and stay with you whenever you like. You can come out and see him. It's only a few hours away, and it will give him some new experiences, new friends. It won't be for ever.' It was easier now, this bit Polly had rehearsed.

'Please don't patronise me. Anyway, we're talking about New York, aren't we? I can't imagine him having any experiences there that don't involve sniffing something out of a bag or holding up a liquor store. Don't you watch *NYPD Blue*?' Maurice was ranting. His voice had risen half an octave.

'I'm sorry. That's all. I can't say anything else. Nothing that would help, anyway.' Polly went to the stove and began draining the vegetables into the sink. Maurice felt the wine bubble up the tube between his lungs. He ran out of the kitchen and yanked open the door of the downstairs toilet. He reached the sink and vomited the afternoon's intake of alcohol against the splashback tiles. Then he stood, shaking with cold shock at the sink. The face he saw in the mirror was grey, his eyes held the hollow, hellish comprehension of Polly's news. They stared back at him, looking for a reason.

Polly called from the corridor, 'Are you all right?'

Maurice bolted the door and sat down on the lavatory.

'The meal's out . . . if you can bear it,' she said.

'I can't.'

'Well . . . well you take your time. I mean . . . yes. You take your time.'

Maurice opened the door and pushed past her. He pulled his coat from the back of a chair, sending it crashing to its side, then pushed past her again and ran out of the house. On the other side of the road he saw the interior light of a car extinguish and he suddenly knew where Val had spent the evening. He crossed the street and stood by her door. She slowly lowered the window. The car was full of cigarette smoke. The radio was on. Val was wearing a coat and scarf, on her knee was the *Telegraph* crossword.

'You've got it all now, haven't you?' Maurice said.

'No. I think we've both lost her,' Val said, staring at the steering wheel, her hands grasping the rim.

'I hope you . . . I . . . I hope you . . . oh, Jesus,' Maurice said.

SIX

WHEN MAURICE'S LIFE came back into focus two days had passed. The floor of his bedroom was scattered with empty lager cans but Maurice couldn't remember how they had got there. He woke on the morning of his party with a new resolve. In this respect, his mind had rarely let him down. Faced with trauma or seemingly insoluble problems, within a few days he would always have the solution – if not to the problem itself, then certainly how to help him bury it. The first time he had been aware of this happening was at the age of eleven when he had an appointment to visit the dentist. Mr Robin, a jovially brutal man, had never considered there to be much reason to provide painkilling injections to his patients. Maurice had had two crowns fitted without the benefit of the needle and had wet his trousers during the course of the treatment (a recurring weakness of his early life). As a result he worried for days when he saw the pencil notification on his mother's calendar that a visit to Mr Robin was imminent. But then, one morning before an appointment, he woke up to find the fear was gone. By examining and imagining every conceivable horror and every nuance of pain he had worried himself free of his anxieties. Even when the jowly face of the dentist was leaning over his mouth and he could feel the drill bit serrating his nerve, he had risen above it.

The pain he felt over the loss of Will and Polly was harder to worry away. It became more bearable with the acknowledgement that it was not a new trauma, merely a continuation of the earlier pain of separation. It was therefore familiar, and familiar horrors he found easier to defeat than unfamiliar ones.

When Maurice got out of bed, he discovered he was already dressed. He found Martha in the kitchen standing by the sink and eating cereal from a packet. She was wearing her shapeless weekend dressing gown which, he now knew, she put on every Friday evening and only removed on Monday morning.

'It's very unhealthy, that,' Maurice said as Martha delved her hand into the cornflake packet and brought out another fistful of flakes.

'I washed my hands, Maurice. At least I don't urinate on the lavatory seat, and floor, and leave huge turds floating in the toilet basin.' When Martha had not spoken to anybody for a while, it always took her a few minutes to set her sights on the conversation. Her first efforts were usually a compendium of the resentments she had been incubating during her period of isolation.

'Don't you?' Maurice said.

Martha pulled a childish face and slammed the packet down onto the sink. The cereal rustled and settled. 'I'm going to have a shower. Grace has insisted that I dress for your hateful little gathering tonight. But don't expect me to be polite to anybody.'

'Wouldn't dream of it.' Maurice picked up the cornflake packet and shook it over a bowl. A false fingernail fell amongst the yellow flakes like a flattened cherry. Maurice handed it to Martha.

'What would I want with that? Give it back to Grace.'
Martha waited by the door, looking for an opportunity to
take another stab at him. Maurice picked up the milk from
the table, sniffed it, then poured it onto his cereal.

'However,' Martha said, 'Grace has insisted that I be polite
to you. She says you've been having a bad time with your
wife. So I'll be nice to you today. I doubt it'll last beyond
that.'

'Thank you for the warning, but I wouldn't trouble
yourself on my account.'

'I'm not. It's entirely on Grace's account. As far as I'm
concerned you can throw yourself under a tube train. But
Grace has decided to save you. She does this periodically
with people and/or animals, so I don't want to upset her.
You'd better not, either. Do something stupid, I mean, like
you were threatening to do on Wednesday night.'

'Oh God, was I?'

'Apparently. I was asleep. Grace said you were standing on
your window ledge threatening to jump into the back
garden. I said from this floor you'd probably only sprain your
ankle, but perhaps that's the sort of gesture you were
intending to make. Was it?'

'Probably,' Maurice said, feeling wretched that he couldn't
remember any of it, though he did remember a woman
leading him to his bed and tucking him in, but the memory
seemed to belong to another time.

Martha said, 'I wish somebody loved me enough to want
to sprain their ankle for me if I chucked them.'

'Unlikely, I'd say.'

'Please lift the lid in future,' Martha said and went to her
room. A moment later the radio was switched on and
Beethoven's 'Ode to Joy' was announced by the velvet voice
of the DJ. The bedroom door slammed. Maurice ate his
cornflakes and tried to reconstruct the previous two days.

With a little effort he remembered leaving Polly's house, talking to Val in her car and going to a pub. After that he had a vague recollection of talking to a man in an alleyway, falling out of a taxi, turning up at work and not being let in by the security guards. The days slowly slotted into place. He put down his spoon and went to the phone in the hall. He dialled Polly's number but the answerphone was on.

After the bleep he said, 'Hello Pol, it's me, Maurice . . . well . . . well, this is hard because I don't know whether we've spoken over the past couple of days. If we have, this isn't an excuse. Honestly. It isn't. If we haven't, well . . . look . . . everything will be . . . I was going to say fine. It won't be fine. It will be OK. And I'm sorry. Not for the other night. Wednesday, was it? I'm not sorry for that. I'm sorry for everything else. I don't know what. But it feels like there's quite a lot. Yes. Quite a lot, really, I suppose. Val, if you're listening to this, stop now . . . now! I mean, Polly, I'm talking to you again, I think things could have been different. I don't think I've been very . . . reachable. Does that make any sense? Anyway, I hope you two can come tonight, well, you at least. If Val can't, then don't worry. If you're still listening Val, then I hope you heard that last bit. And I'm assuming I'm having Will tomorrow as planned unless I've cancelled it, in which case cancel the cancellation. If that's OK . . . Listen, listen, I've decided . . . I don't know why this is. I think I'm going to leave. Work, I mean. I'm going to chuck it all in because I think that's what's been making me.' The tone cut him off. Maurice had had his allotted time. He dialled again. 'Me again. I was saying, I think that's what's been making me so bloody miserable. Not just lately. For years. I've run out of enthusiasm for the place. And now I don't need to work, I mean I do need to work because I want to keep sending you the money for Will, but I don't actually need to do this. I'm going to have a bash at something else . . . not sure what, yet. I might travel, go on the hippie trail, I don't know, get a job as a bus conductor or something. Downsize, or downshift, or whatever it's called. Anyway, it feels better. I feel better. I've been taking these pills from Soames. I was, anyway. I suppose I've stopped now. But he said it's OK to feel sad, I wonder if that's what I feel? Roy said we tell lies just so we can live together. Do we? I don't think we did. At least I don't think I told lies to you. I've lost the thread now. Anyway, I don't want anybody from work to know. I'm just leaving. I'll probably tell . . . no, that's not important. Just don't mention it. If you wouldn't mind. OK. See you tonight. If you can make it. Bye . . . love you . . . bye.'

Polly, sitting on the settee beside the telephone heard it all. It was the ninth message Maurice had left since Wednesday night, and the sixth in which he had announced his resignation from the Corporation. But this was the first time he had called when sober, and certainly the first time he had made any sense. The answerphone bleeped and rewound its greeting for the next caller.

Maurice was sitting on his bed. Outside the door he could hear the raised voices of fifty or sixty people. Periodically somebody would thump on the door and try to open it but it was bolted. Maurice's curtains and window were open. He was looking at the sky and breathing the freezing air. He was dressed in a suit and tie. Warde had commented on it when he came in, shortly before Dawn. Dawn told him that Warde had asked her to come with him on the spur of the moment but Maurice knew it was a lie. He didn't care, whatever he had felt for her was gone. He kissed her like a distant relative and told her to enjoy the party. Warde came up to him an hour later and drunkenly apologised. Maurice accepted the apology in full, forcing Warde to offer his full justification, which was no justification at all. Warde had taken Dawn from him and that was all there was to say.

The stereo in the living room was turned up as 'White Christmas' began to play. The noise level outside the door subsided a little. Maurice imagined fifty people in a huge communal slow dance: arm over arm, cheek to cheek, drunkenly embracing, feeling the spirit of the day before the day before Christmas Eve. The best of Christmas: the joyous hope before the awful reality. Somebody knocked on the door then said, 'It's me, Maurice. Elaine.'

Maurice went to the door and let her in, then he bolted it again. He saw a snatched image of Grace dressed in the split skirt of a chanteuse kissing a man he didn't recognise.

'Here,' Elaine handed him a cold can of lager.

'Thanks.'

She looked tired, there were lines beneath her eyes. She had done her hair with rollers and sprayed it into place. It was tight and old-fashioned like her red dress which was just too long at the knee. She had come as Sleeping Beauty. Maurice wanted to hug her when she told him. She was one of those people who never quite knew enough about how others saw them. For Elaine, this was a blessing rather than a curse. At her throat she was wearing a choker ribbon carrying a Regency silhouette of a woman's head.

'Are you going to come out or are you going to stay in here all night?'

'No. I was just getting a breath of fresh air.' Maurice went to the window and leaned on the ledge, the room in the building opposite was half lit by the pulsing flicker of a television.

'Anyway, Happy Christmas, Maurice.' Elaine went to him and pressed her mouth against his. The pressure pushed him off balance and he held her to steady himself. Elaine

242

interpreted this as encouragement and slid her tongue into his mouth. Maurice felt it probing his tonsils. He dropped his arms down Elaine's back and pulled her closer. Their tongues talked silently to each other until Elaine pulled away.

'Roy's here, you know,' Elaine said, stepping back and wiping her mouth.

'I know.'

'With Caz.'

'Yes.'

'He introduced us. I mean like we were just . . . colleagues. Which of course we are. Were. Will be again. I don't think he understands how important she is to him.'

'I'm sorry.'

'Men like that need people like Caz. I mean to . . . just to give him that stability that allows him to be what he is.'

'Which is?'

'You know what he is.'

'Yes. Do you?'

'Yes. Happy Christmas, Maurice.'

'Happy Christmas, Elaine.' Maurice kissed her again. She undid the lock and let herself back out into the press of people in the corridor. Maurice took a deep breath to calm himself and, when she had gone, followed her out. He pushed through to the kitchen where he found Hardiman and a small dark-haired woman with very large breasts standing against the sink. Lardhead was smilingly inebriated, the woman was rocking backwards and forwards to the music, they were both cloaked head to toe in silver.

'Kitchen foil?' Maurice said. 'Is it?'

'What?' Hardiman said, leaning his ear towards Maurice's mouth.

'What are you?' Maurice shouted.

'Sunday lunch,' Hardiman said, pointing at his girlfriend's chest. Maurice smiled politely, waiting for the punchline.

'Roast chicken,' the woman said.

'Oh, chicken breast is it?' Maurice said.

'What?' The woman looked at Hardiman who shrugged.

'Excellent,' Maurice said, indicating with a head move-
ment that he was going out to the lounge. Hardiman nodded
enthusiastically, then started tapping his feet in time to the
record.

Maurice shouldered through a crowd of people scrummed
sweatily together outside the bathroom. Just as he had fought
free of them he felt a hand catch his and tug him into a
bedroom. The door slammed shut, Grace held a piece of
mistletoe above her head.

'Your turn, Morry.'

'Is there a queue or something?' Maurice said, leaning
towards her and subsiding against her breasts. Elaine had
limbered him up. This time he was ready for it and launched
an enthusiastic attack on Grace's gums with his tongue.
Grace threw the mistletoe away and joined in with equal
fervour. When they finally, reluctantly, pulled apart, Maurice
said, 'I think I have to thank you, don't I?'

'No. Not a word, Morry.' Grace held her finger to her
lips. 'It's all over babe. It's all over now.'

They kissed again. Maurice staggered out five minutes
later. Any longer with Grace and he knew they would have
been in her room for the rest of the evening. When he
looked back round she was pulling an elderly man dressed in
cricket whites by his tie towards her door. His cap fell at her
feet.

'Peculiar!' Maurice said in amazement as Grace's door
slammed shut again.

'Oh, there you are, I've been looking for you for half an
hour,' Polly kissed Maurice on the cheek.

'Did you see that!' Maurice said, gesturing towards Grace's
room.

'Vincent Edwards? Yes, he's here with a man who keeps goosing the women, I think they've come as closet heteros.'

'Blimey.'

'Val's talking to a gloomy girl who's threatening to overdose in her bedroom.'

'Martha,' Maurice said. 'She's talking to Val is she?'

'Will she do it?'

'What? Say again?'

'Will she . . . never mind. Look, can we go somewhere quiet?'

'What?' Maurice said.

Polly pointed towards the front door which had just opened to admit a woman dressed as a tart and a man dressed as a vicar. 'That way?' Maurice said and took her hand to pull her through another small group before breaking free of the mass and escaping into the stairwell. Three men dressed as policewomen ran past them into the flat. The door closed. Polly leaned on the banisters and fanned her face.

'I didn't know you knew so many people.'

'I don't.' He leaned beside her and looked down at the falling perspective of the staircase.

'I got your message.'

'Good. Did I? I mean, had we spoken?'

'Not spoken, no. I talked to Grace on Thursday.'

'Oh.'

'I like her.'

'Yes?'

'That's all.'

'OK.'

'So . . .' Maurice fished in his pocket for his cigarettes. It was empty. 'So what do you think?'

'About you leaving?'

'If you like.'

'I think it's the most courageous thing you've done for ages. Ever done.'

'Do you?'

'Yes, I do.'

The door opened and Roy May and a tall, blonde-haired woman walked out of the party. Roy was helping her on with a long, well-cut woollen coat. He stopped when he saw Maurice, letting the coat momentarily drop away. He regained his composure and when the coat was on, held out his hand and said, 'Happy Christmas, Maurice.' They shook hands. Roy eyed Polly. Caz looked at Maurice as if she knew quite a lot about him. She shook his hand too but didn't say anything. 'Bygones time,' Roy said and patted his cheek with what he seemed to imagine was fondness.

'Absolutely,' Maurice said. 'Did you manage to say goodbye to Sleeping Beauty?'

Roy ignored him, smiled at Polly, took Caz's arm and walked elegantly downstairs. When they were a floor below Maurice heard Caz say something. Only the sibilance reached him, then Roy's baritone answering her.

'Why don't you want to say goodbye to them?' Polly said.

'Because I want to go on. Move on. I don't know, with goodbyes you just get mired in the past.'

'Will you come and see us off at the airport?'

'No. I couldn't. I'll say . . . I'll say goodbye to Will when I drop him off to you.'

'I'll give you the flight number if you change your mind. It will be as easy for Will as you make it,' Polly said.

'Don't tell me how to do it, I know what I want to say.'

'Yes. I'm sorry.'

'No. I'm sorry. About everything.'

★ ★ ★

The 747 backed from its stall and taxied towards the runway. Ten days had passed since Maurice's party. Polly took Will's hand as they passed a procession of tails of other huge planes. Will gazed at the huge confident graphics of the international carriers wrapped round the bodies of the jets; the primary colours of corporate logos blazing against the stark white of the fuselages. The long terminus corridor, tethering the noses of the planes, glowed through the mist. Inside, travellers and their trolleys were shunted on conveyors into the gills of the machines. Engines whinnied, petrol bowsers commuted back and forth, men with ear protectors holding laser wands talked and stamped their feet in small groups, a luggage trolley train sprinted towards a terminus door, low lorries with huge tyres tugged sleeping jets towards their docks. Will watched it all, miniaturising the vehicles, spreading them on a carpet, packing them away in his toy box. Will had a secret. It was an exciting secret and he was sworn not to tell.

'Are you enjoying it, Will?' Val leaned across and patted him on the knee.

'Yes, thank you,' Will said.

The 747 passed beyond the harbour arm of the terminus and into the huge open crosshatched space of the runways. The green and red lights in the tarmac shone on a long path diminishing towards the horizon. The plane slowed and turned and the cabin lights dimmed. An American jet landed right in front of them. The wheels dropped onto the tarmac, dragged and caught the ground. A series of screens were lowered from the cabin ceiling. Polly and Val viewed the safety video while Will craned his neck to see the plane queuing in front of them waiting to go. It lumbered round to shoulder into the wind, screamed and was away. It was their turn. The engines fired. Will felt himself fall into the back of the seat. Polly held his hand until it hurt. The ground rushed and rushed, the terminus flashed past. The runway bumped and bumped under them until Will was sure they would crash and then they were up: free, swinging through space, turning from the airport buildings which were slowly cartwheeling away. Then they were through the clouds and into the light.

The seatbelt sign went out. There was an audible sigh of relief from the passengers, nervous laughter. Seasoned travellers looked up from their newspapers but they couldn't entirely hide their wonder that they were still alive. Polly sighed too, careful to hide it from Val. Maurice was gone, but he was still with her, in a way. Will was too much like him for her to entirely forget him.

'What are you smiling at?' Polly said.

'Nothing.' Will said.

'Are you all right?'

'I need the toilet.'

'I'll take you.'

Val smiled reassuringly as they squeezed past her, then went back to her magazine. Will led the way down the corridor, skirting people who were already standing up to get their bags out of the overhead racks. A stewardess came towards them in a blue hat. Will searched among the faces on the long rows of seats. Some were already bored: a woman listening to a personal stereo, a baby crying, a businessman opening a small bottle of whisky and pouring it into a plastic glass. Then Will saw him sitting at the end of a row and ran and ran, and he didn't care who he bumped into.

When Will reached his father, Maurice took his face and planted a kiss on his forehead. But Maurice was already looking for Polly who had been caught behind the stewardess. She pushed round her and saw him, and stared and laughed out loud as the plane carved slowly, full-sailed, between blue and yellow glaciers towards a wonderful new world.